PRAISE FOR AVA MILES

NORA ROBERTS LAND
Selected as one of the Best Books of 2013 alongside
Nora Roberts' DARK WITCH and Julia Quinn's SUM
OF ALL KISSES. USA Today Contributor, Becky
Lower, Happily Ever After

"Ava's story is witty and charming." Barbara Freethy
#1 NYT bestselling author

FRENCH ROAST
"An entertaining ride...(and) a full-bodied
romance." Readers' Favorite

THE GRAND OPENING
"Ava Miles is fast becoming one of my favorite light
contemporary romance writers." Tome Tender

THE HOLIDAY SERENADE
"This story is all romance, steam, and humor with a
touch of the holiday spirit..." The Book Nympho

THE TOWN SQUARE
"Ms. Miles' words melted into each page until the
world receded around me..." Tome Tender

COUNTRY HEAVEN
"If ever there was a contemporary romance that
rated a 10 on a scale of 1 to 5 for me, this one is it!"
The Romance Reviews

THE PARK OF SUNSET DREAMS
"Ava has done it again. I love the whole community
of Dare Valley..." Travel Through The Pages Blog

THE CHOCOLATE GARDEN
"On par with Ni
Jenn

ALSO BY AVA MILES

The Dare Valley Series:
NORA ROBERTS LAND
FRENCH ROAST
THE GRAND OPENING
THE HOLIDAY SERENADE
THE TOWN SQUARE
THE PARK OF SUNSET DREAMS
THE PERFECT INGREDIENT
THE BRIDGE TO A BETTER LIFE
DARING BRIDES
DARE VALLEY MEETS PARIS
BILLIONAIRE
THE CALENDAR OF NEW BEGINNINGS

DARING DECLARATIONS: An anthology
including THE HOLIDAY SERENADE &
THE TOWN SQUARE

The Dare River Series:
COUNTRY HEAVEN
COUNTRY HEAVEN SONG BOOK
COUNTRY HEAVEN COOKBOOK
THE CHOCOLATE GARDEN
THE CHOCOLATE GARDEN: A MAGICAL
TALE(Children's Book)
FIREFLIES & MAGNOLIAS
THE PROMISE OF RAINBOWS

Non-fiction:
THE HAPPINESS CORNER:
REFLECTIONS SO FAR

Once Upon a Dream Series:
THE GATE TO EVERYTHING

The Gate to Everything

THE ONCE UPON A DARE SERIES

AVA MILES

Copyright July 2016, Ava Miles

All rights reserved.

No part of this book may be reproduced or transmitted in any form by any means—graphic, electronic or mechanical—without permission in writing from the author, except by a reviewer who may quote brief passages in a review.

This is a work of fiction. All of the characters, organizations, and events portrayed in this novel are either the products of the author's imagination or are used fictionally.

ISBN-13: 978-1-940565-48-4
www.avamiles.com
Ava Miles

To Joe—a true hero—for building the gate to everything and pretty much anything else, including trust.

And to my divine entourage, who brings me so much abundance on the other side of the gate.

Acknowledgements

My heartfelt thanks to the special people in my life who support my efforts:

The amazing and uplifting Jade, who has stepped up so brilliantly; Emerald; Angela; Shannon; Em; Hilary; Lori; and Kati.

And to all my readers—I hope you enjoy this wonderful new series.

Author's Note: In case you notice, there was a slight error in THE BRIDGE TO A BETTER LIFE about how Jordan and Grace met. This is the true story...

If a different person were telling this story, they might start it with Once Upon a Time.

But since this story is about tough, good-hearted men who dared to reach for their dreams, I'll start it with Once Upon a Dare.

Eight boys met at football camp decades ago with nothing but grit and hope in their bellies. Like all boys, they had a healthy dose of fear as well.

But their hard-nosed coach told them real men don't give in to fear. In fact, real men do everything it takes to get what they want.

Turns out, playing professional football wasn't the only dream these men had.

They dared everything for love too.

PROLOGUE

"The yellow house you love so much finally sold, Grace. I'm sorry to be the one to tell you."

Her mom's words cut her to the quick, and Grace Kincaid was glad she had stepped away from the party to be alone outside. The December air was cold enough for her to see her breath, and without a shawl, she was shivering in her conservative black dress.

She put her hand under her nose to prevent herself from crying. Even though she thought she was alone, there was no telling if there were eyes on her, waiting to expose her moment of weakness at this NFL party. "I had such hopes for that house, Mom."

"I know you did, honey," Meg Kincaid said softly. "You've pretty much had your sights on it since your dad built it sixteen years ago. But now that Jordan's career has taken off, he won't be returning home to Deadwood any time soon—if ever—and Marcellos is doing so well, too. You're both going to be living there for a lot longer, I expect."

Her mother wasn't wrong. Jordan Dean was the starting quarterback for the Atlanta Rebels, and his fame had skyrocketed last year when he'd taken Atlanta to the playoffs, much like he was doing this year. His talent, coupled with his mega-watt star power and good looks, meant everyone was eating out of his hand. Everyone except Grace, who'd fallen in love with him before all this fame nonsense had arrived at their door.

"If it's any consolation, honey," her mom said, "I've heard the family is really nice. They have two young children and are from Rapid City."

Grace didn't care about that. Those people had bought her dream house, the one she'd hoped she and Jordan were going to raise a family in.

"I'm happy for them," she made herself say because her mom had raised her to be nice. Sometimes, she was too nice. Right now, she wanted to curl up into a ball. That beautiful, yellow colonial had been for sale for three years since it was more expensive than almost any other home in Deadwood, sitting on twenty beautiful acres.

A few years ago, right around when they both turned thirty, Grace and Jordan had discussed the possibility of moving back to their hometown together. He'd been on the verge of early retirement after sitting on the bench for six years as a backup quarterback in New York. The plan was for her to open her own restaurant to cater to the tourists who enjoyed casinos like the Midnight Star owned by Kevin Costner, and for Jordan to build houses with her dad. Their plan had sounded like a dream come true to Grace. But Jordan had decided to give one more team a shot before throwing in the towel. That team had been the Atlanta Rebels.

And now there was no end in sight.

"Try not to be too down, honey," her mom said. "You'll have your own home someday that will be a better fit for your careers."

She made herself say, "I'm sure you're right, Mom," even though she wasn't. She was turning thirty-three next month, and Jordan hadn't proposed. They'd been together for seven years. This news about the house felt like a sign. Maybe it was time for her to give up on her dream of them moving home and making a life together.

"Where are you again?" her mom asked. "I can hear music in the background."

It was her one night off from the restaurant, and Jordan had talked her into joining him at yet another holiday party filled with celebrities and groupies—pretty much the last people Grace would choose to socialize with. "Another party to celebrate the Rebels' undefeated season."

Her mom made a humming sound. "Well, that's a bummer. Knowing you, you'd rather be at home on the couch with Jordan, watching a movie. Must be hard to spend your one night off with him at a party, but maybe the frenzy will die down once the playoffs start up."

Grace hoped so. She and Jordan barely saw each other lately, and the divide between them continued to widen as his star power grew. She'd known him since he was a kid. Had fallen in love with him as a young woman, but with her thirty-third birthday fast approaching, she was seeing him less and less as the man she wanted to settle down with.

Not that he'd asked her.

"Mom," Grace said, "I should get back inside. Thanks for talking to me." She often called her mom from parties like this as an anchor to remind herself of who she was and what mattered to her. But she also did it because she was lonely.

"I'll talk to you tomorrow, honey," her mom said. "Love you."

"Love you too," she responded, and after she hung up, Grace stared across the perfectly manicured grounds of the mega-mansion.

She didn't want a house like this. She didn't want a life like this.

But Jordan seemed to.

She didn't know to do about that.

Heading back inside, she detoured to one of the bars—there were eight of them, for heaven's sake—for a glass of wine. At least the host had catered a fine selection for the guests. She took a sip and tried to settle down, steeling herself to get through the next couple of hours until Jordan was ready to leave. Usually she didn't go home early, but after hearing the news about her dream house, she might make an exception. But she didn't want to explain herself to Jordan. After all, what could he say? *Sorry I didn't want to go home with you and buy that house? Sorry I didn't want to give up on football and marry you?*

"Oh, my God!" Some Valley girl with dyed blond hair, endless legs, and cleavage guaranteed to make a small-town minister blush pushed up next to Grace at the bar. "You're Jordan's girlfriend, right?"

Even though Grace didn't want to encourage conversation, she nodded.

"Wow! You're so lucky. I mean...Jordan is like...so gorgeous and talented. I don't know how you can stand it."

Her eyes scanned to where he was standing across the room with a group of luminaries. His gaze met hers and held it for a tangible moment. He gave her a half smile and raised his beer in a silent toast.

"Yeah, he's pretty spectacular," she said when the woman only continued to stare at her.

Jordan Dean definitely filled a room—tall, toned,

and heart-stoppingly handsome. She had to admit there must have been something special in the air the day he was born. At six-foot-four with sandy blond hair and arctic blue eyes, he was arresting. His muscular body, honed by years of football, looked just as good whether in cheap clothes or carefully tailored fabrics from Europe, while she... Well, she wasn't a "personality."

"Didn't some media person recently call him the David Beckham of American football?" the Valley girl continued. "You've been together a long time, right? If he asks you to marry him, that would make you Victoria."

Victoria Beckham wasn't exactly her role model in life. She was content being Grace Kincaid, a rising chef in Atlanta. Of course, no one at these parties ever asked what she did. All they wanted to do was talk about Jordan.

"It's kinda surprising he ended up with you," the woman continued, sipping what looked like liquid pink bubblegum, "but I guess it's because you grew up together. I mean, you're pretty for your age. And you probably aren't as boring as the tabloids say you are if he stays with you, right? He must be a really nice guy."

Nearly everyone—from the groupies to the media—wondered how one of *People Magazine*'s sexiest men had ended up with her. Until Jordan had become a mega-star, everyone had thought they were perfect together. Now, he was doing beer commercials surrounded by hot chicks in Daisy Dukes and strutting his stuff in major magazine spreads pimping everything from cologne to Italian watches.

Grace didn't wear Daisy Dukes or designer clothes, so a local tabloid reporter named Farley Cooper had dubbed her "Too Dull for Dean." Things had turned ugly, with Farley seemingly making it his life's mission to tell everyone why she wasn't good enough for Atlanta's winning quarterback.

Grace had always prided herself on being a good person and a wickedly talented chef, but the storm of negative comments about everything from her body to her fashion sense had stripped her of her dignity. She'd never lacked confidence before, but the barrage of haters made her feel weak and powerless.

She didn't like who she was becoming in the midst of it all.

Add in the pressure of her upcoming birthday and her ticking biological clock, and she was pretty down on herself. Now her dream house had been sold. She'd let life get away from her on a personal level, and something had to be done about it.

"Excuse me," she said tersely to the woman and took off through the crowd around the bar.

She felt Jordan's eyes follow her movements. He always kept track of her at parties. He was a good guy that way, and while she could handle herself, it was nice to know he cared—even if he wasn't trying to extricate himself from all these shallow people. She just didn't know what he saw in them.

A curving staircase caught her attention, and Grace decided that if she had to be miserable, she could at least stay inside and be warm. She took the steps one at a time, mindful of her three-inch heels. No one was on the second floor, and Grace breathed a sigh of relief when she rested against the balcony overlooking the party.

Kicking the etched glass in front of her wouldn't be wise, but it sure was tempting after that woman's insult. Most people thought Grace wasn't good enough for Jordan in looks or style, but for the past six months, she had been wondering if *he* was the best thing for *her*.

What hurt her most was that Jordan was so dismissive of what people were saying about her. Every time she brought it up, he dismissed it, giving her the cliché, "haters are gonna hate." The bullying—especially Farley's—was a by-product of his success, yes, but it wasn't worth losing sleep over. That was easy for him to say. They weren't making fun of how small *his* breasts were.

She loved Jordan, but she'd fallen in love with the "unfamous" Jordan Dean, the one who loved football like she loved cooking. Few people remembered that Jordan had been selected by New York out of college in the sixth round. Grace had been working in New York City with her best friend and chef de cuisine, Tony Marcello. She and Jordan had renewed their friendship when he'd arrived. Six months of hanging out had turned into something more serious, and he'd kissed her one night after taking her home. Grace had been happier than she'd believed possible.

No one had expected much of him at the time, and he'd gone from the third- to second-string backup quarterback, sitting on the bench for six long years until he'd decided to go to Atlanta as a free agent instead of returning to Deadwood and buying her dream house.

Everything had changed in an instant: Jordan had finally been given his chance. And he had won like crazy. Not wanting their relationship to end, Grace had convinced Tony to move to Atlanta to open Marcellos, a Northern Italian restaurant growing in acclaim. Grace still intended to have her own place someday, but now she wondered when that would be.

Jordan glanced up to where she was standing, and she caught his frown. He shook off the gorgeous women who'd closed in around him and headed for the stairs. The models were scowling now, but their eyes didn't shift away from him. Of course, it was impossible *not* to watch Jordan. He prowled with both a casual and determined energy—each step an assurance that he would get his prize. It didn't hurt that his charm was impossible to resist. Yes, there were plenty of reasons why she hadn't been able to break things off yet.

"Hey," she heard him say as he sauntered toward her, and all it took was that one word to make her shiver.

His voice was like extra chunky peanut butter—dark and creamy with a slight bite. As smooth as it was to her ear, it carried perfectly in low octaves across his offensive line when he shouted a play.

He positioned himself close to her on the balcony, resting his forearms on the metal railing. "I've been watching you all night. You stepped out for a while."

"I needed some air," she said weakly, breaking eye contact with him.

She heard him sigh deeply next to her. "Air, huh? You're miserable, Grace."

Her heart broke at the sadness lacing his voice, and she decided against telling him about the Deadwood house selling. What did it matter now? "I'm sorry."

"I don't like seeing you this unhappy," he said, not looking at her.

Suddenly the weight of all her misery pressed down on her—the media circus he reveled in and she hated, the widening gap between them, and all the lost dreams in that yellow house sold to another family, a family she and Jordan likely were never going to be.

"I don't know what to do anymore," she blurted out, tears suddenly in her eyes.

At his shocked expression, she gestured with her hands. "About us. During the season, we barely see each other."

"We've weathered other seasons before, Grace," he ground out, his own tension rising.

Happier times flashed through her mind, most of them from his years as a second-string quarterback. Like the time he'd rented a horse-drawn carriage for them in Central Park even though he thought it was hokey. Or when he'd waited hours to get tickets to The Nutcracker.

"Last season changed things."

"The more successful I become, the more unhappy you become," he said harshly. "I can't take that."

She put her hand on his forearm, and he finally turned to look at her. There was a rare bleakness in his eyes. "I don't want you to become less successful. I'm glad you and the team are doing so great. I just...don't fit in with all of this. Jordan, you know me. My dad's in construction, and my mom's a nurse. They live a simple life, and they're happy. With my birthday looming next month, I've been thinking about my life a lot. It doesn't look like I thought it would at this age. I don't have..." *My yellow house in Deadwood, a ring on my finger, a baby—you.* She was afraid she never would.

"I know there have been a lot of changes for both of us," he said softly. "Just hang in with me."

"I'm trying, but I'm afraid..." She trailed off, not sure she could speak the words.

He stood and faced her, towering over her like he always did. "What are you afraid of?"

"That we can't...make each other happy any more," she whispered. "That we don't want the same things."

His mouth bunched up like it always did from strong emotion, especially after a tough loss. "I know you want a home and a family—and I do too—but I've waited so long for my career to take off and now that it has...I want to soak up these years before I retire. I don't have much time left to play. Six to eight years, Grace. It's not like being a chef. You can do that for two to three more decades."

"You're right about my career having a longer timeline," Grace said, "but my body doesn't. Jordan, I'm not getting any younger here, as one of the partygoers earlier so kindly pointed out."

His eyes fired. "You're perfect as you are. Don't let Farley or anyone else tell you any different."

"I was talking about my biological clock," she said, her stomach clenching at the words. "Kids."

"Oh," he said, looking away for a moment. "Grace, I want kids too. I've told you that, but not right now. I can't give you and a family the time and attention you deserve. But in a few years—"

"I can't wait anymore, Jordan." She'd been waiting... and waiting...and waiting. What if their paths diverged more? What if he met someone who was more in line with his path and left her?

"So you want to break up with me." He ran his hand through his hair. "Hearing you talk, I don't seem to be good for you anymore, Grace."

That statement pretty much drove a pitchfork through her heart. "That's not true. We're just growing into different people, moving in different directions. Jordan...I still love you. That's what makes this so hard."

He caressed her cheek ever so softly. "I love you too, Grace."

They stared at each other, and Grace could feel the weight of the decision at her feet. "I think we should call it so we can still think back on all the good times we had together."

Swallowing thickly, he lowered his hand from her face. "There were a lot of those."

"For me too."

"Come on," he said, reaching for her hand. "I'll take you home."

The thought of him dropping her off one last time was too much. "I can take a cab."

"Please, Grace," he said, raising her hand to his

mouth and giving it a sweet kiss, a gesture he hadn't used since their early dating days.

"All right," she said and let him lead her down the stairs.

Leaving the party proved a little challenging since so many people tried to delay him, but Jordan managed it with the assertive charm he used on the sports media after a game. By the time his silver Maserati GranTurismo arrived from the valet, Grace was holding on by a thread.

They drove in silence back to her apartment in the historic and charming Virginia Highland neighborhood, the soft strands of Usher playing in the background. When he arrived, he stopped on the street and put the car in park.

"I don't think I can walk you to the door and be a gentleman," he said harshly. "I wish...we'd had one last time."

Suddenly, tears were streaming down her face.

"I do too," she whispered, clenching her fists in her lap to keep from doing something she'd regret.

"At least let me hold you," he said, and then he was unbuckling his seat belt and hers and putting his arms around her.

She buried her face in his chest and inhaled his sandalwood cologne, trying to memorize the familiar feel of his body against hers. He sniffed in her ear, and then he was leaning back and grabbing her face in his large hands. Illuminated by the low light of the car's instruments, she could see the tears in his eyes.

"Be happy, Gracie," he said and kissed her hard on the mouth before releasing her.

She bit her lip to keep from crying out as she opened the car door. "You too, Jordan. I'm sorry. So sorry."

"Just box up my things," he told her, facing forward again. "I'll have yours sent over by courier, and you can send the package back with them."

Digging into her purse, she pulled out her key ring. He swore fluently, something he knew she hated, something he never did in front of her.

"Keep it!" he said harshly. "Just in case you ever need anything."

Anything she might have said backed up in her throat.

"Okay, Grace. Now I've really gotta go."

She stepped back and shut the door, keeping a tight grip on the key he wouldn't let her give back, and watched him speed down the street until he was out of sight.

CHAPTER 1

Three months later...

Jordan privately thought the leather-studded throne was a little over the top. Sure, he'd won his first Super Bowl over a month ago, and it was flattering to be crowned a king at yet another Atlanta Rebels victory party. But the endless celebrations were starting to lose their luster.

Still, he couldn't deny the chair fit his massive frame and gave him a good view of the party. A brunette whose name he couldn't remember had plopped down in his lap to drink her cosmopolitan. Her waist-long hair kept brushing his chest whenever she leaned forward to talk to him. She was nearly as tall as he was in her four-inch stiletto knee-high boots, but while she was gorgeous, she didn't really have anything interesting to say. He was already tuning her out.

He'd been seen with a lot of women over the past few months, which had somehow only made him more popular. He'd been a sex symbol before. Now he was one of the hottest bachelors out there, and women were prowling around him like cats. In fact, his reputation had changed from being a nice guy to a playboy, one his agent and publicist were loving since it was bringing in more endorsements and magazine covers.

What he didn't like was the media asserting he was acting out after being with "Dean's Dull Girlfriend," who must have been crimping his style. He hated them talking badly about Grace and hoped to high heaven she hadn't heard about it. She'd been hurt enough by his fame.

The club's music pulsed a sensual and enthralling beat while a mysterious blue light covered the patrons like fog. He let the music's rhythm wash over him as he absently rubbed the model's hip. After months of a grueling schedule, he was starting to relax. Life was good.

Well, he was working on making it good. After Grace...

Stop it.

He had a nice buzz going, courtesy of a steady stream of Jack Daniel's. He didn't drink much during the season, respecting his body's limits, so it felt good to have a few more than usual.

The model on his lap gave him a smoldering glance, her glistening magenta lips pursing. It looked so much like a cover photo for a fashion magazine that he fought a scowl. God, he'd thought he could get over Grace by plunging himself into parties, hanging out with beautiful women, and living the high life. In the beginning, the euphoria of winning the Super Bowl had made him think it was working, but now he had to admit he was getting tired of all the cloying hands.

He missed her.

The phone in his jeans pocket vibrated, and he angled

the model off to the side to dig it out. His heart stopped when he saw the caller. *Grace.* He blinked, making sure it was really her. Hadn't he just been thinking about her again? Without football to keep him occupied, she was on his mind way too often now. Maybe he was on hers too.

He was assailed with memories every time he scrolled through his call list—the look in her eyes when he brought her flowers, the way she'd laughed and laughed that time she splashed sauce all over the stove after he snuck up behind her and kissed her neck, the sensation of making love to the one woman he loved and trusted and honored more than anyone—but he still couldn't bring himself to delete her from his contacts. How could you delete the love of your life?

Jordan gently pushed the model aside, shrugging off her clingy arms as he hurried to the back balcony of the penthouse.

"Hey," he said when he reached the outside. "I was just thinking about you. How are you?" The words were small compared with what he wanted to say.

"I'm sorry to bother you, Jordan." The voice was familiar but formal, and the sound of it twisted the knife still stuck in his heart. "I wouldn't call if it wasn't important."

He went on alert immediately. "Tell me what's the matter. Are you okay? Is it your parents?" He'd known Meg and Pat Kincaid his whole life, and they were the salt of the earth.

"No, Mom and Dad are fine. Jordan, I need to see you. I'm sorry, but I think it would be better if you came over."

She was inviting him over? His stomach gripped with worry. "Stop saying you're sorry."

Grace cleared her throat. "Okay, I won't apologize— yet. Jordan, can you come?"

He wasn't sure what she meant, but one thing about Grace was that she never exaggerated. He tried to rein in his anxiety. "Name the time, and I'll be there."

"From the background music, I'd guess you're out, but would you be able to come tonight? I know it's late, but I just got off work, and my schedule's been a little crazy…"

Her tone had the Jack in his stomach turning to acid. "I can be there in thirty. Can I bring you something?"

"No, just bring yourself. Thanks, Jordan." She clicked off.

Jordan pocketed his phone and took a moment to settle. Atlanta's city lights glowed mellow orange, and the traffic below him flowed sparsely. He could only wonder what could have compelled Grace to call him. *Now.*

She hadn't called him at Christmas, which he'd spent away from her family for the first time in years. They'd been like a second family to him. Losing them had been almost as bad as losing her. She hadn't even called or texted after the Super Bowl. Though it wasn't something he liked to admit—even to himself—he'd been devastated. Of course, he hadn't contacted her to wish her happy birthday either. He might have worked out in the Rebels' gym all night to fight off the urge to call and hear her voice.

Taking one last deep breath, Jordan straightened and walked back inside to start his farewells. Almost forty minutes later, he stepped out of a private sedan in front of Grace's apartment building. The Virginia Highlands neighborhood suited her and her wish for the quaint, small-town flavor while his modern Midtown residence near Piedmont Park was situated close to Atlanta's nightlife. Even their addresses had shown how different they were as people—a thought that gave him a moment of regret.

He'd arranged for the driver to wait. He needed to be discreet about this stop because the media was following him around like crazy since the win, always eager for a new headline about the Super Bowl MVP for their readers. Grace liked her privacy, and since his fame had been one of the reasons for their breakup, he wasn't going to throw more gasoline on that fire by having the media speculate that they were back together.

The fact that she'd invited him over here anyway, knowing it might create speculation, sent another wave of worry through him as he walked up the red brick path to the glass doors.

God, he'd missed coming here to be with her. Being back here only reminded him how much. In his mind, a vision of her opening the door to him smiling in a simple blue dress came and went.

Since he'd sent her keys back, he buzzed her apartment and heard the lock click moments later. Of course, she'd sent back his keys with the boxes of his things even though he'd told her to keep them. Just Grace being Grace.

When he knocked on her door after taking the elevator to the fourth floor, he heard her yell, "Come in."

He let himself inside. The smell of chocolate chip cookies assaulted him like a cloying perfume. Grace only cooked like this when she was upset. Really upset.

"Hey," he called out.

"I'm in the kitchen."

He followed the voice to the kitchen and stopped in the doorway, stupefied.

"Your hair!"

She'd whacked off her glorious cinnamon-colored hair to short wisps that framed her head. His heart exploded at the sight. *What the hell?* He hadn't seen it this short since second grade, when her mother had let her cut her hair like her older brothers, Mike and John.

She sat at her farm table, clutching her tea mug like it was a life preserver. "I got it cut."

"I loved your hair." The minute he said it, he wished the words back. He stalked over to the table and stood there scowling. She was wearing an old Notre Dame sweatshirt and looked like shit. Was she still upset about their breakup?

He pulled out a chair and sat down across from her. "It looks nice," he lied smoothly. He hated it. She looked fragile. While always petite, Grace had never appeared fragile. She had always bounded with energy and grit.

He gazed around the kitchen. "You certainly cooked up a storm." Every workspace was covered with her large chocolate chip cookies on wax paper with paper towels underneath. "I thought you said you'd just left work."

Her small shoulders lifted in a shrug. "I've been home a while."

Grace didn't often stretch the truth, which made him even warier. Something was really wrong, and he took his time studying her, trying to decipher what it was. Her normally golden skin looked gray. Circles lined her green eyes, and her face was puffy. A wave of fear enveloped him.

"Tell me what's going on."

Grace reached for his hand, and he blinked at her in shock. Her green eyes were pleading, and his fingers curled around her palm of their own volition.

"There's no easy way to tell you this," she said haltingly, "and if I could, I wouldn't for the entire world." She paused, taking a deep breath. "I'm sorry, but...I'm pregnant."

He sat back in the chair. Fell back, more like. "What?" He felt her squeeze his hand again.

"I'm pregnant."

"Wait." His mind clicked on like a backup generator. He did the math. They'd split up in December, over three months ago. Jordan shoved her hand away. "You're just telling me *now*?"

"I went to Italy for a while to work in our sister restaurant." Grace stood up slowly. "I needed some time to think about things."

He shoved out of his chair. She'd been in Italy? "Time? Are you kidding me?"

The pleading in her eyes turned to anger. "Do you think this has been easy? Our breakup *hurt* me."

"It fucking hurt me too! How could you think it hadn't?"

"Please don't swear at me! And maybe I didn't think you weren't affected because of all the women you've been photographed with." She looked down.

"I'm sorry for swearing, and the women were..." Crap, what was he supposed to say? "A distraction. Hype. I can't believe you've waited this long to tell me, Grace."

Her silence was unnerving. "I decided to wait until I was past the first trimester."

His head buzzed as he realized why. She'd been waiting to see if she'd miscarry. "Jesus."

"I told you to stop saying that!" she said in a hard tone. "You know I hate it."

He blew out his breath slowly, reaching for calm. The first chef she'd worked for in New York had bullied her with bad language, and Grace had promised herself she wouldn't be around that kind of ugliness again. Jordan had complied. Mostly.

Grace sat down again and drank her tea, clearly upset if her shaking hands were any indication. He'd bet the bank it was chamomile flavored with lemon and honey, her favorite. He was grateful she hadn't offered him any.

He raised his hand like a white flag. "I'm sorry. I lost it. Chalk it up to shock, okay? It was the broken condom, right?" Frustrated by their separate sleeping arrangements in her parents' house during Thanksgiving—a Kincaid rule—he'd coaxed her into the barn after a midnight walk to make love. It had broken during the heated exchange.

"I was on antibiotics for my sinus infection, remember? It sometimes negates the effects of the Pill." Which was why they'd used a condom.

"I thought you said we'd be okay, that it wasn't the right time of the month."

Her face scrunched up. "I was wrong, obviously. Here I was talking about my clock ticking...I don't know if it's nature's greatest irony or a cautionary tale about being careful what you wish for."

"Ah, Gracie." He swallowed thickly as a wave of emotion rolled through him. "So, we'll get married."

"Like your parents did out of high school with you?" A flash came and went in her green eyes. "That's not the way."

So, his parents hadn't been happy. In fact, the decision had basically ruined both of their lives. His dad's college dreams had been put on hold indefinitely, and he'd ultimately fallen into gambling, women, and alcohol out of resentment. He'd left the family when Jordan was eight. Jordan still had no idea what had become of him.

"We aren't my parents," he said. "Grace, we're having a *baby*. Of course, we'll get married. I thought this was what you wanted." *I still love you.*

She held up a hand like a white flag. "Jordan, the reasons we broke up haven't gone away—despite how much...we might wish otherwise. And now you've won the Super Bowl."

The fact that she looked at his major life achievement as an impediment crushed him. He took a moment to shove back the pain while she drank her tea.

"It's hard for me to believe you're saying this. We both grew up in a community where people still got married if they got pregnant out of wedlock." Again, like his parents.

She glared at him. "Seriously? Are you forgetting that Deadwood was founded on gambling, prostitution, and gold?"

He fought a curse word. "Fine, so Deadwood has a seedy past, but you've always played by the rules. So do I."

She shook her head, and he could see her stubborn streak emerge a mile wide. "Not this time."

"You're really saying no?" He could admit it wasn't the most romantic proposal in the world.

"That's exactly what I'm saying. Jordan, you know I'm right."

She put a small hand on his arm, and his muscles tightened at the contact. He wanted to cover her hand with his own and make everything between them right again. But he didn't know how.

"Do you think I came to this decision easily? I have no desire to be a single mom. And my parents..." Her eyes blurred, and that pretty much devastated him.

"Gracie, have you told them?"

He could only imagine how they must have reacted. Pat and Grace's brothers would want to beat the shit out of him for putting Grace in this position, even if she was a consenting adult. Hell, Meg would want to kick his butt. The Kincaid family protected their own.

"Yes." She sniffed and shook her head like she was shaking off tears. "I told them that marrying you was... not a good idea. They agree with me."

That news tied Jordan's stomach in knots. "I see."

Grace looked up. "Jordan, you've always said I was the wiser one. You have to trust me on this."

He met her eyes. "This is new territory, Grace."

"I knew you'd think you were doing the right thing by offering to marry me," she said, her voice hoarse. "You'd never want to be the kind of father that yours was, leaving his family."

His walls rose up, made of hard, impenetrable steel. His father had been a cheater and a shark, and his abandonment had left deep scars.

"You'll be a great father," she whispered, her mouth tipping up at the corners. "But not a very good husband for me. I'm sorry to say that, but it's true. The fame has changed you, and I don't want to be a part of it."

Tears popped into his eyes. Those words were like the final nail in the coffin of their relationship.

"Please don't be hurt," she whispered. "You're wonderful in so many ways. You know that. But your career demands so much of you. It was hard enough before—and we weren't even living together."

He bit his tongue to keep from saying that her career as a chef was equally demanding in terms of passion and hours. But that wasn't what she was talking about.

Silence reigned between them. The icemaker emptied in the freezer, the sound like the crashing taking place inside him.

He couldn't meet her eyes. "You're right, dammit."

CHAPTER 2

Grace felt her heart crumble yet again. Desperate to soften the words she'd uttered, she rubbed the back of his hand. "I don't know how, but somehow, it will be all right." Those words had become her mantra after the home pregnancy kit had affirmed that she and Jordan would be tied together forever.

She stood to make his favorite coffee, eager to keep herself occupied as the reality of the situation settled into his bones. The simple tasks of grinding the beans, measuring the coffee, and filling the brewer with water helped her settle. She stilled when he came up behind her.

"When did you know, Grace?" he asked softly, and she fought the urge to lean back into him for comfort.

"I suspected at Christmas, but didn't have the heart to check. Mom knew something was up." She'd prayed it was another sinus infection at first, but a part of her had already known. It had seemed like life's cruel birthday present considering how much she'd been stewing about her biological clock.

His sigh punctuated the silence between them.

"I finally took a test on New Year's when I returned to Atlanta, right before I left for Italy." Her trip to Italy had been her salvation. No one had recognized her, and she'd enjoyed being a normal person again—especially knowing the hype around Jordan and the Rebels' Super Bowl win would be insane in Atlanta.

"You didn't have to handle it alone." He put his hands on her shoulders and rested his chin on her head. "I would have been there for you, even with the playoffs. I would have wanted to know."

The tears Grace had tried so hard to hold back spilled out of her closed lids. God, she'd missed his touch, but she'd dreaded the comfort she'd take from it.

"Why'd you really wait until now to tell me?" he asked quietly as the coffee finished brewing.

She'd never outright told him how much she feared that Farley and all the other jackals were right—that he'd be better off without her. The pictures of Jordan partying with other women that had been splashed all over the Internet and tabloids felt like confirmation that freedom suited him. It had only made the breakup harder, as had the embarrassing knowledge that her family and her colleagues had seen them. A little voice in her head told her this baby—their baby—would hold him back too.

"You needed to focus on the playoffs," she said instead, trying to keep her voice even. "This was the last thing you needed to deal with."

His sigh warmed her scalp. When she shivered slightly, Jordan ran his hands down her shoulders, warming her. Awareness was alive and well between them. She'd hoped it would be gone. Being pregnant and not being together was going to be hard. So hard.

Since knowing she was pregnant, every day she'd

feared she'd cave and get back together with him. She loved him. But all the fame surrounding him had only mushroomed, and he'd seemed happier without her anyway.

"The playoffs and the Super Bowl ended early February, Gracie."

"I know," she said, remembering how many times she'd picked up her phone to call him only to put it down. "I didn't just wait because I wanted to be past the first trimester...there was another reason."

He turned her around. "What?"

"You worked so hard to win the Super Bowl," she said, feeling comfortable she could share this one. "It was your dream, like me earning a Michelin star. I wanted you to have some time to enjoy it."

His face scrunched up, and he turned his head to the side, fighting the emotion radiating out of him. "How do you feel about the baby?"

There weren't enough words to describe the seesaw of her emotions. "More than a little scared, but I'm growing used to the idea and doing my best to be happy about it."

He let out a long breath. "And what about Gracie and her needs?"

She shrugged. "What about her? It is what it is. No use crying over spilled milk."

He put his hands on her shoulders and stared into her eyes. "This is about more than milk, Grace. It's a child. *Our* child."

Jordan stepped back to give them space, and she was glad for it. Feeling his hands on her—even in comfort—was too strong a pull toward the past. She knew he was fighting it too.

"Have you been to the doctor yet?" he asked.

She nodded. "Yes, I had the first ultrasound yesterday."

He looked down, his brow knitted, and she realized he was staring at her belly. His hand darted out to touch it, but he jerked it back. Her legs turned to lead at the thought of him touching her there.

"I...um...I'm not showing yet," she said awkwardly.

Jordan raised her chin so he could look into her eyes. "You should have let me come with you, Grace."

She hadn't been able to face the thought of him accompanying her. It would have been too intimate. But seeing the baby on the ultrasound was the nudge that had finally made her reach out to him. There was a baby growing inside her, their baby, and she couldn't hide from that reality anymore.

"Water under the bridge," she simply said.

He pursed his lips, clearly unhappy with her answer. "Do they know what...it is yet?" His gaze tracked to her stomach again.

It was weird, having people stare at her belly. The smell of food had made her violently sick, so while most people waited to share the news until after the first trimester, she hadn't been able to hide it from her colleagues at the restaurant, either in Atlanta or in Rome.

"I hope it's all right, but I want the baby's gender to be a surprise." Waiting to learn about the sex was like waiting to unwrap a present under the Christmas tree. "You can ask the doctor if you'd like, but you have to promise not to tell me."

Those serious glacier-blue eyes studied her for a long moment before he nodded. "If you want to wait, I'll wait."

For Jordan, it was a compromise. He hated to wait. When they were kids, he always used to shake all of his Christmas presents to guess what was inside. In fact, he still did. While she'd always been a pro at waiting.

Hadn't she been with him for seven years with no sign of marriage? She'd been a fool.

"I have a picture." She walked over to the drawer where she kept important papers and drew out what the doctor had given her. "The baby doesn't look very big now, but my doctor says everything is on course."

He took the picture from her with shaking fingers. The black and white photo showed a small form suspended as if in midair. She'd gazed at it a hundred times since yesterday, and it still awed her to see the small head and the tiny fingers and toes.

"I need to sit down," he said, grabbing a chair. "I know you told me, but somehow it seemed unreal until... this. Holy...crap. I really am going to be a father."

She was happy he'd corrected his language this time. "I'm so sorry, Jordan. This isn't...at all like we'd expected, is it?" Visions of them together in that beautiful yellow house in Deadwood flashed and faded.

"I'm sorry too," he said hoarsely. "You...you don't deserve this."

She hugged herself so she wouldn't go to him. "Takes two to tango, as they say. It's not...ideal...but it is what it is."

She poured him freshly brewed coffee as he set the picture of their baby aside as if it were an ancient scroll that could crumble from the slightest force. She made sure their fingers didn't touch when she handed it to him. After pouring herself more tea, she went back to the table and sat down with him.

He set the mug aside untouched. "How are you feeling?"

She gave a dramatic eye roll. "I've been as sick as a dog every morning for more than a month now. Just like Mom, it seems. She tells me it will get better." Grace prayed that was true. Morning sickness sucked.

"When is the baby due?" he asked haltingly. "August, right?"

"August 17, they're saying." She was still having a hard time wrapping her mind around that date being one that would change her life forever.

"I want to be there, Grace. For the birth."

She met his gaze. On some level, she'd hoped he would want to be there. After all the pictures of him partying, she hadn't been sure what he'd want. But faced with his request, she wasn't sure how she felt about it either. Part of her wanted nothing more than to have him urging her on as they welcomed their child together. That image was easy to see. He was a natural coach as a quarterback.

"I'm not sure, Jordan." She wet her lips nervously. "We'll have to see."

His jaw clenched, but he didn't fight with her, for which she was grateful.

"Okay, we'll see," he said after a long pause.

She looked at the table again, tracing the grain of the wood. This wasn't how it was supposed to have happened. When she'd imagined this conversation in the past, she'd pictured a celebration. Non-alcohol sparkling wine and fried chicken and mashed potatoes, her favorite meal.

"What are you going to do about the restaurant?" he asked, taking a sip of his coffee.

The topic of her career was one that added to her nausea. Pregnancy and motherhood were not easy for female chefs, and Jordan knew it. "The doctor thinks I can work my regular hours up until my thirtieth week. Then, I'll need to cut back some and stay off my feet more."

He didn't say anything, which made her fidget. They both knew how demanding the work was.

"Tony thinks he can move me to the lunch shift and let me do more of the prep work, which I can do sitting down. You know Tony. He and the rest of the staff are already making me small dishes to eat, saying it's good for the *bambino*."

A smile flashed across Jordan's face. "Tony will always do right by you. I won't have to worry about you with him around, and that's a relief, let me tell you."

No, Tony and the rest of the kitchen staff's old-world machismo would ensure she didn't over-exert herself or lift any heavy industrial cooking pots. Her biggest concern was the adjustments she'd have to make to balance being a single mother with her career.

He took a deep breath, and she braced herself, knowing what was coming.

"Don't get mad, but I have to ask. Do you want to keep working, Grace?"

"Of course I do. You know how much I love it." Until learning she was pregnant, all she'd truly had was her career. It hadn't felt like enough. Now, she would have a career and a family—just not the way she'd ever envisioned it.

He shifted nervously in his chair, which at other times, she would have found endearing. "I was just checking. Grace, you know anything I have is yours."

"That's all in the past now," she said, hoping he would drop it.

Jordan wagged his index finger at her. "No, it's not! Whether you like it or not, I am this baby's father. I make millions of dollars each year, and I *will* support both of you. I won't have you slaving away like my mother did after my dad left."

Their eyes clashed and held. Money had always been a point of contention between them. Grace had not liked the lavishness his lifestyle afforded. She had resented him for buying her designer clothes so she could comfortably socialize with the rich people in his growing circle. "I'm not slaving away, Jordan. I love what I do, and you know I make good money for a chef."

The more he'd tried to buy her clothes and make her look more polished, the more she'd feared she wasn't good enough in his eyes. Worse, she'd worried he would leave her for someone more beautiful and more interested in sharing the hard-partying, heavy-spending, highly publicized lifestyle he seemed to be gravitating toward. Someone who'd encourage him to do more ads, TV spots, maybe *Dancing with the Stars* one day.

He reached for his coffee, and she could all but hear him growling his frustration into the mug when he remained silent.

"Do you want a cookie?" she asked to lessen the tension between them.

He leaned back in his chair and grabbed one off the island. He took a hearty bite. "No one makes a better chocolate chip cookie than you, Grace. The fact that I can even choke it down at a moment like this speaks to your culinary magic."

Grace sat quietly while he ate. She'd needed to make the cookies to release stress, but she'd chosen his favorite in the hopes of creating a fragile peace between them.

After brushing his mouth with the back of his sleeve, something Grace had watched him do all her life, he rested his elbows on the table again.

"You're right, Grace. I don't know how it's going to be all right, but somehow it will be."

He grabbed her hand, which she squeezed before pulling away. His touch made her want to lean into him.

"So, if we're not getting married, what do you want to do?" he asked.

Details were not her friend right now. All she did was panic in the face of all the decisions ahead. "You need some time to let everything sink in. Are you still going on vacation like you normally do at this time of year?"

Jordan blinked a couple of times, clearly surprised. They had originally planned to go to Italy after the season was over—their usual trip—but she wasn't sure what he'd decided after the breakup. Going to Italy by herself had been another way to reclaim one of her passions. She'd first gone there with Tony Marcello eight years ago, back when they'd worked together at Divino in the Big Apple.

"I'm meeting up with my Once Upon a Dare guys at Sam's house in D.C. for a few days."

The friends he'd made at his childhood football camp were his staunchest allies and supporters—real friends, not panderers—and it warmed her to know he'd be seeing them after hearing this news.

"Please give everyone my best."

"I'll call you when I get back," he said. "You'll call me if you need anything, though, right?"

She nodded to pacify him, but deep down, she didn't foresee calling him for anything—at least not right now.

"My cell will work wherever I am. Any time, okay?"

Grace couldn't help but smile at the pushiness in his tone. He knew she wouldn't call either. "Got it."

Jordan rose from the table slowly, looking like he'd been sacked a record number of times during a game.

"Breaking up was hard, but this... You're pregnant with my baby, and I can't even hold you and be happy about it."

She closed her eyes briefly, trying to hold herself together. "I know."

He gave her one last long glance before walking briskly out of the kitchen. Grace stayed at the table and reached out a shaking finger to touch the crumbs he'd left on the table. Laying her head on her arms, she wept.

For all of them.

CHAPTER 3

Jordan hopped an earlier flight from Atlanta to Washington D.C. in the hopes he could catch Sam Garretty alone before their other buddies arrived. Everyone looked up to Sam, the eldest member of their Once Upon a Dare group and the son of the man who'd brought them all together.

Jordan had first attended Coach Frank Garretty's reputed Ohio football camp as an eight-year-old. His mother had applied for a scholarship, and he'd shown up pretending to be tough, but quaking on the inside. The Coach's annual Once Upon a Dare speech—or, rather, challenge—had changed him.

Playing professional football is not some fairy tale, boys. It's hard, exhausting work. You'll be tested in every way a man can be. There are no daisies and buttercups in this game. If you want everything handed to you like some princess, get off my field right now. If you're going to play football for me or any coach worth his salt, you're going to have to dare it all. So, here's my challenge to you punks. I dare you to be more than you ever imagined...

Jordan had been full of dare—always had been and always would be. And since Coach believed in putting kids of varying ages together to share life lessons and skills, Sam, who was four years older, had been put in the same cabin as Jordan alongside the other six guys in their group. They'd formed a fast friendship that had only grown stronger with each passing year. Now they were all pro football players—an achievement that spoke of Coach's instincts. Jordan considered the other guys his brothers, especially since he was an only child.

And after learning the woman whom he loved—and had lost—was carrying his baby, Jordan needed a brother.

When he arrived at Sam's home in the early morning, the Virginia horizon was hazy, making the large acreage look like a blurred picture, much like Jordan's future. He felt the opposing forces of restlessness and depression war inside him. They hadn't abated since his talk with Grace.

He kept rehashing the reasons behind their breakup in the hopes of figuring out what to do. He and Grace had fallen into a deceptive rhythm over the past few years. They were absurdly happy in the off season and out of sync during the regular season.

His multi-million-dollar salary last year had been a sore spot. Even worse, the paparazzi and tabloid journalists had started to converge on him at all times—even on simple errands to the grocery store—and they'd started to go after Grace, saying she wasn't good enough. He'd told her not to let it get to her, rather like he did when people jawed at him on the field, but it hadn't worked.

They'd started fighting over silly things, like the

expensive clothes and jewelry he'd wanted to buy her to wear out to special functions in the hopes that the media wouldn't make fun of her off-the-rack clothes. She'd thought he was changing and didn't like it. He'd wanted her to enjoy the perks of his success and protect her from their negative comments about her lack of style.

Letting her go had been the most unselfish act of his life. He'd wanted her to be happy—even if that meant not being with him.

Now she carried his child. He was thirty-two, and in a few months, he would become a father. He still couldn't take it in.

When he knocked on the door, he was surprised to see Sam's mom. "Hey, Mrs. G," he said because no one called her Helen.

"Jordan!" she exclaimed, pushing her curly white hair back behind her ear. "You guys aren't supposed to be here until this afternoon. Wait. Why didn't you text Sam to say you were coming earlier? Is something wrong?"

Helen Garretty had been their football camp mom at Once Upon a Dare, always there to prod them toward success like the best mama robin. She and Coach Garretty were divorced now, so she no longer played a role in the camp, but she treated the eight of them just like she had back in the day.

"I needed to talk to Sam before the guys got here."

She had her arms around him before he could blink. "What's wrong, sweetie? Don't make me pull it out of you."

Jordan sighed. No use keeping it a secret when it would come to light soon enough. "Grace is pregnant."

She squeezed him tight and then pressed back. "*Well*...that's a pickle. I was sorry to hear from Sam you two had broken up. Grace is such a nice girl."

"Yeah, she is," he replied.

"I can see why you want to talk to Sam. Come on in. I was finishing up some meals for you guys. He's in the Man Cave stocking the bar for you yahoos."

"You're not going to beat me up or try to give me advice?" he asked, following her into the kitchen.

She gave him an amused look over her shoulder. "Coach dished out the beatings, if you recall, and as for advice, if you want mine, all you have to do is ask."

"I'm asking," he said, unbuttoning his jacket.

"Is there any chance of reconciliation?" Mrs. G asked, taking aluminum foil out of a kitchen drawer and wrapping up what looked like her famous breakfast casserole.

"No," he said, and it still smarted. "She doesn't think I'd make her a good husband."

"Hmm," Mrs. G said, putting the casserole in the Sub-Zero. "Well, that's for Grace to decide, I suppose. You might have some growing up to do, especially now that the country's set a spotlight on you, but you'd make a good husband to my mind. Of course, all the tabloid photos I've seen of you since you broke up with Grace aren't particularly encouraging. I mean, how many women does one man really need, Jordan?"

She could throw a haymaker for an old lady. "Ah, Mrs. G."

"Don't Mrs. G me. I've been around you boys since before you had hair on your chests. Coach and I might be divorced, but that doesn't mean he wasn't right about the trappings of fame. That's not what the game's about. Neither are the women. You're better than that, Jordan."

Well, that put him in his place, didn't it? How could he explain that he'd wanted to forget Grace? That he'd tried in the only way he knew how, and it still hadn't worked?

"The real question is: do you want to be a good father to your baby?" she asked.

"Yes, I do."

"Then do it," she said in her characteristic matter-of-fact way. "I'm going to wrap up the rest of these meals and put them in the refrigerator. Go see Sam. I'll be back at the end of the weekend to see all of you. The Smuck award is a doozy. Sam outdid himself this time, and I helped him execute his idea."

"I can't wait," he said, but he couldn't muster his usual enthusiasm for the contest of wills he and his buddies played every time they all got together.

"Off with you now," she said, and since she made a serious shooing motion, he obeyed her.

Taking the stairs to Sam's lower level, he tried to put a lid on his emotions. Sam was stocking bourbon on the shelves, and Jordan had a flash of his brother giving him other advice over the years.

When he was a new kid at camp, Sam had said, "You're going to do just fine, Dean. Work hard and hit the players between the numbers. The rest will fall into place."

And when Jordan had thought about leaving football altogether a few years back, Sam had said: "You certainly won't play if you quit. How much do you want to play? Hang in there. Your time is coming."

For over two decades, Sam had always given him the most simple, grounded advice that had paid off. Jordan needed guidance now more than ever, and he hoped beyond hope that his brother could help him out.

"How's it going?" he asked, approaching the bar.

Sam turned around and immediately frowned. "What are you doing here early? I get worried when you arrive before everyone else. What's wrong?"

Jordan lifted a shoulder. "I messed up. I needed to talk."

"Why don't I pour us a drink, and you can tell me about it?" Sam asked, setting out two old-fashioned glasses and grabbing the Buffalo Trace. "Who cares if it's early? You look like you could use one."

"It's happy hour somewhere," Jordan said.

They each took a drink and settled across from each other on the leather sectional.

"All right," Sam said, lifting his glass slightly in a salute. "How'd you mess up?"

"Grace is pregnant," he said, fighting the urge to knock back his drink. "I don't want you thinking I didn't take care of her. She was on antibiotics, and the condom broke. We broke up a week later. She just told me about the baby last night."

Sam took his time sipping his liquor. "It's been a few months since you two split. Why did she wait so long to tell you?"

"She says she didn't want to mess with my head during the playoffs and the Super Bowl," he said, setting his drink on the coffee table and standing. "And she was waiting to see if...the baby stayed."

That thought still unsettled him to the core. She would never have terminated her pregnancy—that he knew about her—but it made him wonder if she'd wished for a miscarriage.

"I see," Sam said gravely. "Tough situation all around."

Tough wasn't a mild word when Sam used it. "It makes me feel like crap, knowing she's been shouldering this alone."

"That's in the past. What does she want to do about it?"

"Well, she doesn't want to marry me," he said, pacing in front of the coffee table. "That's for sure. Apparently, I'm not good husband material."

Sam was quiet for a moment—he wasn't one to hurry things—then asked, "Did you imagine marrying Grace?"

He ground his teeth, thinking back to their breakup conversation and how she'd said she was turning thirty-three and just couldn't wait anymore. "We talked about it."

"But you didn't buy a ring and propose," Sam said.

"No, I...I wasn't ready. Everything I'd ever wanted career-wise was finally coming together..." He made himself say it. "I didn't give Grace equal time. And then the media and all the fame stuff—"

"Bothered the crap out of Grace," Sam finished. "They were downright cruel to her, if you ask me. But don't beat yourself up about things you can't change. Focus on what comes next."

"That's the problem. I don't know what to do, Sam. I agreed to break up with Grace because she was miserable and wanted a family. But now she's pregnant with my baby, which seems like the greatest irony of all. She can finally have the family she wants, except she doesn't want me anymore. Sam, I...still love her."

"Do you think you can win her back?" Sam asked, setting his drink on his knee.

"I don't know," he responded honestly. "She thinks I've changed, and the whole fame thing seems like a deal-breaker to her."

Sam snorted. "There's something you need to understand about women, brother. The media didn't throw all those girls at you. You threw salt in Grace's wound, Dean. How would you have felt if she'd done that to you?"

He probably would have punched a hole in the wall. "Everyone has a different way of getting over someone."

"And yet you're not over her," Sam said with a pointed glance.

"You agree with Mrs. G that I've been enjoying the hype a little too much. But I've worked so damn hard to get where I am. The parties and the attention are my payoff for all those years I sweated my guts out in practice and never snapped the ball. Sam, this attention means I'm a master at what I do. That people respect me." The frustration inside him threatened to explode like a shaken bottle of soda.

"Are you really giving your power away like that?" Sam's mouth curved. "You're a master whether someone sees you play or not. Jordan, there's the game and then there's what's important. When you told me you and Grace had broken up, I was sorry to hear it. She's a great gal with real character—not the kind of woman a man comes across every day."

"I can't be a hermit like you, Sam," he said. Sometimes he wondered how his friend could spend all his free time secluded in his Virginia colonial out in the country. "No offense."

"None taken. Why don't you sit down before you wear my floor out?"

Jordan fell back onto the sofa and tried to get comfortable.

"Other pro players have happy marriages," Sam said, shooting him a glance. "I bet if you dig deeper, you'll find there were other reasons for Grace's unhappiness. And yours."

She'd already told them to him, but he didn't see a way to address them now. "It doesn't matter," he said with a bite in his tone. "I don't think she's going to change her mind."

"So how are you playing this?" Sam asked, crossing his arms over his chest.

"I want to be a good father to my kid. I can't be like my dad." Running a hand through his hair, he closed his eyes. The father he'd thought to be a good man had walked out on him and his mother the year before his first summer at Once Upon a Dare. He'd only discovered the extent of his father's sins later, and he'd promised himself he wouldn't make the same mistakes.

"You won't be like your dad, Jordan. That much I know."

Sam's confidence eased some of the tightness in Jordan's chest. His dad had liked to party and be surrounded by beautiful women, but it was different for Jordan. He wasn't an alcoholic or a gambler, and he would never cheat. "Thanks, man. That means a lot coming from you."

Sam set his bourbon down. "Did you tell Grace about the house?"

"No," he said, shaking his head. "It seemed like the wrong move in the moment."

Some people gave jewelry. Jordan had wanted to give Grace her dream house for Christmas—the yellow colonial in their hometown she'd always wanted them to live in together—hoping it might set things right between them. She wouldn't have accepted a car, but a house... Now that his career had taken off in such a spectacular way, Deadwood would always feel too small to him. There were just so many options for him, even after retirement.

Jordan had hoped building Grace a replica in Atlanta would show he still wanted them to get married someday. He'd hoped she would be willing to wait a few more years for him to be ready to settle down. He'd also hoped she might consent to live in the house with him, but she had strong views about marriage and living together... It was why they hadn't lived together before.

Now he was having a more modern house built on the property, one better suited to his style. The other house would serve as a guest house…if he could bear seeing it on a daily basis without being weighed down by memories.

"Why don't you tell her?" Sam suggested.

"I know where your mind's going. You think it might help sway Grace. Besides, Blake bought the house next door to Natalie and talked her into marrying him again."

Sam shrugged. "It worked for Blake, didn't it? And it's Grace's dream house."

But Grace wasn't Natalie. He didn't know all the reasons Natalie had agreed to get back together with her ex-husband, but Jordan wondered how much his friend's retirement had played a role. That was something he wasn't willing to do. Not yet.

"I'm not sure she'll go for the house now—or the idea, which is why I haven't said anything," he said, mulling it over. "She'll probably be upset that I built her a replica without her knowing about it."

"That's what I'm talking about, Jordan. Maybe you should have asked her first. You don't just build a woman a replica of her dream house as a surprise."

"But I *love* to build things," he said, gesturing with his hands. "Architectural design was my major in college, and I used to work construction with Grace's dad. Hell, I helped him build that house she loves." Pat Kinkaid had hired him as a paid helper so he could make money for school, but Jordan knew the older man had also looked out for him because he didn't have a man around the house. Designing and building houses would have been Jordan's backup if football hadn't worked out.

"Personal communication certainly wasn't," Sam said dryly. "You know she doesn't want to stay in Atlanta permanently."

"Sure, I thought she'd be more willing to stay in Atlanta if I gave her the house, but that's not the main reason I didn't ask first," he said, feeling the need to defend himself. "Grace hated me paying for things. I figured...if she saw it, she'd have to accept it."

In hindsight, Jordan could see how his plan might not have been the best. He'd thought she'd want to stay in Atlanta. She loved working with Tony and the rest of her restaurant family at Marcellos. And his career was taking off. But Sam was right—he should have asked.

"Grace is practical," Sam said, nudging him with his boot to reclaim his attention. "Appeal to that side of her. Who knows? Maybe if you're closer to each other, you might be able to work out the reasons why you two broke up. Asking what she wants would be a good step."

"You think it's my fault," he said, staring mulishly at his friend.

"It's never one person's fault," Sam said. "I've been around the block enough to know that. But the way you've been behaving lately isn't exactly a declaration of love."

Jordan looked down in his lap. Now he really felt like shit.

"Maybe this is the Universe's way of giving you two a second chance? A broken condom doesn't happen every day."

Jordan felt all the hairs rise across his skin. "Imagine that. A broken condom as a sign from above."

Sam gave him a playful shove. "Help me finish up before the other guys get here. You can stew and stock at the same time."

"Stew and stock," he muttered, following Sam to the bar. "She's due August 17, by the way. I have time to figure things out." Again, he heard Grace saying she didn't want to wait on him anymore.

"Plenty of time," Sam said as they finished up the duties in preparation for their friends' arrival.

A few hours later, Sam's place was a madhouse in the best way possible. All of the Once Upon a Dare guys were joshing with one another and having a ball.

Jordan was keeping to his seat on the sofa after having successfully defended himself from a pantsing. Grant Thornton was a defensive lineman for the San Francisco Sting Rays, which meant he could pretty much take down anyone he wanted—unless you knew his downfall. The man couldn't stand being tickled. Worked every time. Jordan had needed to get a little more creative with Brody Kellar. As the wide receiver for the Chicago Titans, his buddy could outrun him without much effort. But Jordan wasn't above a well-timed trip—at least off the football field.

Logan Eastwood, wide receiver for the Boston Stars, was prancing around in a rainbow sequins tutu, which Sam had presented as this reunion's Smuck award. Of course, no one truly wanted to win. The "winner" would have to wear that freaking rainbow tutu out in public, and who was down with that?

"Are you going to tell us what the Smuck competition entails, Sam?" Zack Durant, quarterback of the New Orleans Akkadians, called out.

"Yes, I need to know how *not* to win this tutu," Hunter Cahill said. "I'd lose my spot as quarterback for the New York Tigers if anyone saw me in that thing."

Blake Cunningham put his hand on his hips and stared them all down. "If Coach Garretty heard you right now, he'd say you're a bunch of wimps."

"Easy for you to say, Blake," Hunter told him with a slap on the back. "You're retired, and Natalie probably loves you enough to tolerate the sight of you in a tutu."

"Zack Sprat here needs to win it because it would look good on his St. Bernard," Brody said, grinning like an idiot.

"Don't talk about my dog that way, Brody," Zack warned, "or I'll use you for gator bait in the bayou the next time you visit."

"Ohh," everyone cried.

Jordan tried to get into the spirit of things, but just couldn't muster the enthusiasm. His mind kept spinning about what to do about Grace. Was Sam right? Was telling her he'd built her dream house and asking her to live next door to him the best approach?

Someone kicked his feet, and he looked up to see Grant towering over him.

"What's your deal, Dean?" he asked. "You're worse than a bump on a log."

Sam gave him a look as if to say, *Might as well tell them.*

He downed the last of his drink and set the glass down with a clack. "I got Grace pregnant."

Zack and Hunter stopped roughhousing immediately. Blake turned to look at him, and he met the man's gaze. The rest of the guys were soon sitting down around him, all business.

"Tell them what you told me," Sam said.

So he did. The guys mostly had shocked looks on their faces.

"Are you completely sure it's yours, man?" Zack asked when he'd finished.

Jordan leaped up and was in his friend's face in seconds. "We're talking about Grace here," he snarled. "Not one of your Vegas showgirls."

Sam and Blake pulled them apart, and Jordan huffed back to his seat.

"I'm sorry, Jordan," Zack said. Judging from his tone, he meant it. "You broke up months ago. I had to ask."

He bit his lip to keep from shooting his mouth off.

"I like Sam's idea of giving her the dream house you had built for her," Blake said when the silence in the room became overwhelming.

"Oh, yeah?" he asked, feeling way too exposed for comfort. "Sure, moving in next to Natalie worked for you, but not everything has an easy solution, man." He was doubting the wisdom of his plan more and more since talking with Sam. Grace was going to see the house as another stalling tactic on his part, which it was.

"Jordan," Blake said, staring him down. "I feel for you. But don't push it. Besides, I had less of a chance of winning Natalie back than you do with Grace."

"That's the God's honest truth," Logan said. "Grace is a sweetheart, but Natalie..."

Blake turned his gaze on the wide receiver.

"Come on, man," Logan said, not backing down. "Your wife is awesome, but she can be pretty scary sometimes."

"That's the way I like her," Blake said, "but we're getting off point. If you love Grace, you need to fight for her. You find out why things fell apart and you fix it. Do you hear me, Dean?"

Romancing the woman who was carrying his child? "I hear you."

"You don't believe you can do it," Grant said, slapping his forehead. "I can hear it in your voice. Coach would bust your nuts for that wishy-washy response."

"Grace isn't a football play," he said, but even he could hear the wimp factor in his voice. "What if I mess it up more? This isn't just about me and Grace anymore. We're having a kid. Man, I just saw stars like I got my bell rung."

"Put your head between your knees then, Dean," Brody said, demonstrating the move. Sure enough, it helped. After a few moments of holding his head like that, the dizziness passed.

"You'll figure it out," Blake said as Jordan leaned back against the couch. "Just don't wait too long to get your head out of your ass."

Was his head up his ass? It chafed to hear his buddy say so, but he knew one thing for sure. Despite winning the Super Bowl, his lifelong dream, he didn't feel quite right. A part of him had been hollow since his breakup with Grace, and he wasn't sure it would ever be whole again unless he got her back.

"You should tell Grace you built her dream house because you wanted her to be happy—in Atlanta where you both have careers," Zack suggested. "That's pretty romantic, if you ask me."

Would she see it that way? He had to find out. "I might need some help," Jordan said. "You guys love me. Maybe..." No, no one could put in a good word for him with Grace. Not even Natalie, with whom she'd been friendly. He had to win her back on his own.

"If you need help, you ask," Sam said in a definitive tone. "Now, let's leave Jordan to his thoughts for a while."

Grant reached over and shook him playfully. "We're here for you, man."

"Thanks," he said, burrowing deeper into the couch.

"All right," Sam said, rising and going to the center of the room. "Who wants to hear what I've cooked up for the Smuck competition?"

"Me!" Brody called out while others shot their hands in the air.

"I'm almost afraid to ask," Blake said with a playful shudder.

"Only because you won—or should I say *lost*—last time," Logan said, grinning. "I have fond memories of Zeus the boa constrictor, not to mention you screaming like a girl."

Blake walked over and got in his face. "I never scream like a girl."

"Do you want to hear or don't you?" Sam asked.

They all shut up and nodded. None of them could deny Sam for long.

"Your goal is to pick out as many marbles as you can in under a minute," Sam said. "The one who picks out the fewest has to wear the rainbow tutu. Mom made it, by the way, so no cracking jokes about it around her."

There was a catch. There was always a catch.

"And?" Grant asked for all of them.

"The box holding the marbles is filled with crickets," Sam said with a grin.

"Shit!" Brody said, shuddering. "I hate bugs, but especially ones that jump."

"Me too," Zack said. "You need to have your head examined, Sam."

Their host gave him a mischievous smile. "You forget. My dad used to play for the Nebraska Cornhuskers. Anyone know what they were called before that?"

Everyone looked at each other.

"The Cricket Busters?" Zack asked, throwing his hands up in the air. "Oh, please put us out of our misery."

"The Bug Eaters," Sam said. "I won't be wearing that tutu. I've got strong blood running through these veins."

But Jordan didn't. Either that or his concentration was shot.

He ended up wearing the rainbow tutu.

Chapter 4

The day Jordan returned from vacation, he headed to Marcellos to see Grace. His time away had helped him decide on a plan of action. He only hoped Grace would listen.

In the past few days, he'd ordered all the most highly recommended pregnancy, fatherhood, and baby books. He was in full-on preparation mode, but it chilled him to the bone how much the books couldn't tell him. How was he supposed to take care of a kid? How was he supposed to know what to do when it cried or asked him the big life questions? He was so going to screw things up.

When he pulled his Maserati to a halt at Marcellos' valet stand, he eyed the young man barreling toward him with a ferocious scowl instead of his usual smile.

"Hey, Johnny, how's it going?" The kid hailed from Florence and was in his third year at Georgia Tech's mechanical engineering program. He worked two jobs to pay for school. Jordan had always tipped him well.

The boy ripped the valet card off, nearly tearing it in

half. "Fine, *Mr. Dean*. I'll try not to dent your ride."

Jordan winced. He wouldn't be surprised if there *was* a dent in his car when he reclaimed it. Johnny adored Grace. Hell, everyone at the restaurant did. And given that the vast majority of the wait staff was either Italian or Italian-American, they protected her like a sister in the old neighborhood. He couldn't imagine they'd be happy with him—even if Grace had mostly initiated their breakup. They were blindly loyal that way.

After struggling with the best way to approach Grace about the house, he'd finally texted her and asked to meet so they could chat. Jordan had suggested Marcellos after her lunch shift. They'd be on her turf, which would give her an added sense of protection. And when he left, there'd be plenty of people around to support her. He'd read some scary articles about the effects of stress on a pregnant mother, and he wanted to minimize it at all costs. Grace already looked fragile enough.

Walking through the elegant glass doors of the restaurant, he headed toward the back. The smell of rosemary, lemon, garlic, and basil mixed with roasted meat hung in the air. On other days, it would have made him hungry. Today, it made him feel more nauseated.

Adriana, the sultry, black-haired hostess, saw him coming and muttered something biting in Italian, making a rude gesture with her hand.

"Hello, Adriana," he said warmly. "I'm here to see Grace."

"Testa di cazzo," she replied.

"Yes, I'm an asshole," he agreed with her, "but I'm here to make things right."

"Imposibile," she responded. "You've been seen with more women than Don Giovanni—and right after you two broke up. You're a pig!"

He bit his tongue, deciding it would be futile to try and explain. Plus, he had other problems. He'd been spotted by the only patrons left in the restaurant—an older couple dawdling over an afternoon espresso and a slice of ricotta and golden raisin cheesecake. The last thing he wanted was for Grace to be reminded of his fame.

He blew past Adriana and continued toward the back of the restaurant to the kitchen.

Ricardo, another waiter, glared at him and muttered something in Italian. Angelo, the busboy, stopped what he was doing the moment he saw Jordan. He flew back to the double doors of the kitchen. Jordan knew he was warning Grace.

God, he'd hoped things wouldn't be so dramatic.

Before he could follow Angelo into the kitchen, Tony came through the doors.

Jordan didn't bother trying to go around him. He knew the man would tell it to him straight. Tony's honesty and general lack of interest in Jordan's fame had made him a good friend. Jordan used to swing by the restaurant to pick up Grace after her shift, and he and Tony would have a nightcap more often than not. They'd even been to Italy together a few times.

"Let's go to the bar, Jordan." Tony stretched out a hand to direct him even though Jordan knew where it was.

Jordan nodded and followed him. Grace would come out when she was ready.

"I've missed the bar," he said to be amiable...and also because it was true.

Made of stained glass, it depicted a Tuscan sunset, fields of sunflowers, rows of fat, purplish grapes on old vines, and an olive grove with young children playing amidst the gnarled trees. Tony had commissioned it in Italy, and despite all his traveling, it was still the most unique bar Jordan had ever seen.

He slipped onto a leather barstool. Tony slid his lean,

runner's frame onto the next stool. He wore a white chef's apron over a black shirt and jeans. Tony didn't wear the ugly chef's pants from the catalogues. Like Jordan, he was a fashion snob and made no apologies about it.

Jordan nodded at Alfonso, the bartender, who was topping off some lemon-infused grappa. The guy muttered something in Italian before giving Jordan his back.

"Alfonso, give us some room," Tony said in English.

The man scowled, but walked to the end and slipped out of the bar. Tony didn't offer Jordan a drink. For a man famed for his hospitality, the gesture spoke volumes.

Jordan decided to bring it out first. "So, everyone's pretty pissed at me."

"An understatement," Tony snorted, his aquiline nose lifting slightly. "Bodily harm was mentioned when Grace said you were coming today. Victor was more creative. He suggested poisoning by bad mushrooms. Apparently it's particularly long and painful. I thought that was personally the best of the lot."

"I'll be sure not to order any food today," he said, half jokingly.

Tony turned to face him. "Do you have any idea what this is doing to Grace? She is a proud woman. You two break up, and then she discovers she is with child while you're off gallivanting with a bunch of groupies. You know what the media used to say about her. She is humiliated."

Jordan ran a shaking hand through his hair. "Don't you think I know that? Do you think I wanted this for her? Jesus, Tony. I was trying to get over her and took things too far. I didn't know about the baby until last week. If I'd known earlier, I would have shut the rest of that down. I'm not a complete asshole."

Tony went around the bar and pulled out two glasses

and a bottle of Jordan's favorite grappa infused with lemon. It held the makings of a truce.

After pouring a larger portion for Jordan, Tony slid the glass across the bar. They both downed their drinks. The alcohol and lemon hit Jordan's tongue, burning all the way down.

"Grace tells me she will not marry you, although I am glad you were willing to do the right thing. As you said, you're not a complete asshole, just a misguided one." Tony poured another round. "I would have poisoned you myself had you not offered. Since Grace is a wise woman, she must have her reasons. She tells me that we cannot all have a traditional family. I know she does not mean it."

Jordan did not answer. Staring into his glass, he frowned.

Tony traced the bar's wooden grooves after setting his glass aside. "She was planning on moving to Rome temporarily. After you broke up, Piero Ferantini from La Timora in Rome and Grace were going to exchange places for three months. We've been talking about a swap for a while now, but no one thought Grace would be the one to leave. When you broke up, she asked me to send her, and days before she left, she told me she was pregnant."

The emotion in Tony's voice gave Jordan a flavor for how difficult that conversation had been. "She told me about the trip. She's always loved Rome."

"I expressed my concerns since she was pregnant," Tony said, "but she insisted on going anyway, saying she needed to get away and think."

"I'm glad she came back early," Jordan said, his relief enormous.

"Although she didn't say so, I suspect she didn't want to be in the States during the playoffs, especially since you—and your *friends*—were already making the news every other day. And no one makes cruel comments to her in Rome." He made a dismissive gesture with his hand. "She didn't come back until a few weeks ago."

Probably right around the time she made it past her first trimester. Things were starting to make more sense. "She was trying to escape for a while," Jordan said. "I understand the feeling, but we need to deal with what's in front of us."

"She did good work in Rome, but she did not come back better, Jordan. Maybe she didn't have enough time. Maybe it's because she's started to realize that her life will be different with a baby."

Jordan felt sweat bead at his temple. "Yes, it will be. For both of us."

Tony slapped him on the back. "She is not taking care of herself. Her morning sickness has been fierce. Working in a restaurant did not help. She could barely keep anything down. The sight of food caused her much upset." Tony looked back toward the kitchen.

"I've read about the side effects of pregnancy, but I... don't get it," Jordan said, feeling like an idiot.

"She does not want to eat! I can barely coax her to eat three bites of her favorite sandwich. I thought there was something wrong with the prosciutto and Parmesan when I saw that she had not touched it. But it was fine." Tony frowned. "We are trying to take care of her. I make her leave early, but she goes home alone, which is not good for her."

No, it wasn't good for either of them to bear such weight alone. The time he'd spent with his Once Upon a Dare brothers had buoyed him up some, but he knew Grace had been burrowing into her work.

"I make Grace sit and cook as much as possible so she is not on her feet all day," Tony said. "You do not want to know how that suggestion went over in the beginning."

All he could do was nod. Grace had always resisted special treatment, why would this be any different?

"She does not have that healthy glow that pregnant women are supposed to have, Jordan."

"I'll do something about it, Tony." Standing up, Jordan set his glass on the counter. "Thanks for the grappa, and thanks for looking out for Grace."

Jordan wasn't willing to wait for Grace to come out any longer. He headed to the kitchen doors. The minute he walked in, everyone paused in their prep work. Grace looked up from smoothing mustard over a piece of beef tenderloin she'd sewn closed with a large needle. A visible tremor ran through her body when she saw him.

Carlo set aside the ladyfingers he was using for the tiramisu. Victor let his hands rest on the sea bass he'd been slicing open. Roberto ceased deveining plump, gray-and-black-striped tiger shrimp near the industrial sink. He let his blade wink in Jordan's direction.

It was quite clear what would happen to him if Grace sent him away. He nodded to the guys, not planning to engage in some macho fest.

"Hello, Jordan," Grace said, wiping her hands on her white apron and easing out of the chair Tony had mentioned.

"Hey, Grace," he replied, studying her.

She was pale and drawn, and there was a glob of mustard dotting her middle like she'd been playing paintball.

"Can we go somewhere and talk?" he asked.

"Sure," she said cautiously. "Tony said he'd come get me when he was finished speaking with you."

Since Tony hadn't stopped him, he supposed he and his old friend had made some progress. "I guess the plan changed. He's still at the bar."

That news seemed to settle the rest of the kitchen staff, and Grace nodded and led Jordan to the break room. Cookbooks and magazines lined the shelves on one wall. Posters from Italy graced another. Grace pulled out two sparkling waters from the small mini-fridge beneath the shelves, and they sat at the table in the middle of the room.

He opened the bottle she gave him, the hiss sounding between them as the carbonation released. Jordan wasn't sure where to start, so he went with his biggest concern. "How are you feeling?"

He watched her throat work as she swallowed. The new haircut made her neck seem more vulnerable. It was still a shock to see this new Grace.

"Fine. I hope you and the guys had fun." She clenched her hands in her lap.

Fine? He put his water down, shaking his head. Sometimes straight up the middle was the only way to make the play.

"We did, but I had trouble relaxing because all I could think about was you...us...the baby. I even won the Smuck award, so I had to parade around D.C. in a rainbow tutu. So, let's not beat around the bush. I'm not fine, and you're not fine."

Her green eyes widened.

"Look, if Tony hadn't said something, I would have seen it for myself. I thought it was the stress of telling me the other night, but you look pale and fragile. I've never seen you like this." And it made his stomach clench.

She glared at him. "I know how I look. Do you think I'm happy about it?"

He hated to push her buttons, but maybe it was the only way he could get through to her right now.

"Do you really want this baby, Grace?" he asked harshly.

"What?" she asked, blinking.

"I know it's a little late, but I would understand if you didn't. I mean, it sucks, right? We break up after you tell me you can't wait for me to ask you to marry me and start a family, and then *boom*, you find out you're having my kid. This certainly isn't your dream life, and here I am again, making you miserable."

"You have a nerve, talking to me like this," she said, the words close to a snarl.

"Do I?" He kept his face straight. "I mean, you deserve credit for that type of thing. It must be awful, being such a martyr."

He watched her raise her hand and waited for the shove.

"A martyr?" she cried. "Where do you get off calling me that? Or telling me that you'd understand if I don't want this baby? Of course I want this baby! You do too."

"You're damn right I do!" he said, raising his voice.

Grace leaned back in her chair as if the wind had been taken out of her, eyes suspiciously wet. "Then why are you saying all of this?"

"Because I want you to start taking care of yourself. Grace, it kills me to see you like this. And it makes me feel even guiltier than I already do." He paused, putting up both hands. "That's my problem. But this isn't going away. We need to deal with it."

"I know that, Jordan. Do you think I like feeling like this?"

He took her hand out of instinct. She froze and started to pull it back.

"*Stop.*" He pursed his lips, fighting emotion. "I can't take you pulling away from me like that. Okay, I've done a lot of thinking. I know you won't marry me, but I have a suggestion. Will you just listen?"

Her hand went lax in his, but she didn't let go. "I'm listening."

"You and I used to be best friends. Hell, we grew up together. Your mom and mine were close. I worked for your dad. I was part of your family. I'm not saying that we can get back to that, but we've got to find a way to be friends again, Grace. We have a baby coming."

She blew her breath out slowly. "I know."

"I spent most of my vacation thinking about what we were going to do. I know you'll want to be a good mom and spend lots of time with the baby when you're not working." He leaned forward, watching her high cheekbones redden with emotion. "I want to spend lots of time with the baby too—when I'm not on the road for a game. It'll be hard to make arrangements around our schedules, so I want you to think about what I'm going to say."

He paused, watching her pull herself together. He didn't continue until she nodded.

"I don't know how you're going to take this, but I built your dream house here in Atlanta—a replica of the yellow colonial in Deadwood. I was going to give it to you for Christmas."

She blinked at him, her mouth dropping open. "You what?"

"I was hoping it would make you happy. And that it would show you...hell, that I intended to marry you...in a few years. I knew we...I wasn't going back to Deadwood anytime soon, if at all."

Her face completely bunched up, and she put up a hand as she fought for control. "I don't know what to say to you right now. Part of me wants to hit you for doing this without talking to me. Jordan, you know what that house means to me."

"I know, but you know me. No sense sometimes. I didn't know what else to do. I...didn't want to lose you, but in the end...it didn't matter."

She continued to stare at him. "The night we broke up, Mom told me a nice family had finally bought the house."

Suddenly everything made sense. "You were crushed. Why didn't you say anything? I had another house exactly like it—well, plus some improvements—ready for you."

"Are you kidding me?" she asked. "Jordan, I'd been waiting seven years for you to propose. We were supposed to start our life together in that house years ago, but we came here instead."

"Grace, I know you had this whole life planned out for us. That we'd go back home. You'd open your place, and I'd work with your dad. We'd buy that house and raise a family. I couldn't give up on football, and once I realized that returning to Deadwood probably wasn't in the cards, I knew I needed to give you what you wanted most. That house."

A couple of tears streaked down her cheek. "I wanted that house, but I wanted you more. Jordan, when my mom told me that house had been sold, I thought it was a sign."

"And now you're pregnant," he said softly. "Why can't that be a sign that we're supposed to be together?"

She looked down and released a harsh breath. "Because you don't really want to be married to me. Otherwise you would have asked. I understand what you said about your career. I do. But you weren't willing to prioritize having a family before. I don't see that changing, and besides, you've...lost yourself in all this fame. I don't want to be a part of it anymore."

Jesus, so nothing had changed. "Fine. We're not getting married, but the house is there, and it's still your dream. I...couldn't sell it, and because I love the property, I decided to make your house the guest house instead. I'm building another house on the land, and it's going to be finished in a few months. I plan to live there." He'd paid a lot of money to make that happen. Crazy money—the kind that had helped drive a wedge between him and Grace.

"You want me to live in a replica of my dream house while you live next door?" she asked with an ironic shake to her head. "Sometimes your thought process defies common sense."

But he heard the catch in her voice.

Desperate to press his advantage, he stared into her eyes. "We'll be neighbors. It'll be like our own family compound."

She narrowed her eyes at him, all wary now. "You're really serious?"

"Grace, don't you see? This way I can pop over to see the baby whenever I want. And he or she can come and see me whenever." He'd dreamed about his son running up his sidewalk after school, football in hand, or his little girl asking if he'd teach her how to pitch the ball.

He refocused on Grace. She looked like she had stopped breathing.

"I don't want to be some deadbeat dad who only gets to see his kid a few days a month."

When she squeezed his hand, he reached out to tentatively touch her face. God, he craved a connection with her, any connection. "I need to be involved, Grace. Please don't shut me out."

Chapter 5

Grace couldn't seem to form a complete sentence. He'd built her dream house in Atlanta without telling her and wanted her to live next door to him?

"Jordan, I know you want to be involved with the baby," she said, trying to ignore how handsome he looked in his cream Italian knit shirt and designer jeans and boots. "And you will. I'm just not sure it's this way." She wasn't certain she could live in that house—here—without him. Every vision she'd had of it had included him.

He leaned toward her. "Yes, but how, Grace? That's the part that I don't like. You'll be living in that small apartment of yours with the baby, taking him or her to day care when you work. You know Tuesday's my only day off during the season, and even then I show up at the stadium for a while. Sure, I'll see the baby more in the off season, but I want more, Grace."

He was describing their life pretty much as Grace had envisioned it, and she had to admit she didn't like it either. But the house...

"I'll miss so much during those other eight or nine months," he said, "and that's not counting us making the playoffs again. My season didn't end until February this year. It's not enough time."

"I don't know what to tell you, Jordan," she said honestly. "You have a time-consuming profession." So did she, but her situation was a little more flexible.

His frown bordered on mulish. "That's true, but Sam Garretty said lots of players manage to play football and have happy marriages and families."

She bristled, and he held up his hand as if sensing it.

"You've made your feelings known about marriage. I'm not trying to change your mind, okay? I'm only trying to show you a different way. If you live in your dream house, you'll have privacy and your own life, I promise. We'll be friends again. Somehow. And I'll be able to see the baby a lot more because you'll only be a shout away."

She couldn't deny that there was some appeal to the plan. Her heart had hurt from the thought that their son or daughter wouldn't see much of Jordan for most of the year, and shuttling the baby around through Atlanta's infamous traffic would not be ideal.

"We'll hire someone to take care of him or her when you go back to work," Jordan continued, his blue eyes intent. "And when he or she gets older, he or she can come over and see me anytime I'm home. We can play after school and do homework together, Grace. Like I always wanted to do with my dad."

Well aware of how Jordan's dad had wounded him, Grace found herself softening.

"Please, Grace."

Their eyes locked, and she could see the pleading in them. She rubbed the tension in her neck, thinking it through. Beyond being a replica of the house she loved, the proximity would be distressing. How could she live next door to him when he seemed to have moved on with other women? Surely they'd come home with him. The pictures of Jordan with an increasingly attractive parade of gorgeous women had devastated her enough. To actually see him with one of them?

"Jordan, it's too much," she exclaimed.

"Dammit, Grace, don't let this be about money," he said, misunderstanding her. "I'm rolling in it, and you won't let me spend any of it on our baby? Come on, Gracie, what kind of logic is that? Please let me give this to you and the baby. *Please.*"

Jordan was close to begging. Grace's chest tightened at the realization.

"Okay, I'm willing to give it a shot, Jordan," she heard herself saying. It wasn't a decision she'd intended to make on the fly, but that look on his face... Plus, she loved that house—even if it was in Atlanta. She wanted her baby—their baby—to have a yard to play in.

His face broke into a relieved smile. "Thank you. You won't regret it! I promise."

"We need to have ground rules," she said, feeling swept away by her own agreement.

"Yes, I know. I'm mostly good at following rules." He punctuated the joke with a wink.

Her mouth twitched. That was one thing he was not. "Always the kidder."

His smile slowly faded. "Not always, Gracie. Not about this. I know what you think about my reasons for building you this house, but I really... I only wanted you to be happy."

To Jordan, sometimes things were too simple while she overanalyzed everything. She bit her lip, knowing she had hurt his feelings. "I'm—"

He raised his fingers to her mouth. "Don't apologize to me, Grace."

Her lips burned at the touch, so she eased back. "Okay, I won't."

"Speaking of rules, how about this one? I want you to take better care of yourself and the baby. Promise me."

"I promise." Of course, she wasn't sure it was a promise she could keep. She couldn't recall getting a good night's sleep since the breakup, and it wasn't for lack of trying.

Jordan took out his phone, punched something on the screen, and handed it to her. "I thought you might want to see the house. I can take you for a tour whenever you're ready. It's...I got the floor plan from town hall."

Grace's breath caught when she saw the photo. It did look *exactly* like the one in Deadwood. Painted in a warm yellow, it was two stories with a smaller third story punctuated with dormer windows. He'd even added an identical cushioned swing to the white wrap-around porch. She realized it would be the perfect place for her to rock the baby—like she'd always imagined doing. The front door was the same bold red of the original and captivated the eye. Large windows sparkled in the sunlight. The shingles were wood and a natural brown.

Just like in her dreams, the house looked homey and pretty, exactly the kind of place where she could spend the rest of her life. With him. Her heart pretty much shattered.

"Oh, Jordan, you...you...it's perfect." God, she was going to start crying. He'd built this for her before the breakup? What must he have gone through, knowing it was still sitting there, waiting for her, but she'd never know about it? "Why didn't you tell me about the house the night we broke up?"

He was silent a long time. "Because I could see how unhappy you were. Then you started talking about turning thirty-three, and you told me you wouldn't wait for me anymore. This house... You were right. It was a holding pattern."

She fought tears and shook herself to regain control. Rehashing the past wasn't going to help anyone. "You mentioned improvements."

"You needed a chef's kitchen," he said, a smile rising and falling on his face.

From the look of it, that's exactly what he'd given her. The Viking range that dominated the one wall made the stove in her current apartment look like an Easy-Bake oven. The island was a sizeable workspace flanked by more cabinets, a bookshelf for her cookbooks, a grill, and a deep fryer. The stainless steel sink was industrial but sleek. And there was an enormous Sub-Zero refrigerator, its metallic finish gleaming like mercury, a subtle contrast to the kitchen cabinets done in a warm cherry.

"I love the kitchen," she said, enlarging the image so she could take in more of the details like the sand-colored countertops. "This is much better than the one in Deadwood." It was hard to admit that.

"I hoped you would think so," he said.

Suddenly all of the hurt she'd felt the night of their breakup was back between them. She put her hand on his arm, and he looked over sharply.

"Thank you...for doing it—even though you really are crazy. Building me my dream house..."

She forced herself to pull away before the touch could mean anything, because if she lingered for much longer, she'd start wondering if she'd misjudged him. If maybe he'd planned on a future with her after all.

"Come on," he said after a tense moment. "I need to let you get back to work."

Jordan made a joke of trying to pull her out of her chair even though he could easily lift her with one arm.

When they got to the door, he put his hand to her back. Feeling his gaze, she looked up at him, trying to hold herself together.

"Thank you, Grace."

"For what?" she asked.

"For agreeing to live in that house and be my neighbor." He leaned down and gave her a quick kiss on the cheek and left her standing there as its warmth faded from her skin.

Grace started to break her life down into weeks—how much of the pregnancy she'd already experienced, how much she had left. She checked out a prenatal Pilates class, but had quickly decided it wasn't for her. It was one thing for the women to constantly eye her bare wedding ring finger, but one of the women—a stranger—had recognized her and asked how Jordan Dean was handling his impending fatherhood. Grace spent enough time avoiding the stacks of tabloids that infected every grocery store, not to mention the click-bait headlines on the Internet. Worse, every now and then there would be a reporter waiting for her outside her apartment or the restaurant, hoping for a photo of Jordan's "baby mama." She didn't say anything to Jordan, hoping to keep the fragile peace between them.

A part of Grace wanted to share more of the pregnancy with Jordan, but if they were together and the baby moved, she did her level best not to show it on her face. She couldn't bear to have him touch her—even like that—afraid her resolve would weaken. All she needed to do was see a random photo of him at a local party to remind her of why she'd made her decision.

He hadn't asked her again about wanting to be with her during the delivery, and she was glad. Part of her felt bad about not wanting to include him, but she didn't think she could handle the emotions or the intimacy. It was hard enough to live in the "friends bubble" he was weaving around them. It was like artificial sweetener. It didn't taste like the real thing, but it made her want it.

So, Grace signed up for birthing classes and asked Tony to be the "stand-in" for her mom, who had happily agreed to be present at the birth. Her parents were still a bit wary about this whole neighbors scheme, but she'd told them she could always revisit it if it didn't work for her and the baby. Of course, she hadn't told Jordan that.

Jordan kept up a steady stream of presents, nothing too lavish to get her back up. One day a gift package arrived that included saltines and gourmet chicken broth. Even though she was in her second trimester and felt wonderful now, the gesture both touched her and made her laugh. He sent a basket of prenatal vitamins and a body support pillow wrapped up in a bright green bow. Only one of the presents had made her close to tears—a little yellow baby jumpsuit decorated with cartoon-like butterflies and worms.

As for the house, she didn't go there again. She told him she wouldn't move in until right before the baby was born. It was unconscionable to think of walking the halls all alone with nothing to take her mind off her lost dreams. Once the baby came, she'd be too busy to cry over spilled milk.

When Jordan visited her at the restaurant to check up on her, he chatted about inconsequentials—like how she managed to make her Italian meringue so tall or whether it bothered her to roast "Bugs Bunny" in a balsamic prune sauce.

Maybe it was his attentiveness, but she found herself wanting to take a bite out of him whenever he walked into a room. Grace had never been fully comfortable with the power of her attraction to him, especially as he had grown more famous, surrounded by women who made a living on their looks. Somehow it was even weirder now that she was pregnant.

If Jordan noticed the covert glances or flushed cheeks, he never said a word. Besides, sometimes she caught him staring at her breasts. Truthfully, she couldn't blame him. She'd grown two cup sizes. Even the guys at the restaurant had noticed. It was embarrassing. Her body was more foreign than it had ever been.

He asked to be involved in the plans for the baby's

room, and she agreed that they'd go shopping together—on the stipulation that they each would pay for half. It felt like the victory it was when he agreed.

Grace told herself it was no different than him meeting her at the restaurant, but somehow it was. After insisting on meeting him at the store—it had been too weird to have him pick her up—she realized why. There would be people at the showroom, and they would be together. She almost backed out.

He was waiting for her in his car when she arrived in the parking lot. He immediately exited his Maserati and walked toward her with that powerful, sexy stride. It was difficult to ignore how flat-out gorgeous he looked in designer jeans and a navy button-down shirt. His Super Bowl ring winked on his hand as he waved at her.

"Why did you suggest this when you knew we'd have to deal with fans?" she asked when he reached her. "I must have pregnancy brain because I didn't even think about it until today."

The corners of his mouth turned up. "Pregnancy brain? I've read about that. I called the manager of the showroom and asked for a private showing. I took care of it, Grace."

Of course he had. She glanced at the showroom's door and noticed the Closed sign hanging there. "It's probably not good for your image to be seen shopping with your baby mama." The media's nickname for her was more salt on her wounds, especially since a few of them had said she still looked dumpy. With her growing tummy, it was sometimes how she felt.

"You're not my baby mama," he said with a growl. "Dammit, don't let them get to you like that. If I could stop them from talking about you altogether, I would. You know that."

"Jordan, please don't swear," she told him gently,

getting that anxious feeling she always experienced when someone swore out of anger. All these years later, the scars from her old boss's verbal abuse lingered.

"Sorry," he said, taking a breath. "It upsets me."

"Me too. Tony showed me the statement you gave about me and the baby a few weeks ago," she said. "I never thanked you for it because...it was—"

"Awkward," he finished for her. "I know. But people needed to know the breakup was my fault."

"But it wasn't," she said. "It just...was."

"I wanted to deflect any negative comments from you, so I said it was. I also needed people to know that this was an unexpected surprise, but we're dealing with it as friends."

He'd also said in the statement how happy he was about the baby. That had touched her more than anything, particularly since she'd seen the truth of it in his behavior.

"Come on," he said, putting his hand to the small of her back. "I've never shopped for baby stuff before. It's going to be fun."

He threw on his favorite sunglasses, and the sunlight glinted on the lenses, making his star power amp up a few watts.

"How's our little one doing?" he asked, studying the baby bump she now had. "I hope you can see how great you look. You're finally... I'm about ready to be cliché. You're glowing, Grace."

She didn't see it that way when she looked in the mirror, and the media certainly didn't agree. "I feel pretty good. I have a doctor's appointment this week, but everything should be on target."

"Oh. Good." The smile faded from his face. "Shall we go shopping?"

She could sense the change in his energy. "I'm

still not comfortable having you come with me to the doctor's. I'm sorry."

"Don't be," he said, rubbing her back quickly before dropping his arm. "I want you to be comfortable."

He meant it, she knew, even if he wished it were otherwise.

They took off toward the store's entrance. After rapping on the door, the manager opened it with flourish. "Mr. Dean! Ms. Kincaid. Welcome to Baby Land. Please, come in."

The fifty-ish man was overdoing it, but then again, most people behaved that way in Jordan's presence.

"I'm Charles," he said in that same exuberant voice, "and I'll be giving you my *exclusive* attention today. Thank you for sending over those signed jerseys, Mr. Dean. Everyone who works here was over the moon about them."

"You're most welcome, Charles," Jordan said, flashing a winning smile. "I appreciate you opening the store just for us. If you don't mind, we'd like to wander around for a while and see what's available. I'll holler at you if we have any questions."

Phew, Grace thought. She had hoped Charles wasn't going to hover.

"Of course, of course," the man said, immediately backing away. "Anything you want, Mr. Dean."

As soon as they were out of earshot, Grace cast Jordan a look. "Usually you correct people when they call you Mr. Dean."

He rolled his eyes. "I'm learning some people overstep by a mile if I get too casual with them. Since the Super Bowl, it's been...never mind. We're not talking about me. We're here to buy baby things. So, where do you want to start? Cribs? Lamps? Car seats?"

In all their interactions, he never did talk about

himself, but she'd seen glimpses, of course, being that the media covered his activities like eager vultures, everything from what party he'd attended to what designer clothes he'd worn to an event—and who he'd been seen with. There weren't as many women, according to Adriana when they talked at the restaurant, but they still flocked around him like moths to a lamp. She'd tried not to think about it since she no longer had the right.

"You always say, 'Go big or go home,'" she said. "Let's start with cribs."

"Please tell me you're thinking about a white one," he said, walking the showroom with her.

They passed everything from strollers to high chairs until they found the displays of cribs. Just looking at the soft baby blankets and stuffed animals was enough to put tears in her eyes. Pretty soon, she was going to hold this little miracle inside her and lay him or her to sleep every night. She still couldn't believe it—even though the baby was kicking more now. Usually about the time when Grace wanted to go to sleep.

"Hey," he said softly. "Are you having another baby moment? Tell me about it so I can join you."

It was his catch phrase for those moments when she would spontaneously tear up. Part of her wanted to be annoyed by it, but she kind of thought it was cute.

"I was just thinking about the baby and how I can't wait to hold him or her. The baby's moving more, and I'm getting excited."

As if the baby had heard her, Grace felt it uncurl inside her. She cupped her belly and smiled down at the mound. *Hello, little one. Yes, we're out buying things for your room. It's going to be so beautiful. I promise.* A few weeks ago, she'd started talking to the baby, and the love and peace she felt in those moments made everything she was going through worth it.

When she glanced back at Jordan, she noticed he was staring at her stomach.

"I've never asked, but...what does it feel like?" he asked her quietly. "When the baby moves... It did just now, right? You always get this awed look on your face. Sometimes...I feel a little cheated. It's...not as real to me yet as it is to you...and I want it to be."

When Jordan decided to be vulnerable, he didn't go for half measures. Her hand shook a little as she took his hand and laid it against her baby bump.

"Holy crap! It *is* moving." His blue eyes flew to her face. "I feel it. Oh, my God. Wow! Just wow."

His fingers curved around the mound, and before she knew it, she was moving his hand a couple of inches over. "I usually feel the baby more here."

There was another kick, and Jordan's mouth dropped open. "Holy shit! I mean, sorry. It's just...that's so crazy. I mean...I can finally feel him...or her. That's our baby, Grace."

When their eyes met again, her heart felt bruised. Yeah, this was their baby—the one they'd made together, not knowing they would soon choose to be apart.

His touch made heat break out all over her body, and suddenly she was desperate to wrap her arms around him. To listen to the steady beat of his heart with her belly resting against his middle, feeling the baby move as he held her.

Awareness of him flashed through her. God, it had been so long since he'd touched her, and she missed it. Missed him and how good things used to be between them. And darn it all if she didn't miss sex. Lots and lots of sex.

She made herself step back, and his hand had no choice but to fall back to his side. A sheen of wetness entered Jordan's eyes as he stared back at her.

"I know this is hard," he said, "being together like this, but...thank you for sharing that with me, Grace. I'll never...forget it."

He headed toward one of the cribs, giving them both a moment. She watched him run his hand almost reverently across the top of the crib.

When she joined him, he released a deep breath and gave her a quick smile.

"This is one of the top models," he said, clearing his throat. "I did some research."

He seemed almost sheepish about it. "Research, huh?" she prodded.

"Well...yeah," he said, ducking his head. "Baby shopping isn't only about buying for looks and fit—like clothes. We need to keep things like safety in mind."

Every time she thought she had him figured out, he managed to surprise her. "You're going to be a great father, Jordan. You're already being responsible."

"You sound surprised," he said, picking up the teddy bear in the crib. "I can change, Grace. This baby... It's changing everything."

And the baby hadn't even been born yet. How much more would Jordan change? Moreover, how was she supposed to handle him growing into the family man she'd always hoped him to be? She didn't think he would revert back to his old ways of putting football above family, like he had with her, but she still feared it.

"I like this crib," she said, running her hand over the railing. "It has safe corner posts and the slats are no more than two and three-quarter inches apart, if my eye is right. Plus, it has nice lines and an adjustable mattress height."

His eyebrow rose as he held the bear against his massive chest.

"You're not the only one who's been doing research," she told him.

"I wouldn't expect anything else from you, Grace," he said. "But this time, I'm not going to let you down."

It was like he'd read her mind. She looked back at him sharply, not knowing what to say.

CHAPTER 7

Jordan saw the shocked look on her face and knew his comment had struck home. How many times would he have to show her he was stepping up? For a moment there, he'd thought she was remembering how it used to be with them. He'd found himself growing aroused by the mere touch of his hand to her belly. He felt a little guilty about desiring her as he felt their baby move for the first time, but he couldn't seem to compartmentalize his emotions.

She looked so achingly beautiful right now, and though he had to battle with himself constantly, it was hard to ignore the changes in her body. Her curves were becoming lusher...and her breasts. He'd always thought they were spectacular, but they were bigger than ever. And he wanted to touch them. He wanted to touch *her*. Not just to feel their baby move—which was still blowing his mind—but to connect with her on that deep level he'd always felt with her.

If he had to settle for just one thing, it would be to

see her smile at him again. She did it so rarely now. Her once easy smiles had become less and less frequent in the last months of their relationship, and it had killed him to believe he was the cause.

"I didn't expect you to let me down, Jordan," she said softly.

He gazed at her steadily, knowing she wasn't telling the full truth. "You didn't expect me to step up. That's different. I might have let you down in the past, but I promise you that I won't let the baby down."

Her beautiful eyes grew troubled. *"Jordan."*

"Grace, I won't let you down going forward either. I promise."

She started to have a baby moment, and he clenched his hands by his side. When she got weepy like this, he had to fight a million battles inside himself to keep from reaching for her.

But then she stepped forward and put her arms around him, shocking the hell out of him. He hadn't held her like this since the night of the breakup, and his heart swelled in his chest. God, he loved her. Still. So much.

He cautiously slid his hands around her back, and when he felt her nestle her head against his chest, he tucked her close. Except it wasn't as close as they used to get. Not with the baby cushioned between them.

The changes in her body filled his awareness. Her stomach was a lot harder than he'd expected it to be... but her breasts were still soft and the new size of them pretty much blew his mind.

His hand rose to cup the back of her neck, bared by her current hairstyle. She shivered and lifted her head, and in those luminous green eyes he'd always loved, he saw the desire there—and the love she tried so hard to hide from him.

"Why aren't we together?" he asked in a whisper. "It's

not over between us, and we've been circling around it for months. Grace, I still love you, and I want us to be a family. Feeling the baby move just now...I'll do anything to make that happen. Tell me what you need from me, and I'll do it. Anything."

She pressed her head back to his chest, but she didn't leave his arms. Her muscles tensed up like she was fighting sobs, and he rubbed her back.

"Maybe we should talk about it," she said when she looked up at him. "I...still love you too, but I keep thinking—"

"Don't think," he said, desperate to reach her. "That's what got us into trouble. Love should be enough. We should agree it's going to be enough. That the other stuff doesn't matter."

She looked away. "The other stuff makes it hard. And Charles is watching us discreetly from the high chair section."

"Dammit!" he said with heat as Grace moved away from him.

"*Jordan.*"

"Sorry," he said, but seriously, he was about ready to march off and tell Charles to take a hike. He'd seen the man checking on them from a distance.

She put space between them, walking through the rows of cribs, and he gave her the time. They could talk about the future after they left. He would ask her to come over or offer to follow her home. Then they could find a way to move forward—together.

When Grace rejoined him a few moments later, he felt a million times lighter, and the smile she gave him was somehow both wary and warm. Yeah, she was thinking about it.

They agreed on a crib, and Jordan suggested he take photos of their final selections so they wouldn't have to find Charles every time they came to a decision. He wasn't so sure he could maintain his civility with the guy. Grace's relieved sigh made him laugh as they continued on to the next aisle.

Other than the two car seats—one for her car and one for his—they selected a single high chair, a stroller, and a bassinet. Jordan let Grace choose her favorite lamp, joking that he didn't have enough parental experience to know whether a lamp with a giraffe or a lion was better for childhood development. And he might have punctuated the comment with a flirtatious wink that made her smile.

Their final selection was a white baby dresser with star-shaped hardware. Grace was smiling non-stop by the time they made their way to the front, and Jordan's whole chest was filled with warmth. Sharing this experience had shifted things between them—more than he could have hoped for.

The store manager tried to chat Jordan up about next season while ringing up their purchases, but he kept his answers curt. Jordan pulled out his credit card at the end and gave Grace a pointed look. He could just imagine the media getting hold of that gem. *Jordan Dean splitting baby costs with his baby mama?* It was a headline they didn't need.

She stared back at him mulishly, and he leaned in so only she could hear and said, "Later." And he couldn't keep the heat out of his tone because he wasn't only talking about settling up after they left. Her blush told him she wasn't either.

After saying goodbye to Charles, they headed to the front door of the store. Jordan caught sight of a reporter standing next to a familiar white van in the parking lot. He swore silently. Farley Cooper was out there, which meant other tabloid journalists were undoubtedly with him. Either they had tailed Jordan without making it obvious or they'd received a tip from someone in the store. If it was Charles, the man was going to get a piece of his mind. Jordan put a hand to Grace's back.

"What?" she asked, coming to an immediate stop.

"I don't know how he found out I was here, but Farley is lurking by that white van."

"No!" She immediately tensed up. "Farley is the worst."

"I'm so sorry, Grace. There may be more of them out there."

He rubbed the lower part of her spine when she closed her eyes and pressed her fingers to the bridge of her nose.

"We can do this two ways, Grace. If I leave alone, there's a chance Farley and any others will follow me. But I can't be sure one of them won't stay around to photograph you. In that case, you'd have to face them alone. I don't like that idea, by the way."

He could feel her closing up, reverting to the unhappy woman she'd been months before—and it made him want to tear something apart in frustration.

"We should go out together," she said, her voice cracking.

"You know I'll have your back, right?" he asked.

She bit her lip. "I hate that I'm already afraid of them taking pictures of our baby—even in my belly. This is never going to go away, is it? Even though you and I aren't together, this baby will always be the son or daughter of the Super Bowl winner Jordan Dean."

All the ground they'd gained seemed to have vanished right before his eyes. His hand fell away from her back. "I don't want our kid to be harassed any more than you do, Grace. I'll do my best to keep him or her out of the media. I can't promise more than that." He wished he could. He wished he could rip every camera away from every reporter. If he had his way, he'd make a bonfire of them.

She was silent for long enough to make him sweat. "I know you can't promise more than that. All right, let's go. I might hate this, but I won't cower."

Before he could say anything, she pushed open the door and strode into the street. He jogged to catch up with her.

Farley rushed forward, already snapping pictures, and a couple more reporters popped out of their vans like gophers, cameras at the ready. His stomach sunk when he caught sight of the man with the professional grade video camera. This was going to be on the news, not just in the newspapers.

"How does it feel to be shopping for the new baby, Jordan?" Farley called out, his bald head gleaming in the sunlight.

The son of a bitch always wrote a little puff article to accompany his photos. Every single one of them squeezed the First Amendment for all it was worth. "Wonderful."

Grace was walking swiftly like she'd done before, heading to her car.

"Grace! Can we have a picture of you and the baby bump with Jordan? Every Atlanta Rebels fan wants to see Jordan's baby mama and her cute little bump."

Jordan gritted his teeth and kept his hand on Grace's back. "Not today, guys."

The reporters swarmed around them, flashing more pictures. Jordan and Grace kept moving, even though they had to slow their pace. He noted Grace already had her keys in her hand, ready to jump into her car.

"Everyone knows you put out a statement saying you're the father," Farley said, crowding way too close for comfort, so close, Jordan could see the pattern of broken veins across his bulbous nose. "But did you have a paternity test, Jordan? It's a little weird to learn you're going to be a daddy after you break up with someone."

Jordan staggered to a halt, and Grace stopped beside him. This time she put her hand on his arm, warning him.

"The baby is mine," he said in all but a growl.

"What's it like not being together with your baby mama?" Farley said, and the reporters surrounding them were all grinning now. "You sound a little touchy, Jordan."

Farley knew how to rile him up to make better pictures. "Stand aside, guys, so I can escort Grace to her car."

Grace started forward again when Jordan increased the pressure on her back. The reporters were forced to walk backwards as they advanced.

They were thirty yards away from her car when Farley shouted, "Come on, Grace! You might be too dull for Dean, but you've never been a bitch. Show us that baby bump Atlanta's QB gave to you."

Jordan was in the man's face immediately. "Don't you dare talk to her that way! Now back up, Farley, or I'll call the police."

Farley was still taking pictures as he jeered at Jordan. Since he had his camera on rapid speed, he'd have hundreds of them by now. Great.

"Show us that baby bump, girl," another reporter called out from behind Jordan.

"Don't touch me!" Grace cried, and Jordan turned to see her slapping at a man's hand. He'd been reaching toward her belly.

He saw red. "Leave her alone!" He shoved the reporter away, wrapped his arm around Grace, and led her away from them.

The reporters followed them, smelling blood in the water. Jordan had lost his cool completely, and Grace was holding her belly like she was protecting their baby from jackals. He noted a few of the reporters had accomplices, men waiting in running cars, ready to follow them.

"We're taking my car," he said, changing their course and leading her to the passenger side of his Maserati.

She didn't argue with him. When they were both in his car, she huddled in her seat to prevent them from taking a good photo of her. He turned on the car and had to gun the engine to get the remaining jackals to move out of his way.

And then the chase began. They followed him out of the parking lot. Normally he would have raced off— ignoring the speed limit—but Grace and his child were precious passengers.

"What are we doing, Jordan?" she asked finally, her breath choppy. "I need my car tomorrow."

"I'll get your car, Gracie. Don't worry about it." He looked in the rear-view mirror and counted at least three cars behind him. "What do you want to do? Do you want to come over to my place for a while and sit this out?" They'd done it before, and both knew it could take hours.

"No," she said, and her voice sounded expressionless now. "Take me home. They'll camp out for a while, but hopefully they'll be gone when I leave for work tomorrow."

"Have they been coming to your apartment?" he asked. "Dammit, Grace. You didn't say anything."

"Don't swear," she told him. "I can't take it right now. And yes, a few have shown up at my place. Thankfully not Farley. I think he's just happy I'm not with his precious quarterback anymore."

The bitterness in her tone had his jaw locking. "I'm sorry about this, Grace. You have no idea how much."

He turned onto the interstate to take her to her apartment, filled with the sick sense that this was it—he'd never win her back. The media would always be a part of his life while he played football, and she couldn't handle that. And who could blame her after a scene like that? But he still planned to ask her.

By the time he pulled up to her apartment, he felt as hopeless as he'd been on the night of their breakup. Since the reporters weren't far behind, he jumped out to walk her to the door. She was already out of the car and striding to the front with her key out.

"I'm fine," she barked out when he lurched forward to open the door. "Don't worry about my car if it's a problem. I can take a cab or ask Tony to pick me up."

"I'll get your goddamn car, Grace," he said, his frustration spewing out of him. He paused when she jolted, then said, "I'm sorry. I'm just mad."

"Me too," she said, letting him come inside the apartment lobby with her—away from the reporters. "I'd hoped…"

He took her by the shoulders. "Let me come up so we can talk. What happened at the store between us—"

"No," she said, stepping away. The new distance drove into him like a knife. "I had a weak moment, but this only confirms my decision. I won't have the baby go through this, Jordan. It's not fair. I just want our child to have a normal life. Like you and I did growing up."

That was impossible. What she'd said earlier was true—their child would be the daughter or son of a famous football star. It was out of his hands. "I told you I'll do my best to protect you both."

"Maybe I shouldn't live next door to you," she said. "I'm only making it easier for them to get what they want."

Every nerve in his body tensed up. "Don't say that, Grace."

"Proximity might only makes things worse," she said. "Look at today. If we'd just ordered things online, this wouldn't have happened."

"We can't live in a cave, Grace." He ran his hands through his hair. "Listen, I know this isn't ideal. I hate it too. But it's going to be okay. Just don't..."

He had to take a moment to reel in his emotions. She released a long breath.

"Please don't go back on what we've agreed is best for all of us," he said, staring into her troubled eyes. "Not because of one bad moment. Besides, if you and the baby are apart from me, I can't protect you as easily."

"Jordan, how can you be so blind? You can't protect me—us." She put her hand to her belly. "Not when you're the only reason anyone's interested in us."

His heart broke into a million pieces. "Don't say that. Not that."

"I'm going up," she said, firming her shoulders. "Text me when my car is back if you manage it."

After handing him the keys, she left him standing there with the reporters waiting for him outside.

He had no idea what he was supposed to do now.

Chapter 8

Grace spent a sleepless night lying in bed cupping her belly. Whenever the tabloid journalists surrounded her and Jordan, she felt caged in. Exposed. Now she realized their baby was going to be exposed as well. The worst part was that she had no idea how she was going to protect their child.

She reaffirmed her resolve not to get back together with him. She'd slipped up yesterday. It wasn't going to happen again.

Jordan texted her early that morning, saying her car was back in her parking lot. He asked to come up and talk, but she couldn't face him yet. She was too raw.

When she finally got out of bed, she received another text from Jordan.

Can you call me? The media is all over what happened yesterday. I bet reporters are outside your place and at the restaurant. I don't want you going out alone.

A sharp spasm shot across her belly, and she took

a moment to breathe through the fear. Heavens, she'd prayed it was over, but Jordan had lost his cool—and so had she. Of course the sharks would come, Farley in particular. Heading over to the windows that faced the street, she cautiously looked through the blinds and gasped. There were at least five TV vans out there with a host of twenty or so reporters camped out.

She texted Tony.

I know you're not at the restaurant, but expect some reporters. There was a thing yesterday.

He immediately texted back.

I saw it on the news this morning. I was just about to text you. Are you okay?

She responded.

Working on it. Do you want me to stay home? I don't want to make things tough for everyone.

It wouldn't be the first time reporters had lingered outside the restaurant. She usually stayed home in these situations—it was easier for everyone that way.

Probably for the best. Rest. I'll come over with something special later.

Tony always made sure she ate well.

Her belly gripped again, and she felt something damp between her legs. Alarmed, she headed into the bathroom and froze when she noticed some heavy spotting.

"No, no, no!" she called out, cupping her belly. "It's okay. We're okay. Don't..."

Don't leave me.

She called her mom in a panic. Though her mother did a good job of hiding the worry in her voice, Grace could sense it. Her advice was to call her doctor without delay, which Grace did. When she reached the nursing assistant, she relayed her symptoms and was told to come to the office immediately.

Since the reporters would likely recognize her car, she called for a cab and asked it to pick her up in the underground garage. She didn't text Tony because she didn't want to worry him until she knew more.

She didn't text Jordan because they were following him around too, and he would insist on meeting her. Besides, her mom had said it was best to keep calm, and she just couldn't deal with so many confusing feelings right now.

No one followed her to the doctor's office, thank goodness, and she was immediately ushered into an exam room. Dr. Jessica Saunders arrived moments later and examined her thoroughly. The spotting was serious, it turned out. Grace had placenta privia—a tear in the placenta. With full bed rest, Dr. Saunders was hopeful Grace would be able to carry to term.

Grace hung her head, trying not to cry. It was her fault for reacting to the press like she had—she knew it. Dr. Saunders recommended as little stress as possible until she reached full term, not wanting to risk an early delivery. Right now that stress involved Jordan—and Grace's heart broke for all of them. She was going to have to tell him she couldn't see him for a while, especially given the media's renewed interest in them. There was no way she would risk losing their baby.

It finally sunk in that she wasn't going to be able to work, the one thing that had always given her joy. And it would put Tony in a bind, which made her feel guilty. She knew Tony wouldn't care about that, but she did.

In the cab on the way home, Grace called her mom and gave her the update. Her mom said she would fly out to see her as soon as she could get a ticket. The relief was so staggering, she almost wept. Then she called Tony and told him the news. His sigh was heartfelt, and he said he would come over to her place shortly.

He arrived with Italian wedding soup and Grace's current addiction—freshly made chocolate Italian gelato. He assured her that everything at the restaurant would be fine. She could work on their new menu while at home. That soothed her a bit. Right now, she couldn't imagine lying in bed all day, every day, doing nothing but worrying if she would miscarry.

She knew she should call Jordan—she owed him that much—but she was in full-on avoidance mode. To his texts, she responded briefly that she was taking care of herself. She wasn't sure of what else to say.

Her mom arrived the next day, and Tony picked her up at the airport. She heard them enter the apartment together, but Tony must have realized they needed some time alone because her mom appeared solo in the bedroom doorway. Grace fought tears at seeing her. Her mom's red hair was streaked with gray and cut in a fashionable bob that fell to her chin. Shorter than Grace and just as petite, she usually had a smile filled with sunshine, but her expression today was all concern

"Hi, honey," her mom said and then crossed to the bed and pulled Grace into her arms.

"Oh, Mom," she said, snuggling her face into her neck and bursting into tears.

Her mom didn't say anything, just rubbed her shoulder. After a few minutes, Grace lifted her head and dashed at the tears streaming down her face.

"I'm so glad you came, Mom."

"Where else would I be? Now, let me look at you." Her mom gently rested her hand on her belly. "You're still pretty small for thirty weeks. You're not eating enough."

"You sound like Tony. This media thing...it knocked me flat on my back. Literally."

Her mom's eyes narrowed. "You father and I watched

the video clip on YouTube. I wanted to tear their hearts out for hounding you like that. I won't say what your dad and the boys wanted to do."

"Worse than tear their hearts out?" she asked, feeling the briefest smile touch her lips. "I got scared, Mom. They surround you and push you and call you names... when that guy tried to touch my belly..."

"No one should subject you to that kind of harassment," her mom said, "and when I see Jordan, I plan to tell him to do a better job of protecting you and my grandbaby."

Grace hated that they had to be protected at all. "I was scared for me, but then it hit me that they might hound our baby like that. I can't stand the thought of it, Mom. It's not the kind of life I want for my child. I had so much freedom when I was younger. Riding my bike in the street with other kids or running through the fields."

Her mom reached for her hand. "You don't live in South Dakota anymore, Grace, and there's no use hoping for what might have been. Don't do that to yourself—or Jordan."

She knew it wasn't fair, but she couldn't seem to help herself. "I haven't always wanted this baby, Mom. Without Jordan...I thought we would get married and *then* have a baby, but he never asked me. Well, not until he found out about the baby, and we both know that doesn't count."

Her mom's frown spoke volumes on that subject. "He's an idiot."

"But as it's grown and moved around inside me," she continued, "I've started to imagine what he or she will look like. I see other kids when I'm out running errands and I think, I'm going to have one of those. It overwhelms me sometimes. But then I think about being alone and wonder if I can do it by myself. I'm afraid I can't." It was one of the toughest things she'd ever said out loud because it meant admitting her own weakness. She felt like she was swimming in them these days.

Her mom lifted her chin and looked her straight in the eye. "Gracie, you listen to me. I'm not saying it's ideal, but you're strong enough to do anything you set your mind to. Did you believe you could go to the Culinary Institute of America and work for not one, but two award-winning restaurants?"

She shook her head. Plenty of people in their small town had thought she was a big dreamer who needed a strong dose of reality. The same had been true of Jordan.

"Being a mom involves juggling a lot of balls—more so when you don't have a partner—but you can do it," her mom continued. "Besides, Jordan's idea to have you two be neighbors gives you a 'type' of a partner. I might not like how things turned out between you two, but I've known him since he was born. He'll pull his weight."

Grace nodded because she knew it to be true. "I haven't told him about my condition yet, Mom. I was afraid of the stress. For the baby. He's going to blame himself for what happened with the press. I hate this."

They rested against each other in silence for a while, and Grace was comforted by her mother's rock-solid presence.

"You look wiped out," her mom said. "Do you think you can rest now? I'll talk to Jordan for you. I'm here to help, and Tony's going to stay a little longer too. You're not to worry about anything."

She had secretly hoped her mom would offer to talk to Jordan, and she'd tried not to feel guilty about that as well. "Tell Jordan, I'm sorry...and that I'll call him when I can."

The baby's safety had to come first. She knew he would understand.

CHAPTER 9

Jordan was close to leaving the stadium after a pre-season afternoon practice, and honestly, he couldn't wait to get home. The press had been hounding him, and his easy-going demeanor was shot. Grace had responded only briefly to his texts. He could feel her pulling away from him, and that one moment from their shopping trip kept playing over again in his mind. They'd been so close to giving it a second try. He knew it. A part of him was depressed by it all, and since the media was everywhere these days, he basically went to practice and then back to his apartment. He didn't like how caged in it made him feel. Not one bit.

For the first time since he'd become famous, he understood Grace's feelings about the invasion of her personal privacy. The media was keeping him from doing what he wanted, from what he needed to do. That couldn't continue.

His phone rang as he was changing, and when he noticed Grace was *finally* calling, he hurried out of the locker room without a shirt on to take the call in a more private setting.

"Hey!" he said, pitching his voice low. "How are you? I've been worried."

"Jordan, it's Meg."

"Meg?" Then it sunk in. "Something happened. What happened?" He pressed a hand to his forehead as tension shot through it.

"Grace is okay, but she needs to be in bed for a while with the baby. I came to stay with her."

Oh, God, no. Not this. "Are they all right? Dammit, Meg, when did this happen? Why didn't Grace call me?"

"I'll explain more when I see you."

Meg's familiar voice had soothed his hurts when he was a boy and cheered him on in his football games in more recent years. Now it was slightly stilted, and it was yet another slash to his aching heart. "I'm finishing up now. I'll be there as soon as I can." He strode back to the locker room.

"Jordan, I think it's better if I meet you at your place. I'll leave here shortly. Tony is going to stay with Grace."

"What? Why can't I come over? I want to see Grace." *I need to see her. And the baby.* If Grace was resting with the baby, it meant there was trouble. Had she almost miscarried from stress? He doubled over and had to fight to breathe. This was all his fault.

"Jordan, she's resting. And she needs it. I'll explain the particulars when we talk."

Shoving his own issues aside, Jordan took a moment before responding. "Okay, I'll be home shortly. I can text you the address or send a car for you. Whatever you'd like."

He wouldn't ask if there were reporters still camped out at Grace's. He knew there were. He'd hired a security service that watched over celebrities to wait outside her apartment in case she needed anything. Had she called him back, he would have told her that. But she hadn't, and he hadn't pushed it.

"I can find my own way there," she said, ever the tough-as-nails Midwesterner he knew her to be. "I'll see you soon, Jordan."

Jordan clicked off, staring down the hall. The energy buzz he always felt after a workout died away. It didn't matter that things were going well for the team. He felt old and tired. And helpless.

Jordan finally made it to his car in the parking lot. As the QB, he had a reserved spot right next to Coach Humphrey's 1992 blue weathered pickup. The truck was like his coach—unassuming, durable, and tough. The trade to the Rebels had been the start of his success. Grace had made him veal scaloppini instead of letting him take her out to celebrate his new, hefty contract. They'd made love after consuming way too much of an expensive Brunello he'd brought to her apartment.

Those days seemed eons ago right now.

Ignoring the team of reporters and scantily dressed women calling to him a short distance from the parking lot, he put his car in gear and sped out of the lot. The media followed him, of course, giving him that same hemmed in feeling.

When he got home, he rushed to tidy the house. The maid was coming over in a few days, everything was in shambles. When it was mostly presentable, he shaved and changed into khakis and a button-down shirt.

Jordan eyed his hair in the enormous slate-gray framed mirror in his bedroom. Even though she hadn't said so, he knew Grace didn't like it when he wore his hair a little long. Meg would hate it too. He licked his fingers and smoothed the hair back behind his ears in the hopes of making it more presentable to her. When he was finished, it was slightly more in keeping with his past look, but the hair curling at the collar couldn't be concealed. With a sigh, he headed to the family room.

Eyeing the carved teak bar forlornly, he headed to the kitchen instead to prepare tea and coffee and wait for Meg to arrive.

The security guard in the complex finally called him to say she was downstairs. Noticing a pillow slightly out of place on the buttery Italian leather couch, Jordan darted to straighten it. There were more nerves licking in his stomach than before the Super Bowl.

He jumped slightly when his discreet doorbell chimed. Jordan walked down the foyer, which was lit by a French chandelier, and opened the door.

"Hello, Jordan." Meg made an attempt to smile, but the corners of her mouth fell slowly. The sea-foam blouse she wore matched her eyes, but her white capris and low-heeled brown sandals made her seem even more petite than he remembered.

"Hey, Mrs. K."

Meg awkwardly stepped forward and embraced him. Surprised, he slid his arms around her. She patted his back as she always did before releasing him.

"Please come inside. We can get you some tea."

She hadn't been to his new place before. Neither had Grace. He had sold the old one and bought the penthouse after the breakup, needing a change in scene. There were too many memories of Grace in his old apartment, even though this one was still in Midtown. He planned to keep it—even when his new house was finished. It was closer to the action downtown and a good investment.

Meg took in the surroundings. He knew what she was seeing. His penthouse boasted an incredible view of Atlanta's downtown and bespoke of restrained wealth, an eye for beauty and comfort. It suited him to a T. He caught her wringing her hands, and since she was not a woman prone to nerves, it bothered him that his wealth would affect her like it did her daughter.

"I see you've been reading up on being a father," she said, gesturing to the stack of books neatly arranged on the Italian tile coffee table.

"You know how I like to prepare for things," he said, aware of the tension between them—one he didn't know how to alleviate.

He wanted more than anything to demand that she tell him what had happened with Grace and the baby, but it seemed she wanted to take her time. Pushing her would get him nowhere. She was like Grace that way.

He led her to the kitchen. It was smaller than his old one, which had been designed and stocked for Grace. He had intentionally gone simpler this time around.

Jordan had already warmed the water in the stainless steel teakettle, so he simply turned on the gas to reheat it. After turning on the coffee maker, he turned around. Her green eyes were lasering into him. He felt as if she was reading his mind. She would guess about the kitchen. God knew what else she was picking up on.

"Please sit down." He gestured awkwardly to the bar stools by the marble countertop.

"Do you have a few telephone books I can stand on to get into it?" she asked, attempting to use levity to break some of the ice between them.

He couldn't have been more grateful.

"Nope. They don't really make those anymore—even for short ladies like you."

They shared a smile, and he was able to take an easier breath.

"Let's sit at the table. I'll get your tea."

He took the teapot he'd pulled out of a back cabinet and poured in the water. Like Grace, she loved chamomile with lemon and honey. The movers had packed the tea up with the rest of his stuff. His heart had lifted at the sight of it, and he'd kept it in the hopes she might surprise him sometime after his Super Bowl win. He'd been an idiot. Sam was right—he'd shamed her by letting himself be photographed with those other women. Grace never would have come to him if not for the baby.

Meg sat quietly as he brought over the teapot and mug. He smiled and then poured the coffee he'd made for himself.

When he sat down across from her, he said, "So, tell me about Grace."

She told him the doctor's prognosis in simple terms. He held her eyes the whole time, listening intently, while his stomach pitched in terror. She really could lose the baby. From his reading, he knew how vital the placenta was to a healthy pregnancy.

"I'm so sorry, Mrs. K. This is all my fault."

"Oh, Jordan," she said, her voice breaking a little. "I'm sorry too. For all of you."

"You must be so mad at me," he said, his voice breaking. "And Pat and Mike and John."

She placed her hand on his forearm. "We wish things were different for you both. This is hard...on everyone."

He clenched his fist. "I hate this, you know? All of it. I don't know how to make it right. I'm trying to do what I love, but my career keeps hurting Grace. And now our baby. *Oh, God.*"

"Jordan, I've known you since you were born. The Jordan that grew up in Deadwood had a life I understood. But all the VIP treatment and those women who flock around you." She waved her hand. "No one can understand all *that*. I won't pretend to. Only you can know if it's making you happy."

Of course she would have seen pictures of the extravagant parts of his lifestyle. Did she also wonder why he hadn't asked Grace to marry him before? He was too afraid to ask.

"You and Grace are going to have to make it work for the baby's sake. I don't know how, but you will. You'll soon learn that in order to be a good parent, you have to put what you want behind what's best for your kids. It's not easy, let me tell you."

His mother had told him the same thing many times after his dad had walked out on them. He hoped he could be as good a parent as she'd been to him. And if she managed to help him a little from heaven, he wouldn't look a gift horse in the mouth.

Meg traced the rim of her mug. "You're trying to do what you think is right by Grace. The idea of being neighbors is a good one, if you ask me."

"That means a lot to me, coming from you," he said harshly, taking a drink of his coffee to wet his throat. "Especially when I didn't ask your daughter to marry me before." All right, he was putting it out there.

"That's not my business." Meg paused. "Grace has to find her way through all this too. I hate to say this, but she's broken under this, Jordan. I've never seen her this vulnerable. Being a mom is a big thing, but losing you and her dreams for the life she wanted... It's like she's lost a piece of herself."

He could only nod. He didn't know what else to say.

"She'll face it because that's what a Kincaid does. I know my daughter. It's unimaginable to me how she must feel. The media spectacle only made it all worse."

"I wish they'd never shown up." He wanted to pound the table in frustration. "I want to obliterate all of them."

"You're not alone in that," she said coldly. "But let's focus on Grace and what's best. Being pregnant takes a lot out of the body."

And yet, before the recent media event, she'd been glowing. He'd felt her coming back to life and hoped their near reconciliation was one of the reasons. "I'm glad she's resting, Meg. But I can't imagine how upset she is about not being able to go in for work. She loves her job."

"It will be hard on her, but she'll do it for the baby. That's all that matters now."

"I couldn't agree more," he said. "What can I do to help?"

She clenched his hand hard, and his chest grew tight with foreboding. "The doctor thinks it might be best to let Grace rest without seeing you right now. Things between you are stressful, and stress isn't good for the baby."

Oh, Jesus. Not see her? I'm like Typhoid Mary. "If that's what the doctor thinks is best. I want... Oh, God." He felt tears burn his eyes. "I just want them both to be okay."

"Give Grace some time to heal and get this baby out of the woods. In the meantime, you can work on a plan to keep the media away and allay her fears when she moves into the new house."

"I've already hired a company. You have my word that I'll do my best to handle the situation." He couldn't stop them from doing their job, but he could do a better job of protecting Grace and the baby.

She patted his hand. "I know there's a lot of...stress and sadness now, but the joy of seeing your baby when he or she arrives... Jordan, it will change everything."

Everyone said that, from the experts to his fellow players. He still didn't completely know what it meant. But he planned to be as ready as he could be. They could all use a little joy.

"I'll stay away, Mrs. K, until Grace and the baby are

better," he said, feeling his throat grow tight. "But you'll tell her I'll miss her. I've gotten used to...seeing her again. And the baby growing..."

He watched her blink tears away for a moment. "I'll tell her, Jordan."

"I was sorry you weren't at the Super Bowl," he made himself say.

Her eyes darkened. "We were too, Jordan. The boys came over to watch it with Pat and me. We were proud of you, Jordan. Your mother would have been too if God hadn't seen fit to take her from us so young. You worked so hard for so long. You deserved it."

Jordan found that he couldn't respond. Man, he missed his mom. On days like this, all he wanted to do was dial her number and talk to her.

They sat quietly, drinking in the silence until Meg announced she needed to get back to Grace. When they reached the front door, Jordan moved first, holding onto her tightly until she pressed back. As she walked to the elevator, he had to bite his lip not to call out to her and ask her to tell Grace that he loved her.

CHAPTER 10

Grace's spotting didn't stop over the next few weeks, but it didn't worsen either. Her mom arranged for a leave of absence from the hospital to stay with her longer. The bed rest was a constant frustration, but her mom's presence helped. She didn't know what she would have done without her.

Her mom called Jordan with periodic updates at Grace's request, but whenever she listened to her mom talk to him on the phone, she had to fight the tears that wanted to streak down her cheeks. And the urge to grab the phone and talk to him. She missed hearing his beautiful voice.

His Once Upon a Dare guys showered her with well wishes and presents, everything from giant teddy bears and cashmere baby blankets for the baby to French copper pots and white truffles harvested near Alba for her. She suspected Jordan was behind the ongoing encouragement—that it was his way of staying connected—and it made her miss him even more.

As more days passed, Grace relaxed, knowing the baby was further out of the woods. They were going to make it, and sometimes, she gave in to the tears of relief at that thought.

An oppressive humidity hung over Atlanta on a Wednesday evening in early July just two days after America's birthday when she felt it: a huge tugging in her womb. She put her hands on her belly.

"What's wrong?" her mom immediately asked, setting her knitting aside and rising from her normal perch in the rocking chair they'd brought into Grace's bedroom.

Her gaze flew to her mother's. "I'm not sure. There was this tugging. Didn't feel like the usual."

"Hmm..." her mom said, falling into nurse mode. "Let's hang out a little while and see what happens."

Her mom placed her hand on the watermelon shape that had become her belly.

A few minutes later, there was another tug, this one stronger than the last. The pain seemed to shoot up her side. "Ow. Are these contractions?" *Please no. I'm not full-term yet.*

"They might be," her mom said. "Could be Braxton Hicks. Any back pain?"

Her alarm was rising, and she could feel the urgent beat of her heart in her chest. "Yes, for a few hours now. I thought I was just uncomfortable. Lying down all the time makes me feel like a beached whale. Mom, I'm scared."

"Don't be," her mom said, cupping her face and staring into her eyes. "I'm here. Everything is going to be fine, Gracie."

But soon the pains sharpened.

"Why don't you call your doctor?" her mom said finally. "I think she's going to want you to come to the hospital, but let's confirm."

Sure enough, after a short call, her doctor asked her if she wanted them to send an ambulance. Her mom shook her head when she asked her, saying they didn't need the fanfare.

"I think we should call Jordan and see if he can take us, Grace," her mom surprised her by saying. "You don't have to have him in the room when the baby is born, but he'll want to be at the hospital. He'll feel more included that way."

Just the thought of seeing Jordan again in the flesh had her insides churning, but it was the right move. "Will you call him?"

"Sure thing, sweetheart," her mom said, grabbing her phone. "Hi, Jordan. Don't freak out, but Grace is having some contractions, and the doctor wants her to come to the hospital. Can you come and pick us up?"

Her mom listened for a moment and then said, "Good. See you soon."

While they waited for Jordan, her mom helped her change out of a cotton nightgown and into a T-shirt and stretchy pants. The hospital bag they'd packed together weeks ago came out of her closet, and Grace tried not to panic.

Jordan must have broken every speed limit because he arrived ten minutes earlier than she'd expected from his new digs in Midtown. Her hands curved around her belly when she heard him knock on the door. Her mom rose from the bed and went to greet him.

When he arrived in the doorway, he was smiling. She knew a game face when she saw one, and apparently he'd practiced one for her.

"Hey there, Gracie girl. Are you ready to see if our baby plans to come into the world today?"

Grace took her hand off her belly, noticing how his eyes darted to it quickly before looking back at her. She tried to return his smile. "Sure, let's get this show on the road."

She moved to sit up on the bed, and Jordan darted forward. "Here, let me help you. You might be a little off center from being in bed so long."

He reached a supportive arm around her back as she scooted awkwardly from the middle of the bed. Grace didn't shrink away from his touch, but a shiver went through her. She blamed it on the contractions, but knew it was a lie.

"Maybe it would be easier if I carried you to the car," Jordan said, frowning at her. "I don't want you tiring yourself out. You might need to conserve your energy."

"Okay. Good idea."

Jordan lifted her easily. "Just like I thought. Even with the baby, you're still a lightweight."

"I don't want the baby to come early," she whispered to him suddenly, letting the safe feeling of being in his arms wash over her.

He met her eyes, and in them she could see the worry he was trying so hard to hide. "I know, sweetheart." He pressed his cheek to hers in a gesture of pure comfort. "What did your mom tell you, Gracie?"

She could feel tears well up in her eyes. "She said the baby is far enough along."

"Has your mom ever been wrong?" he asked, casting a glance at her mom, who was watching them by the door.

Her mouth tipped up slightly. "Not usually."

"Well, then there's no reason to worry, is there?" he said matter-of-factly.

She nodded. "Are you scared?"

"A little, for you," he confessed harshly. "If I could take this from you, I would. You've already gone through so much."

"You would look silly with this watermelon belly," she teased, trying to bolster them both.

"Oh, but think of all the new clothes I could wear," he said, teasing her right back.

She burrowed her face in his shoulder, inhaling his musky aftershave. And then she felt another sharp pain in her back and made an anguished sound. Grace gripped his arms as the sensation built.

"Breathe, Grace," he said in his team voice. "Deep breaths. Like me, okay?"

If the pain hadn't been stronger this time, she might have teased him for knowing about breathing during labor. More research, no doubt.

Her mom picked up her bag by the door. "We'd better get going," she said in a calm but firm tone.

Cradling Grace against his chest, Jordan followed Meg out of the apartment. She locked it behind them, then continued on ahead, giving them some space.

"So, what's it like having your own personal nurse?" Jordan asked.

"Wonderful. An angel in disguise."

"I'm so glad you had her," he said, walking briskly through the lobby. "It helped me worry less."

As they reached the door, Grace felt a rush of panic surge through her. "There's no press out there, is there?"

He shook his head. "No, Grace. I have new ways of diverting them. I'd never let them close to you and the baby."

The absolute certainty in his voice calmed her, but when they arrived at the front door, he stopped. "Do you trust me, Grace?"

She nodded, and her mom pushed the door open. The sunlight was harsh on her eyes, and the humidity was oppressive. He led them to a black SUV parked with its hazards on in the fire lane.

"What do you think of my daddy mobile?" he asked.

Grace's mom opened the back passenger door. "Beats that old minivan I had to drive with you kids."

Jordan gently lowered her to the back seat, and her mom rearranged the fluffy pillows piled there to help her get comfortable.

"You brought pillows?" Grace asked Jordan.

"This is a full service ride," he said, handing her a blanket from the front passenger seat.

She gave him a look. "It's almost a hundred degrees out."

A shadow crossed his face, and for a minute she could see the helplessness he was fighting. "I thought... Right. Let me turn up the air."

Jordan stowed her bag while her mom settled beside her in the back.

He drove slowly down the street. "What hospital are we headed to? I forgot to ask."

Her mom told him to go to Northside. "The hospital has a celebrity entrance we're supposed to use. Dr. Jessica told me where to go."

Grace looked over at her. "You didn't tell me that."

Her mom shrugged. "You didn't need to worry about it. I took care of it."

When they arrived at the hospital complex, her mom gave Jordan directions to the side entrance. The minute he parked and exited the vehicle, two hospital workers rushed out with a wheelchair. Before she knew it, Grace was being wheeled into a private elevator, her mom and Jordan following right behind her. Dr. Saunders was waiting for them when the doors opened on the third floor. She had on chartreuse tennis shoes.

"Hey, Grace," she said with an intent look. "Meg, it's nice to see you. And you must be Jordan. It's good to finally meet you."

Jordan nodded, resting his hands on Grace's shoulder. "Yes, thank you for taking such good care of Grace and our baby."

Our baby, Grace thought, and hearing him say those simple words was enough to put tears in her eyes.

"It's a pleasure," Dr. Saunders said. "Well, Grace, you just made it to thirty-three weeks. That's all we could hope for, given what's happened. Let's get y'all settled in so we can see if we're dealing with the final performance or the opening act. We have a private suite waiting for you."

As they wheeled her down the halls, Grace could feel herself tightening up. She hated hospitals, and even though they were bringing her to the maternity ward, she was still nervous.

"Grace." Jordan extended his hand to her. "You got this."

She nodded and grabbed the comfort he was offering.

When they arrived at the suite, the nurse wheeled her into the room, and they got her into the hospital bed with Jordan's help. The room was decorated warmly in the same soft yellow as the hallway. High-backed chairs sat like an old couple across from a purple print couch and rocking chair. It was friendlier than the average hotel room, but Grace still couldn't pretend she wasn't in a hospital.

"You might want to step out a sec, Jordan," her mom said, patting his arm. "They're going to get her into a gown and examine her."

"There's a private room off to the right," Dr. Saunders told him, pointing. "That way you can be close enough to call."

Jordan's eyes sought hers one last time before he smiled at her and left.

Her heart clutched, and she had to admit the truth. It hurt to see him go.

CHAPTER 11

Jordan had mixed feelings leaving Grace. The private birthing coach he'd consulted in case Grace wanted him present at the birth had shown him videos and walked him through the process—either a natural birth or a Caesarean. Either way, Jordan was prepared for both. He would just take his cue from Meg and Grace. They would tell him how much they wanted him around.

The private waiting room was smaller and decorated with a burgundy printed chair rail. There was a medium-sized television mounted on the wall in front of two high-backed chairs in navy. He sat in one and sorted the magazines on the small coffee table, feeling the need to organize and control something. He noted that over half were about parenthood and babies. Some Jordan had already read. He'd subscribed to a few on the advice of his coach.

At first the magazines and books had read like a foreign language—who would have thought there was so much lingo specific to childcare?—but he'd learned from them. Some of the information felt a little off given how his mother raised him. But he figured that's what made parenthood individual. Everyone did it differently. It was clearly not a science.

He texted a few of his Once Upon a Dare brothers while he waited. They were all eager to hear the news about Grace. A few of them asked if he wanted them to fly out, but he told them to chill until he knew more. Although he appreciated their support, he could barely focus his attention on texting. All he could think about was what was going on with Grace and their baby. Besides, if they all showed up at the hospital, the media would certainly put together what was going on.

Autocorrect kept messing up his words, so he finally stopped texting and let himself process how it had felt to see Grace today. His heart had stopped. She had looked so scared and yet so beautiful. And her belly. The sheer size of it blew his mind, and when he'd felt her contraction while holding her in his arms…

Shit got real.

Meg came in about fifteen minutes later. He knew because he'd checked his watch at least twenty times. He jumped to his feet, spilling the magazines he'd arranged. The smile on her face might have been perfectly believable if not for the worry knotting her brows.

"Jordan, Dr. Saunders thinks it would be safer to do a Caesarean given everything Grace has gone through. There's some increased bleeding now that labor's started. They're prepping her right now. Dr. Saunders gave permission for me to scrub in and assist."

He'd felt nauseous watching the scalpel cut across the woman's belly in the video. How much worse was he going to feel knowing that was happening to Grace? "I'm glad you're going to be in there with her, Meg."

She gave him a short smile. "Would you like to join

us? Grace said she was okay with it if you are."

His knees almost buckled. She was trusting him. Grace was finally trusting him. "Yes...that would be... great...just great."

"Well, let's get you in there." She rested her hand on his arm for a moment. "It'll be fine, Jordan."

He took one of her hands and squeezed it. "I'm so glad you're here, Mrs. K. What would we do without you?"

Meg led the way. Some medical assistants helped them both scrub up and don hospital gowns. When they walked back into the main room, he stopped short. There was a white shield across Grace's chest to prevent her from seeing the procedure. Her engorged belly was bare and brightly lit under the lights.

He swallowed before cautiously angling closer, immediately intimidated despite the video he'd seen. Nothing could have prepared him for this. He was afraid they were going to hurt her, that the scalpel was going to do permanent damage. And there was nothing he could do.

"Welcome to the party, Jordan," Dr. Saunders said, her dark eyes the only part of her face not hidden by the mask.

His head was buzzing so much he couldn't form a response. Then Grace turned her head to look at him, and his legs went rubbery. That instant connection between them seemed to fill the room. Her moss-green eyes were scared and frantic.

He rushed forward and grabbed her hand. "I'm here now," he told her, reaching deep for his strength. "It's going to be fine, Grace. They're going to take great care of you and our baby."

She nodded frantically. "I'm glad you're here, Jordan."

"I wouldn't be anywhere else," he told her, his heart rapping against his chest.

The nurses pulled up a chair for him by the head of the bed. Had she feared he would faint? The chair was too small for him, so he sat on the edge. He was tall enough to see over the screen and couldn't look away as the scalpel flashed under the bright lights. If Grace could endure this, the least he could do was bear witness.

Biting his lip under the mask hard enough to taste blood, he watched as the scalpel found its mark and drew a line across her belly. Blood followed in its wake.

Grace gripped his hand, and he feared she was feeling pain. "Are you okay?"

"There's some tugging," she said, her voice charged with emotion.

"It's okay, Grace," Meg told her. "Pressure is common even though the epidural numbs from the waist down."

Suddenly Jordan's eyes flew back to Grace's belly. There was a lot of blood, but there was also a little baby being lifted out.

Holy shit.

"It's a girl," Dr. Saunders announced, holding up the baby for them to see.

She squalled at the top of her lungs, and Jordan was suddenly glad he was sitting down. His head exploded. *A girl.*

Grace started crying, and soon he was pressing his cheek against hers, crying too.

"We have a girl, Gracie," he said, his voice hoarse. "We have a daughter."

"Oh, God," she whispered. "A little girl. Oh, Jordan."

He watched as the nurses took his daughter over to examine her and clean her up. They allowed Meg to help.

"She's passed the Apgar test," Meg said, swaddling her in a pink blanket one of the nurses handed her. She picked up the tiny bundle and brought her over to them. Tears were wetting Meg's mask too.

Grace held out her arms, and her mom settled the baby down on her chest. Filled with wonder, Jordan released Grace's hand so he could reach out to finger the blanket holding their daughter.

"She's so beautiful," Meg said softly. "You couldn't have done better, you two."

They huddled together as a unit, eyeing the small face protruding from the swaddling. Her eyes were slightly open and dark blue. She had small, cupid-shaped lips and a good crop of brown hair with a tinge of red. Delicate fingers barely rested outside the blanket, so small and transparent Jordan could barely comprehend it.

"Just look at her," Grace said, tears running down her cheeks unchecked.

"She's perfect." Jordan reached out a shaking hand and gently ran a finger along his daughter's cheek, amazed at how soft her skin was. "She's so tiny."

"She's tiny because she's early," Meg said. "She weighed in at six pounds, two ounces. Not too shabby after everything she's been through."

He and Grace didn't seem to know what to say after that. Both of them stared at their daughter and gently touched her face, their hands uniting in a mission to make sure she was real.

Meg smoothed a hand over Grace's head. "They need to sew you up now, honey. Then they'll take you to recovery. I'll stay with you. The baby needs to go to recovery too, but you'll get her back soon, I promise."

"Wait!" Jordan said when he saw the nurse headed their way. "They're taking her away?" No one had told him that. He felt a spurt of anger.

"Would you like to go with her, Jordan?" Meg asked.

"Would that be okay, Dr. Saunders?"

"Sure," the doctor said. "We need to put her in the NICU to keep her warm. But you can hold her for a few minutes beforehand, I think. Get to know your daughter."

Grace grabbed his hand. "Go with her, Jordan. I don't want her to be alone."

The hoarseness in her voice had him fighting tears. "I won't leave her alone, Grace."

She sniffed. "I know we didn't talk about names because of...stuff, but if it's all right, I thought we'd call her Ella Allison. For your mom."

Pain flashed in his heart. *"Grace."*

Allison had been his mother's given name, but she'd gone by Alice most of her life. Jordan felt more tears spill. He quickly knuckled them away. "It's a beautiful name. Mom would have loved it."

Grace gave him a soft smile, and her green eyes seemed to glow now. He was mesmerized. "I think she knows, Jordan. I feel her here. Don't you?"

Goosebumps broke out across his skin. "Yeah," he agreed. He wasn't a spiritual man, but he'd felt her presence at big games before. And he felt it now. That sense of peace and love that surpassed regular moments in life.

The nurse cleared her throat. "We need to take her to recovery."

Jordan leaned down to kiss Grace's cheek. "We'll see you in a bit. I'll take care of her, Grace, I promise."

When she nodded fiercely, he carefully took the baby from her arms.

Ella Allison fit perfectly in the crook of his arms. He'd practiced with a doll at home, wanting to be ready. But she wasn't a doll. She was his daughter, and the most beautiful thing he'd ever seen in his life.

"Follow me, please," the nurse said, and he gave Grace one last look before heading to recovery.

Jordan sank into the rocker the nurse suggested he use. He was still trying to relax his arms, but he couldn't stop staring at her. She barely moved, but when she did, it was to stretch—like she was expanding into all this new space after being tucked away in her mother's womb for so long.

"You have that deer-in-headlights look that most first-time fathers have," Meg said, making him look up.

She walked quietly across the room and placed a hand on his arm.

"It's..." He struggled to form a sentence.

"Yeah, I know," Meg said, patting him. "You did a good job in there."

"Jesus." He cuddled Ella closer. "I didn't do anything. Grace did it all. Sorry I cussed. I'm...not myself. I've been working on cleaning up my language."

Meg chuckled. "You came. You stood up. You comforted. That's all fathers can really do anyway." She looked down at her granddaughter's face. "I can already see both of you in Ella's features. She has the shape of Grace's eyes and your nose."

His eyes gazed down at his daughter, and suddenly he could see it too. He leaned his head against Meg's arm, needing the connection to her. "Oh, Mrs. K."

"Yeah, it's pretty awesome stuff, Dad."

"Dad," he muttered hoarsely. "That's going to make me either freak out or cry. Not sure which right now."

"Oh, you're going to do just fine. I need to get back to Grace."

He didn't look up from his daughter's face. He realized Ella's hair had the same reddish tint as her mother's. "Tell Grace I..."

His throat seized up as he heard the ticker tape

in his brain play again. *I love her*, it seemed to shout. Anguished, he looked at Meg.

"Tell her I love her and that Ella's okay," he said finally, unable to stop the words from swirling out of him.

She looked down, and for a moment he was afraid she was going to say something, but then she simply walked out.

Jordan blew out a breath. It had been dancing on his tongue for months now. Whether Meg delivered the message or not was her choice. Right now, he was feeling all the love in the Universe.

All too quickly, they took Ella to the NICU.

As he waited alone, he grew restless. He flipped through magazines. He got up and sat back down. He paced. He wanted to see his new daughter. He wanted to see Grace. He felt bereft without them.

Meg finally came back a little while later to tell him that Grace had finished nursing, and he could return to her suite. He was caught off-guard, so he muttered, "Oh," like an idiot.

Nursing. Breasts. Milk. Yeah, Grace wouldn't want to share that with him. She'd always been modest, and he didn't expect a baby would change that. The whole nursing thing was a mystery to him despite all he'd read. The articles and books all indicated it was an important element of the bonding between a mother and child. But he'd also read how much fathers enjoyed being included in that bonding, and he'd hoped Grace might let him be a part of it. He'd have to wait and see.

When Jordan entered the suite again, his bones melted like wax. Grace was lying back with Ella tucked into her arms, her head tilted so she could gaze down at the little face. He walked over, feeling time slow. Grace looked up when he pulled a chair next to her bed. Her smile was so radiant that he could only grin right back at her.

"Isn't she the most beautiful thing you've ever seen?" she asked, pure joy cascading out of her like sunlight.

He nodded. Words were inadequate.

Grace handed him the baby, and he blinked down at her. Her little face, so peaceful, peeked out of the soft pink blanket. She seemed to be sleeping.

"You don't have to share her," he heard himself say.

Grace only smiled all the brighter. "Sure I do. Ella needs you too."

Jordan cuddled her close to his chest. "Ella," he said directly to his daughter for the first time and felt her stretch like she was already responding to her name.

When his eyes met Grace's, he couldn't look away.

CHAPTER 12

Grace ended up staying in the hospital for four days because of the C-section, and after weeks of bed rest, she was chomping at the bit to get out.

But Ella made everything worthwhile. She seemed to eat all the time. And when she stretched her little arms or cracked her eyes open, Grace felt so much love well up inside her, she was sure she would overflow with it. Then there were the practical matters of learning how to breastfeed and change the baby's diaper carefully with the umbilical cord still intact, but Grace reveled in it.

When he wasn't at the hospital, Jordan oversaw the rapid moving of Grace's things from her apartment to the new house with Tony's help. The baby's room was already set up—had been for weeks—which was all Grace really cared about. So long as she had a bed to sleep in, it didn't matter.

Jordan mentioned his house next door had just been finished as well. He seemed a little stressed about his own move, but Grace couldn't be sure if it was because the reality of their new living arrangement was upon them.

Even though Ella had arrived early, the doctor said she could come home with Grace; her lungs were developed enough, thank God, and her birth weight was solid. Truth be told, if they'd made the baby stay, Grace would have stayed too. There was no way she was leaving her baby girl.

The doctor also said Ella needed to put on more weight, and Jordan agreed, commenting that she weighed less than a football. She certainly wasn't much bigger than one. She seemed so small in Jordan's massive hands, but Grace loved the way he looked down at her with a sense of wonder.

Of course, she did the same.

Leaving the hospital proved nerve-wracking considering all the press the Dean baby was generating. Word had leaked out, but Jordan had promised he had a plan to keep them out of the media's grip.

They snuck out the back of the hospital as Jordan's PR person gave a press conference near the front entrance. Black SUVs flanked their vehicle when they were a few blocks from the hospital. Jordan had told her he'd hired professional bodyguards for their family and asked her to trust him. Grace didn't feel like she had a better option, but it was all a bit intimidating.

They sailed along the interstate, and a little tension eased from Grace's chest when she realized they hadn't been followed. Jordan took the exit to their new place and wound around two-lane highways before turning onto a side road named Georgia's Place. Their compound was buried well behind the main road, but Grace knew that wasn't going to stop the jackals. They would be lying in wait.

Grace reached for her mother's hand as they neared

the gated entrance. Media trucks were camped outside, just as she'd suspected, but beefy men in all black with ear mikes herded the animated press corps back as the black wrought-iron gate swung open.

"It's all right, Grace," Jordan said, catching her eyes in the rear-view mirror. "The press can't see inside the car, and they won't get onto the property. You and Ella are perfectly safe here."

In that moment, she couldn't ask what would happen when they tried to leave.

"There will always be a guard at the gate, okay?" Jordan said, a hard edge to his voice.

Her mom bumped her in the shoulder. "If the guards don't do their job, we'll just call Jordan's teammates. They'll put the fear of God into any would-be pursuers."

Jordan gave a fake laugh. "You know it. My Once Upon A Dare guys can't wait to meet Ella once the season is over. They've got our backs too."

Grace could only muster a weak smile.

They passed through the oaks lining the lane. Grace loved that the property was large and mostly wooded. The trees looked like happy giants eager to protect them.

As they drove further down the road, Grace took in all the changes from the last time she'd been here. Before it had been early spring, and now it was mid-summer. The grounds looked lusher somehow. Grace recognized a variety of trees she hadn't noticed before: magnolias, cherry, Bradford pears, dogwoods, and some lovely Chinese maples clustered in an artful display.

When they reached the fork in the lane, Grace let her gaze follow it. Jordan's house rose from the ground with such majesty that her chest tightened. If her house's purpose was to attract visitors, his was to wow and impress. The design of the two-level house was sleek and modern. There were balconies and arches cascading across the front as if in perpetual motion. To Grace, it was reminiscent of Barcelona's architecture, which she knew he loved.

Crepe myrtles flanked a small rose garden leading from Jordan's house to hers, separated by a cheery yellow garden gate. She could tell the installation was recent from the freshly planted grass, the square sod lines still visible. More crepe myrtles flanked the fence along their properties. Their blooms were bright red and white.

He drove down the lane to her house and pulled to a halt in the circular driveway. Meticulously groomed bushes and hedges rode low on the ground before her front porch.

Grace's diaphragm tightened. This was her dream house—no, it was hers and Ella's. And that modern one only a short distance away was Jordan's. Seeing their two places, so different and yet so close together, only magnified the sense of separation between them.

For years, Grace had wanted to raise a family in this beautiful yellow house—yet her new home was in Atlanta and not Deadwood, and she was going to live there as a single mother with her new baby. It took effort not to give in to tears.

All her old dreams were gone, and if not for Ella, she wouldn't even be here with Jordan.

"My goodness," her mom whispered, releasing a slow breath. "It's the exact image of the house in Deadwood. I...wasn't prepared for that. Despite what you told me. Oh, Grace."

She gripped the hand her mom held out and let her gaze rest on Ella. They would make it a home together. Even if Ella's daddy lived next door instead of at home with them. She was already worrying how she would explain that to Ella as her daughter grew older.

To Grace's relief, Jordan came around to help her with the car seat. The bed rest had made her a little weak. Or maybe it was walking into her new home with her baby and Jordan.

"We can put Ella in the bassinet upstairs after I've given you the tour," Jordan said, holding Ella in her carrier. He forced a smile and led the way down the flagstone path to the front porch.

He opened the door and let Meg and Grace precede him into the house. Her mom muttered, "My goodness," as Grace's mouth dropped open. She knew Tony had helped him, but she hadn't expected her things to be arranged with such care and skill.

It already looked like home. Her farm table was arranged in front of bay windows to the left of the kitchen. Her couch and loveseat were situated in front of a fireplace on the far wall. Her coffee table sat in the center, her cooking magazines and coffee table book of Italy arranged amidst her assortment of vanilla-scented candles. A sizeable flat-screen television, which had not come from her apartment, stood across from the couch. She would have to talk to Jordan about that later. Her pictures of Italian bridges and Parisian café scenes hung on the walls. Of course, there were some blank walls. Jordan had told her he and Tony wouldn't fill the house beyond what they thought appropriate, saying Grace needed to make her mark.

But the two men knew her so well, there wouldn't be much for her to do. The style fit the open floor plan to a T.

"So, what do you think?" he asked, easily holding Ella's carrier. "Did we do okay?"

He seemed as nervous as the rest of them. They all knew what this house meant to her—and what it wasn't.

Grace caught sight of her mother's face as she turned

to look at him. Her mom looked as stunned as she felt. "It's..." She searched for the right word, seeing how tight his shoulders seemed. "It's beautiful, Jordan." *Like I'd always imagined the house in Deadwood looking.*

He smiled and let out a breath. "Whew! What a relief. Tony and I were sweating bullets. Let me show you the rest."

She followed him through the rest of the bottom floor, which sported a gym, a small office, and a cozy sunroom filled with houseplants from her apartment. It looked out onto an impressive gray flagstone patio with a fire pit. A collection of wrought-iron patio furniture with thick red cushions fanned the area. Candle pillars of varying sizes and potted plant arrangements spilling from exotic containers complemented the inviting space.

"Those aren't mine," she said, loving what he'd done, but worrying about the boundaries she felt they needed to set. "You know how I feel about you spending money."

He gave her a playful wink. "Ella wanted it for you— for taking so much time off to make sure she arrived so beautiful and healthy."

So that was how it was going to be. She felt her heart tear a little. "You get a pass this time."

"Being a new daddy with the best little girl in the world makes me feel pretty exuberant," he said, leading them to the main staircase. "I want her to have everything."

Even though she knew the upstairs had four large bedrooms, it still seemed huge after her small two-bedroom apartment. The two guest bedrooms were both tastefully decorated in styles Grace would have chosen.

"I'm going to take the navy room while I'm here, Grace," her mom told her as they walked down the hall.

"I'm glad you're staying for another month, Mom," she said, relieved she wouldn't have to adjust to two huge life transitions alone. Being a nurse, her mom's reasons for staying had been more practical. She'd wanted to give Grace's incision enough time to heal.

"I have to see you and Ella settled," her mom said. "Does this room face east, Jordan? I like having the sun stream in when I wake up."

"It does," Jordan said.

A farm girl at heart, her mother liked to rise with the sun. "I'll make sure not to sleep on that side then," Grace added. "After working late at the restaurant, I'll want the dark in the morning."

"Oh, I know," Jordan said, and the timbre of his voice reminded her of all the mornings they'd awoken together in total darkness and made love only to discover it was late morning when they rolled out of bed.

Her mom snorted, and Grace felt her cheeks burn with embarrassment.

"Let's check out my room," Grace said, wanting to give him a playful shove for that comment. In the old days, she would have, but things were different between them now.

"This way," he grandly gestured, and so she entered the master suite ahead of him.

The room had a recessed ceiling with a plantation-style fan above Grace's bed. Her furniture was largely arranged like it had been in her old bedroom, although this room was much larger.

"You'll sleep with the angels in here, Grace," her mom said. "It's beautiful, Jordan."

"Yes, it is," she said, running her hand along her comforter, eager to ground herself in the familiarity of her things. The familiar floor plan intermixed with her treasures made her feel small and somewhat uncomfortable.

"You made some adjustments here too," she said,

seeing the master bath with a Jacuzzi tub, a sleek vanity with not one but two sinks, and a steam shower. The walk-in closet was two times larger than her last one and lined in cedar.

"Stop thinking about the money," Jordan ordered curtly and walked out of the room with Ella.

She wasn't just thinking about money. Grace realized she was going to have to stop comparing it to her dream house in Deadwood. And so, she said goodbye to it in her heart, resolved to make peace with *this* house and *this* life she was living. Otherwise she would be miserable, and that's not how she wanted things to be.

"I still can't get over this, Grace," her mom said in an undertone, putting her arm around her. "Seeing this house will give your father chills."

"I don't want to speak about the house in Deadwood again, Mom," she told her.

Their eyes met, and her mom nodded.

"Grace, come look at how the nursery turned out!" Jordan called.

When Grace walked in, she pressed her hand to her mouth. She'd seen pictures and given her input from the hospital, but it moved her something fierce to see her new daughter in the room she would call her own.

Jordan set Ella's carrier down on the white frilly daybed lining the wall and sat beside her. "See, she's smiling. I knew you'd like your room, sweetheart."

Tears spilled down Grace's cheeks as she took in the scene. However they had arrived here, they were a family—not a perfect family, but a family nonetheless.

"It's so beautiful, Jordan," she said in a hoarse voice. "All of it. Thank you."

He looked up, the corners of his eyes tense with concern. "You're welcome. I just want you and Ella to be happy. That's all I care about."

She gave him a teary smile, and he quickly looked away, his ears red with emotion.

"Be hard not to be happy in this room," her mom said, touching the white crib. "It's like baby dream land in here. I wish we could have given you kids a room like this growing up, but we did the best we could."

She hugged her mom. "We had each other, and that's all that mattered." And it was true. She'd been happy growing up in the old house that blew a fuse if someone ran the dishwasher and microwave at the same time. She and her brothers had managed to share one bathroom without too much conflict. It was the only life they'd known.

But Jordan's life was bigger than that. So was hers, by association, if she was being honest with herself.

Grace picked up a giraffe from the various stuffed animals in the toy chest and hugged it. The pillows decorating the room were shaped like numbers and letters. One group spelled their daughter's name and another spelled love. Grace liked that best of all.

The wall mural Jordan had insisted on had turned out great. As they'd discussed, it depicted a cartoon-like safari scene. Giraffes, elephants, monkeys, and cute little lion cubs stood in artfully arranged poses near trees or out in the savannah grasses. They all had smiling faces, and Grace couldn't help but smile too over the fullness in her heart.

"It will be a while before she can appreciate all of this," her mom said, sitting beside Jordan on the day bed. "But when she does...oh...she's going to have a lot of fun in here."

Grace walked over to the rocker she'd bought for herself from a local carpenter. When she sat in it, the wood seemed to hug her body. "Oh, I like this."

Her eyes tracked to the changing table stocked with

little baby diapers. She still couldn't believe how small they were. Ella suddenly stretched and yawned without opening her eyes, melting Grace's heart. Jordan reached down to adjust her pink baby cap, stroking her cheek like he simply couldn't believe she was his.

"Let's go downstairs and make some lunch," her mom said, crossing to the door. "Why don't you put her in her bassinet and turn on the baby monitor?"

Grace was reluctant to leave Ella upstairs, and her mom seemed to know it. She gently pulled her out of the rocker.

"Come on, Gracie," her mom said. "I know she's just out of the chute, but you can leave her to sleep for a few hours. Trust me, in a couple of months, you'll wish she still slept this much. Plus, you need to eat and go for a walk to regain your strength."

Her mom was right. "Okay."

Jordan hesitated too, and her mom crossed her arms.

"You too, Daddy."

His mouth turned into a frown, but he lifted Ella from the carrier and put her in the bassinet in Grace's room. After they set up the baby monitor, Grace's mother crooked her finger at them. They left Ella sleeping—sometimes there was no saying no to Meg Kincaid—but shuffled their feet the whole way out of the room.

Back in the den, Jordan explained that the baby monitors worked long-distance. They'd work in his house too, which would make it easier for him to come over and help if Ella was crying.

Grace wasn't sure how she felt about that. Couldn't she just text him? But he seemed so happy, she didn't say anything. They could talk about it another time.

Grace's energy was flagging, and her incision was itching some, so she agreed to sit at the table while her mom and Jordan put together sandwiches like old times. They ate together, and Grace tried to hold off feeling weird about Jordan eating lunch with her and her mom. He'd been around the hospital all the time, but somehow it felt different here.

When Ella started fussing over the monitor, Jordan immediately jumped up.

"I'll get her," he said, and she watched him race off.

"He's going to be a good father," her mom told her, handing her a peeled orange. "I know it's a bit awkward, but give it time."

She ate her orange because she didn't know how to respond. They all had a lot of things to get used to, and today seemed to be a big transition marker.

When Jordan brought Ella back freshly changed, he was beaming, cuddling her close to his chest. The love emanating from him was palpable, and she had to admit she'd never seen him this tender before. She'd seen him around kids, sure, but this was a whole new level of softness. And it looked good on him.

She had to steer herself to remember the past and all that stood between them. It would be easy to slip—like she had while baby shopping.

She realized Ella needed to nurse, and it wasn't like she could ask Jordan to go into the other room like she had in the hospital. Bucking up, Grace situated herself on the couch and reached for a crocheted blanket to pull over her shoulder.

"Okay, I'm ready for her," she told him.

Jordan brought Ella over and handed her over carefully, a frown on his face. Fumbling with her nursing bra, she waited for Ella to latch, trying not to be embarrassed.

Jordan stood over her for a minute while she fussed with Ella's little yellow socks peeking out of the blanket.

"Are you always going to be this weird about nursing in front of me?" he finally asked. "It doesn't have to be this way, Grace."

She looked up. "I'm not completely comfortable with you around."

"I'll go get your bags," he said and walked out.

Her mom started to clean up their lunch, oddly silent.

"Mom, please don't say anything," she whispered.

When Jordan returned with their luggage, there was a line between his brows. "I know you're uncomfortable, Grace. This arrangement will be an adjustment for both of us. All I'm saying is that we both want Ella to be happy. I'm willing to do anything to make that happen. That's...all."

He left before she could respond. When he came back downstairs, his movements were stiff. Guilt clawed into her, and she wanted to make things peaceful again between them.

"You can burp her if you'd like," she told him.

He approached hesitantly, not meeting her eyes, and took Ella from her. "Thanks."

"I'm willing to do whatever it takes too, Jordan," she said softly. "Being here is proof of that."

There was a long pause before he nodded, and she wondered if he was thinking about her dream house in South Dakota too. She forced herself to stop thinking about it as he set himself to burping their daughter. When he finished, he handed her back to Grace.

"I'm going to see if everything is still good at the security gate and next door. I'll be back in a while. Text me if you need something."

Grace knew a retreat when she saw one and felt guilty that she was looking forward to having some time to acclimate.

"Perhaps you can give me a tour next door when Ella goes down for a nap again," her mom said. "I'd like to see your house."

A smile flickered on his face. "I'd be happy to, Mrs. K."

Her mom gave him an encouraging wink. "We'll see you later, Jordan."

"Of course." He approached Grace awkwardly. "I'd like to give Ella a kiss goodbye...if that's okay. I know she's too little to remember it, but my mom always did that with me when I was a kid, and it...I remember liking it."

Grace had to firm her lip to stop the sudden trembling. "It's a nice gesture."

He leaned over and kissed Ella softly on the head. "I'll see you later, sweetheart."

Grace caught his scent. Felt his warmth. And made herself stare straight ahead until he'd left the room.

Then she closed her eyes and cuddled Ella closer, telling herself the two of them were enough on their own.

CHAPTER 13

The short distance to the yellow gate dividing their properties was the hardest yardage Jordan had ever needed to cross. The architectural perfection awaiting him at his house didn't offer any comfort. He couldn't stop thinking about the life they might have had if he'd given up on football and they'd moved to Deadwood and gotten married like Grace had wanted.

But regrets were useless. He had to make the best of what was. They both did. At least his daughter was a stone's throw away. But opening and closing that gate only made the division between him and Grace feel more pronounced.

He shook his head, trying to banish the dark feelings and focus on Ella. She was the most amazing gift he'd ever received—and she was his. For the rest of his life, she would be his daughter, and he would be her dad. He still couldn't get over how much that thought had transformed his life and all the visions of his future. She would be in the stands cheering him on before he retired from the NFL. And they would spend holidays together and go on vacation together.

He wouldn't be alone anymore. Like he had felt when his dad had left. Like he had felt when his mom had died suddenly of a heart attack at fifty-five. Like he had felt when he and Grace had broken up.

And his daughter would never feel alone either.

Thankfully, he had an ally. Meg did her God's honest best to orchestrate the next steps for them all in the days after their return from the hospital.

Like some kind of family magician, she managed to weave him into the family fold with ease, calling him over for breakfast when Ella awoke or when he got home from practice after her nap.

His daughter seemed to sleep all the time, which frustrated him. He knew she wasn't going to be able to play with him for a while, but he'd hoped for more interaction. Still, her mere presence was enough to move him—he loved to watch her sleep, her little chest rising with her breathing, even if it felt like a weird thing to do. Grace seemed to feel the same way, and sometimes they simply sat together on the couch as she slept in her carrier, conversation unnecessary.

He wanted to pull his weight, and he discovered he was a champion burper. Meg taught him how to place Ella high on his shoulder and pat her with just the right rhythm and pressure. It still baffled him that Ella weighed less than his shoulder pads, but since she was growing like a weed, he wasn't worried.

At first, he'd come over all decked out in his brand-new Italian threads, wanting to look attractive to Grace, but that had come to a quick end. Ella had spit up all over his designer silk-blend shirt. He'd felt the warm liquid run down his back and uttered a heartfelt, "Shit." Grace had called him on his cussing and hastily taken Ella from him, but Meg had barked out a laugh and handed him a burp rag. Before Grace had turned around, he'd seen the grin on her face and heard her whisper, "Good one, sweetheart."

Meg taught them both how to bathe Ella in the sink on what Jordan referred to as the "baby sponge." She felt like a greased pig when wet, which terrified him. But he came to love the way she smelled after a bath, so he held her firmly as he washed her while she fussed and grunted in the water.

He grew distracted at practice and earned a good chewing out from the Rebels' offensive coordinator. The guys had given him some slack over being a new dad, but they had their first pre-season game coming up in early August. He needed to get focused, but fretted over the thought of leaving Ella for road games. She was so little and growing so fast. He was worried he was going to miss something.

Already she'd become his whole world.

While he dreaded leaving, he wasn't looking forward to seeing Grace's father and brothers. Jordan suspected Meg had arranged their visit to coincide with Jordan's departure for his first game in Seattle. They would only overlap for one day. It was likely all they could handle. Meg planned to leave a week after they did, and Jordan would be sorry to see her go. She'd been a Godsend.

Meg was oddly restless when the Kincaid men arrived. Jordan was burping Ella, and it was impossible not to feel the shift in the air. He immediately handed Grace the baby and stepped back. Part of him wanted to head for the hills, but he stood his ground.

The Kincaid men bore a remarkable resemblance to one another—they all had heavy stubble on their strong jaws, tough-guy dents in their chins, lanky frames, and strong shoulders. John and Mike ran together in the mornings with their father three times a week, Jordan knew, since he'd run with them whenever he'd gone back to Deadwood with Grace. While Patrick's hair had gone salt and pepper, his sons' hair was still dark-coffee brown.

Patrick was filled with warmth as he greeted his wife and Grace, and he delighted over Ella. All that warmth slid away as he looked across the room at Jordan.

"Patrick," he said, crossing to shake his hand.

"Jordan," the man replied crisply.

There was no mistaking the disappointment radiating from the man he'd admired, and it cut him deep. Jordan hadn't known if Patrick was going to comment on the house—especially since he'd built the original one in Deadwood—but when Patrick looked away, Jordan knew the topic would remain closed.

It was probably for the best.

Jordan turned to Mike and John, who had finished embracing Meg and Grace as well. Instead of hugging them, like he would have done before the breakup, before Ella, he shook hands with them too.

Patrick took Ella from Grace's arms and cradled her to his shoulder like an old pro. The family chatted like a unit, acting as if Jordan weren't in the room. Mike had two little boys who were too rowdy for plane travel, so he'd come without his wife, Bev, but she'd sent a lovely baby blanket knitted in yellow and sage. John's wife hadn't been able to make it either, which meant there was no one around to cut the tension.

He had never felt more outside the circle, and it didn't help that the Kincaid men stood across from Jordan like an opposing team. Patrick planted his feet, rocking on his heels. His sons seemed to mimic the stance.

Jordan saw the nervous glances Meg and Grace were trading and decided that he had stayed long enough. He walked across the room to John, who was now holding Ella. Everyone froze at his movement, as if he were some stranger who'd wandered into the room, which only added to the tension already knotting his shoulders.

"I'm going to take off," he said, running his hand over Ella's silky head, careful of the soft spot.

He gazed at his daughter before meeting John's hard stare.

"Have fun," he said, forcing a smile.

As he walked out, he felt everyone's eyes on him. When he was halfway across the drive, he let out the breath he'd been holding. He felt like a lineman had knocked the wind out of him. He couldn't stay in his new house tonight. Not with the whole Kincaid family this close. He'd stay in town and pop back to see Ella before he left for Seattle.

"Jordan!" he heard Meg call from behind him as he reached that frickin' yellow gate, the one he saw as both his curse and his saving grace.

Turning around, he steeled himself. "Yeah?"

She crossed the distance to him with narrowed eyes. "Give it time. With the men. It was hard with me too in the beginning. Especially seeing this house. Remember? It will get easier."

Would it? Meg had a more open heart than her husband and sons—always had. "Okay," he said, not wanting to debate the matter. "I'm going to stay downtown tonight, but I'll text you when I'm on my way back to see Ella before I leave."

She frowned. "You don't have to stay away."

"Yes, I do," he said, kicking at the ground. "It will give us all some space."

"Fine," she answered briskly. "But text Grace. I'm leaving pretty soon, and you two will need to get used to talking without me in the middle."

He watched her walk swiftly back to the house and felt darkness sweep over him. The sound of deep baritone laughter from inside the house made him hang his head.

Besides his Once Upon a Dare brothers, one of the most precious relationships Jordan had ever had was with the Kincaid men.

It grieved him to realize Ella wasn't going to bring it back.

CHAPTER 14

Grace found herself a little teary-eyed the day of her mother's departure. Jordan had asked if Meg could leave on a Tuesday so he could pop back from the stadium to say goodbye. Technically Tuesday was his only day off during the season, but like most hardcore football players, he worked some that day too.

She watched her mom bathe Ella on the final morning and talk to her in that sing-song voice reserved for babies. "I don't know what I'm going to do without you," she said as her mom transferred Ella from the water to her bath wrap decorated with giraffes.

Her mom gently dried Ella off as the baby stretched and let out a little cry from the change in temperature. "You're going to be fine, Grace. It's been nice spending all this time together, hasn't it?"

"Yeah, it has," she said in a small voice. Gratitude didn't begin to cover it.

"A mother doesn't often get to spend this much time with a daughter once she leaves home," her mom continued, wrapping Ella in the cloth and picking her up. "I'll always be grateful for it."

She hugged her mom's waist, mindful of the baby. "Me too."

"It's time to make your family your own, Gracie," her mom said, carrying Ella back to the changing table in the nursery. "From where I'm standing, you and Jordan seem to be doing pretty well so far."

Grace couldn't deny it was true. She was able to go for more days now without remembering that this house was a replica of another she'd loved, and that was a victory. And Jordan... Well, even though he was traveling for pre-season games and working like a mad man, he still checked in whenever he could. The video messages he sent for her to show Ella pretty much melted her heart. Jordan had also asked her to take videos of anything special Ella did and send pictures of her, of course. Her mom had commented on how adorable it was that Jordan went so gaga over his daughter, and Grace couldn't agree more.

"Every time I think we have a schedule, it changes," Grace said, grabbing a diaper and handing it to her mom. "And it's going to change again when I go back to work in two weeks." She'd decided an eight-week maternity leave was reasonable, especially after all the time she'd taken off for bed rest. Thankfully, she and Jordan had already hired a woman to look after Ella. The nanny they'd chosen was a young woman from a big family in St. Paul, Minnesota. Amy had attended Emory University and majored in childcare. Jordan had asked to handle the details of her employment, and because her mother had advised her to pick her battles, Grace had allowed it.

"When you have a baby, things constantly change," her mom said, finishing off the diaper and then dressing Ella. "Get used to it."

Grace grabbed the damp bath wrap to take into the bathroom. "I love being a mom," she said. "But I'm still a little scared when I don't know what to do."

Her mom put Ella to her chest, rocking her. "Join the club. Do you think I know how best to help you and Jordan? All I can do is do my best. Remember that with this little one here. As a mother, there will always be moments when you don't know what to do."

The bath wrap fell to the floor. "I didn't know you felt that way. You're like super mom."

Her mom made a raspberry with her mouth, startling Ella. "Sorry, sweetie. Your mommy was being silly. There's never going to be some light-bulb moment where you figure it all out. If anyone tells you that...I'd call horse puckey."

Grace's mouth twitched. "Horse puckey, huh?"

"Exactly," she said, cuddling Ella close. "Oh, I'm going to miss you. Both of you."

"We might have to send you the pictures and videos we send to Jordan," Grace said, feeling bereft already.

"I'd love that," her mom said, smoothing the little brown hairs on Ella's head. "Why don't you shower and get dressed while I'm still here? That way I can spend a little more time saying goodbye to my granddaughter."

Grace fingered her ratty white robe. Laundry hadn't been a priority lately. "Good idea." She stooped to pick up the damp wrap before leaving.

Out in the hallway, she paused by the door to listen to the song her mom had started singing. "Somewhere Over The Rainbow" had been her favorite lullaby growing up, and she planned to continue the tradition. When her mom finished, she started to head to her suite.

"Listen up, young lady," her mom said, and because Grace thought for her a moment that her mother was talking to her, she paused. "Your mommy and daddy are going to need you to remind them why all this back and forth between the two houses is necessary. I know you're going to be up to the task. You have the best mommy and daddy any little girl could ever ask for. I hope you can help heal the hurts between them. Who knows what might happen then? Maybe your daddy will grow up a little more and your mommy will forgive what was."

Grace put her hand to her mouth as pain flashed in her heart. *Oh, Mom.* They hadn't talked about it, but did her mom still hope she and Jordan could reconcile? Of course, she did, Grace realized.

"But mostly, Ella," her mom continued, "I hope you can teach them how to laugh with each other again. They used to laugh so much when they were together, and somewhere in this whole hullabaloo, they forgot how."

When her mom resumed humming, Grace padded to her bathroom, thinking over what she'd said. She and Jordan *had* stopped laughing. When he'd put her on the back burner to focus on his dream job as the starting quarterback for Atlanta, they'd stopped laughing. And as more people had started watching them and photographing them, Grace had forgotten how to laugh altogether.

She'd felt like every moment of their shared life was being dissected. But it had gotten worse. While she'd always been complimented for being pretty in a tomboy way, the media had declared her "Too Dull for Dean." She wasn't thin enough. She didn't dress well enough.

Pretty much, they'd said *she* wasn't good enough.

And the fear that Jordan would one day agree with them had drilled down to her very bones.

As she undressed, she looked in the mirror. She still had a little baby tummy, and her breasts really were huge, but it was her body—the body that had brought Ella into this world—and there was beauty in that.

She'd allowed other people to start telling her who she was toward the end of her relationship with Jordan. That was going to have to stop. She needed to be more empowered for her daughter. As she stepped under the spray, she made a pledge to be herself—and not care what anyone else had to say about it.

Easier said than done, perhaps, but it was a start.

A couple hours later, her mom was ready to go. When Grace caught sight of Jordan jogging over, she felt like she'd grown a new skin. It might still be thin, but it was there.

"Not too late to change your mind, Meg!" Jordan called out as he approached. "How are we going to putter along without you?"

"Get a golf cart," her mom quipped, rocking Ella. "I'm only a phone call or a text away. For both of you."

He put his arms around her, careful not to squash their daughter. "Thanks for everything, Meg. You're the best. First, last, and always."

"You're welcome, kiddo," she said, kissing his cheek. "You give it to San Francisco this weekend, okay?"

"Already done," he replied with his Jordan flare. "Let me have Ella so you can say goodbye to Grace."

"I need to give this little one a special kiss," she said, repositioning the baby so she could look at her. "One that's gonna last your grandma."

Ella squinted in the sunlight, and it made Grace smile when Jordan immediately raised his hand to shield her from the bright light.

"You've got good daddy instincts," her mom told him. "And you, precious little girl. You're going to be so much bigger when I see you next. I'm going to miss you like you wouldn't believe, but I know you're in great hands. I love you, pumpkin."

She gave her a kiss and then snuggled their cheeks

together, closing her eyes. Grace thought her mom might cry, but then she smiled and handed the baby to Jordan.

"All right," her mom said, turning to Grace. "Now you."

She closed the distance and wrapped her arms around her mom. "I'm going to miss you too. So much." She felt tears leak out from her eyelids.

"Yeah," her mom whispered, rocking her. "Me too."

"Tell Dad and the boys I love them," she told her mom as she hugged her tight one last time.

Her mom gave an audible sniff and nodded. "Count on it. Pretty soon, it will be the holidays, and we'll see each other again."

She and Jordan hadn't discussed that yet, and she saw him glance over sharply. "Can't wait."

Her mom gave Ella another peck before heading to the car. "I'll text you when I land. Love you!"

"Love you too," Grace replied.

After the car pulled away, Jordan came over and gave her a gentle nudge.

"Are you going to be okay?" he asked, bouncing Ella gently. "You know you can go and see them anytime you want. I'll make it happen."

Already he was anticipating her needs. He'd always encouraged her to visit home more often when they were together, but she'd rarely taken him up on the offer. Work kept her busy too. Honestly, she could buy her own ticket, and he knew it. He'd wanted to do it for her because it made her happy.

"Thanks," she said as a few more tears streaked down her face. "I must still be a little hormonal and overtired." Man, she hoped that crap would be over soon.

Jordan transferred Ella to the crook of his arm and wrapped his other arm around her. "If that's why I've been so emotional lately, I must be hormonal too."

She elbowed him in the side, and he gave a reluctant laugh. "Funny."

"No, I'm serious," he said. "I take one look at Ella sometimes, and I get all choked up. She's...amazing. I knew I'd love her, but..."

She looked up and found herself falling into his arctic blue eyes. "What?"

He lifted his shoulder. "I never imagined loving anyone like I love her. She's everything. You know?"

It took Grace a moment to swallow. "Yes, I know."

"I mean...you were everything too," he said, his eyes meeting hers for a split second before darting away.

Once. Before all your football dreams came true.

"You don't have to be embarrassed," she said, feeling that all-too-common tension return. "I understand."

"Do you?" he asked, his grip on her tightening.

Suddenly Grace was all too aware of the male strength he exuded. Its power to liquefy her insides with desire hadn't abated—if anything, it was stronger than ever. It had been a long time since he'd touched her like this. It didn't matter that he was only trying to bestow comfort.

"It's less complicated with her," he continued, his gaze flicking back to her.

The heat in his eyes told Grace she wasn't the only one remembering what it had been like between them.

All too quickly, his eyes fastened on their daughter. "Ella is just...this precious little person I've been given to cherish. I can't imagine what I've done to deserve her, but I'm grateful for her. Man, my teammates were right. When you become a daddy, you blabber like a moron over your kid."

Jordan had always been emotional. It was what drew people to him, Grace included—and it had made him a great football player. When it came right down to it, there had always been a sweetness in him.

"I'm glad you've fallen so hard for her," Grace said softly. "I have too."

"Did you think I wouldn't?" he asked, his brows slamming together.

She eased out of his grip because...well, if she didn't, it might mean something. "No one could have told me how much love I'd have for her. I don't think we had a clue."

He held up one hand. "Clueless. Yeah, that's me. But I'm starting to feel more confident about doing daddy things. Your mom was a great teacher."

She stilled for a moment, surprised by his choice of words.

"What?" he asked, always tuned in.

"It's a little strange, hearing you talk about being confident. You're so confident I never think you worry you can't do something. Even those six years you rode the bench in New York, you still thought you could be a marquee quarterback. You were right."

His eyes darkened. "I put on a good show. Maybe that was part of the problem between us. I never told you when I wasn't feeling up to the task. Some days back in New York, I had to force myself to get out of bed and go to practice. And when we moved here, I...worried all the time about making you happy...once things took off for me."

His admission hit her full force in the chest. "Why didn't you say anything?"

He shrugged. "Because I'm a guy. I try to fix things. When I could be a free agent, I left New York for Atlanta. Heck, that's why I tried to give *you* things. That's why I built your dream house as a surprise. I hoped you would be satisfied being here with me since I wasn't going back to Deadwood. And I was right to be worried. In the end, I couldn't make you happy—despite everything."

"Oh, Jordan," she said, feeling tears spring into her eyes.

Ella started to cry softly. "Look, she's already got a knack for timing," Jordan said, bouncing more now.

Grace wished she could find a way to soothe the tension emanating between them. Her chest was tight, and his ears were red with emotion.

"She's hungry," she said softly.

He kissed their daughter's forehead and then handed her over. "That's your department. I can burp her when you're done. I'd actually really like to—if that's okay. I was hoping I could spend the rest of the day with her. Even when she's asleep. That's weird, right?"

"Not a bit," she said, watching as he took a few more steps back to give them both space. "I love to watch her too."

Ella's cries were increasing, so Grace bounced her a little, but she knew that wouldn't appease her.

"Okay, I'm off," Jordan said, turning around and walking backwards toward his house. "Text me."

He turned around and took off toward the yellow gate between their houses. "Jordan!" she called out.

As smooth as a cat, he spun around.

"Thanks for telling me that. What you said earlier."

He nodded and then he was jogging off. When he reached the gate, he gave them one last look. His shoulders seemed to sag, like he had lost his mojo.

This time she found herself transferring Ella so she could wave.

Even in the distance, she could see him smile.

CHAPTER 15

While their family wasn't exactly conventional, Jordan didn't think they were doing too badly. He measured his weeks by two dates: Ella's checkups—which he'd asked Grace to schedule for Tuesdays so he could attend—and game day.

So far his team was winning decisively, but it was only early October. They'd be facing tougher opponents later in the season. Grace seemed happy to be back at work, even though she said she missed Ella like crazy—something they had in common. She'd decided to work the lunch shift to ease into the transition, especially since Ella was still nursing, but she covered the dinner rush on Tuesdays, the nights he could come home early to be with Ella.

They were balancing schedules, and so far, it was working.

The baby monitor lay next to his bed every night. He listened to it like Grace's grandfather used to listen to the police scanner.

Then, a few days before Jordan's weekend game in Buffalo, Ella went from being a good sleeper to an insomniac overnight. For two solid nights, Ella woke up almost every thirty minutes. She'd cried before, but these weren't cries. They were wails. And they broke his heart as he listened to them in the confines of his house. How could something so little, so beautiful, cry like that?

But Grace didn't call him, so he stayed put, unable to sleep but powerless to do anything. Grace was the one who brought it up the next morning—she'd talked to her mom about it, and Meg was certain Ella was just going through a spell. There was nothing physically wrong.

On the third night, Ella kept to her new crying schedule. Jordan came awake, as if in a fog, and glanced at the alarm clock. 3:33 a.m. Deciding it was time for the reinforcements to arrive, he reached for his phone and called Grace.

She picked up on the fourth ring. "What?" she asked, Ella's cries piercing in the background.

"I'm coming over," he said simply.

He pulled on a T-shirt and boxers. Stuffed his feet into some tennis shoes and headed out of the house. He let himself into Grace's house with his key and turned off the alarm. Ella's cries hadn't abated, so he took the steps two at a time. He found Grace in the rocker with their daughter. Lamplight from the princess nightlight they'd bought her colored mother and daughter like pink champagne.

Grace had a blanket over Ella, covering everything except for her little feet. Clearly his daughter wasn't interested in nursing if she was making that racket, but he gave Grace points for trying.

"What are you doing here?" she asked, frowning at him. "Go back to bed. I have enough on my hands right now."

Jordan stood over the rocker. "You've been up like crazy the last couple of nights. Let me help. She's my kid too, and I take that responsibility seriously. So, from now on, we take shifts. Maybe then we can both get some sleep."

Grace shifted Ella closer when she started to cry again. "If Ella's keeping you awake, why didn't you shut the monitor off?"

He leaned over her, seeing the bags under her eyes in the soft light. "Like I said, she's my kid too. I'm not turning her off at night."

"But that's silly. You can't help."

He gestured to her chest. "I might not be able to nurse her, but I can damn well help out. And don't tell me not to cuss. I know! But Ella's not herself, crying like this. She doesn't seem hungry."

"No, she doesn't," Grace said with a heavy sigh. "I've tested her belly for gas and checked for a fever. Nothing."

"Then maybe you take her to Dr. Madison tomorrow just to make sure," he said, seeing she was close to tears. "Despite what your mom said. I love Meg, but she's not here."

A piercing cry erupted from under the blanket, and then a little hand thrust out angrily across Grace's lap. She eased Ella out of the blanket with one hand while reaching for her nightgown with the other.

Jordan nearly ground his teeth. "For heaven's sake, let me have her if you're going to be so damn modest. It's not like I haven't seen your boobs. And I'm sorry I swore again, but I'm upset."

He reached for Ella, and his hands brushed Grace's stomach and chest. His skin burned from the contact, but Grace actually recoiled. He fought another curse word.

Jordan cradled the crying baby to his chest and

started bouncing in the soothing motion she liked. Her cries pierced his ears. She didn't settle down.

When Grace had her nightgown buttoned up, she stood. Her short hair looked wild and matted at the same time. "You're being stupid," she snapped. "I'll just have to nurse her later."

"I understand that, but I'm going to pull my weight. Especially when she's like this." He patted her tiny back in a consistent rhythm and brought up a solid belch. "Good one, honey."

The cries reduced to fussing.

"It's not gas," Grace said again, and Jordan decided it would be best not to reply.

She made no move to leave.

"Go to bed." Jordan inclined his chin toward the door, but she kept hovering like a worried mama. "Look, we'll work this out. We just need to be creative. I'll come over when I hear you get up to nurse her. Or you can text me when you're finished if it's that big of a deal to you. I still don't understand why in the hell you have to be so private about it. Women have been nursing babies for centuries."

She put her hands on her hips. "Well, that's too bad. I think it's private, so it'll stay private. And stop cussing!"

Sometimes she made him so mad. "Fine, you do what you have to, but I'm still going to help."

She blew out an aggravated breath. "You can sleep in one of the guest rooms. It's stupid for you to shuttle back and forth every time I nurse her." Grace put a hand to her side and stretched her back, yawing. "Plus I'm too tired to text you."

Jordan tried not to watch the way the nightgown tightened over her petite shape, which was quickly returning to its normal curvature, with one exception—her glorious new breasts. The shadow of her cleavage was visible, and he started to sweat.

Oblivious to his sensual regard, she crossed the room and ran a hand over Ella's soft head. "Since you're going to be stubborn, I'm going to bed. She's all yours. There's breast milk in the freezer if you want to give feeding her a try."

A smile started to creep across his face at the thought, but then another struck him. "Hey wait, how am I going to know when she's hungry?"

"Trust me, you'll know. She'll start rooting around, looking for her next meal."

Since Jordan had already experienced that first hand, he calmed. Ella's fussing and grunting continued after Grace left. He tried everything. He sat in the rocker. They laid on the daybed. He danced with her on the soft carpet and sang lullabies from his childhood, mixing up many of the words.

When she finally fell asleep against his chest what seemed like hours later, he was afraid to lay her down in the crib. He eased into the rocker and closed his eyes. When she started to cry again, he wanted to weep. If some baby whisperer had offered to lull Ella to sleep in exchange for the secret game plan for this weekend's contest against Buffalo, he would have coughed it up. How did people get through this?

Ella continued to cry on and off. As morning light appeared under the window blinds, she went to sleep again. After thirty minutes, she was heavy in his arms, and he thought it was safe to put her in her crib. He transferred her with the care of a man holding a stick of dynamite and then gently covered her up. When she stretched her fist over his head, he silently chanted, *oh please stay asleep, baby.*

She settled, and he breathed a sigh of relief. He barely made it to the daybed. The guest room was too far. His feet hung off the end, but he didn't care. It was a flat surface. He needed to catch some Zs before he headed to practice.

But he'd done his part as a dad, and that thought sent him to sleep with a smile.

***

Grace awoke groggy sometime later. All she wanted to do was surrender to her exhaustion and sleep some more, but then she remembered how Jordan had insisted on staying and helping with Ella. She made herself sit up and scrubbed her face. Ella hadn't eaten since around three unless Jordan had fed her. She would be hungry soon, except there was no noise from the monitor.

She donned a robe before padding down the hall. When Grace reached the doorway, she stilled at the sight before her. Laying on his stomach on the girly white daybed, Jordan was snoring softly. His muscular arm hung off the mattress. Since he wasn't prone to snoring, she knew he was beat.

Grace walked quietly over to the crib. Their little angel was asleep with a smile on her face. Figured.

Jordan's soft groan had her jumping. She pivoted like a ballerina as he flipped onto his back, resting a hand on his chest. That daybed couldn't be comfortable given his height. His hair was matted down in tufts, but he was still gorgeous. No one could pull off the grunge factor quite like Jordan.

What in the world was she going to do with him? This side of him was one she'd never imagined. Her brain was too fried to think about it. She crept across the nursery and let herself out.

Grace was sipping her second cup in front of the morning news when she heard Jordan come down the stairs. His face was haggard and slightly off his usual tanned hue. He put a hand to his back and stretched as he came forward.

Grace took mercy. "Why don't you pour yourself a cup of coffee?"

"Thanks. I'm going to need a jolt to get going before I head to the stadium."

After pouring his coffee, he joined Grace at the farm table and sat across from her. "No one makes better coffee than you."

She pulled a muffin out of the basket and passed it to him on a white napkin. He smiled before he took a bite. His eyes closed.

"Pumpkin spice muffins!" he said with reverence. "I've missed you."

She couldn't help smiling. "Thanks for last night."

He stopped chewing for a moment, surprise flickering over his face like the morning sunlight streaming through the windows.

"You're welcome." His tone was hesitant, almost unsure.

Grace felt the need to give him a little more credit. "I really appreciate everything you've been doing."

He choked, which turned into full-blown coughing. "I'm fine. You did all the hard stuff—carrying her, having her, feeding her. I'm just the clean-up guy."

Running a hand over her brow, Grace watched him closely. How many times had they shared a morning cup of coffee before heading off to work? Here they were again, and all because they had a daughter upstairs. "You're more than that. I'm grateful for it."

He cleared his throat again. "Even though I don't have the boobs?"

She fought a smile, knowing he was hoping to lessen his embarrassment. "Trust me, they're not all they're cracked up to be."

His eyes flicked down, and her breath stilled.

"They seem pretty perfect from where I'm sitting."

And didn't *that* turn the tables? When Farley Cooper had started making fun of her little angels, as he called them, saying she stood out in a party of breasty beauties, she'd lost confidence in her body. Were they only perfect to Jordan now because they were bigger? She couldn't bear to ask, so she picked up her coffee cup and took a sip.

"Sorry, just making an observation." He frowned. "So, are you okay sharing the Nightly Terrors of Our Young Babe if she keeps up this schedule? Man, that sounds like an Edgar Allen Poe story."

The sexual tension between them shimmered like the tide before going back out to sea.

Grace forced herself to relax. "Yes, I'm okay with that."

He drank the last of his coffee and stood. "We both work and have a baby. It's going to be challenging sometimes. Everyone says to take things one day at a time with an infant."

She wondered if he'd read that somewhere and found she couldn't hold back the smile.

Jordan flashed her a wicked wink. "But she's pretty freaking special, so I'm willing to undergo serious torture to have her around."

"And this from a man who makes his living being tortured by big fat men in colored tights."

He chuckled softly. "Don't let the defense guys hear you call them that."

Jordan headed to the door, and she found herself wishing he could stay longer. Which just wasn't a good idea.

"I have to take issue with the colored tights comment," he said at the door, rubbing the stubble on his face. "I wear them too, after all."

And he looked incredibly good in them, Grace couldn't help but recall.

"Kiss our girl for me when she wakes up. I'll pop back over to say goodbye before I head to the stadium." He flashed another smile before walking out.

Our girl?

Yeah, that's exactly what Ella was, and right now, Grace wouldn't want it any other way.

CHAPTER 16

The experience of sharing night duty with Grace for the next week deepened the bond between Jordan and Grace as parents. Their friendship started to reemerge, anything from her teasing him about snoring on the daybed to him teasing her about her spiky pixie hair, which he finally admitted looked good on her.

He was exhausted, but he was happy. His friends had tolerated his brief texts over the busy weeks following Ella's birth, but perhaps it was time to give one of them a holler. Blake Cunningham could let the other guys know how he was doing. He called him from the car on the way home from practice.

"Hey!" Blake answered right away. "I've been hoping to hear from you. How are things with that beautiful daughter of yours? She's growing like a weed."

He wouldn't trust too many people in the world with pictures of his daughter—not when the media had put out a bounty for the first picture of her—but his Once Upon a Dare friends were like brothers.

"Don't call my daughter a weed. She's way too cute for that."

"You know what I mean," Blake said. "What do you want to talk about first? Being undefeated or Ella?"

"While it feels great being undefeated, it's only October. Plus, nothing can compare to fatherhood. Blake, it's...better than I could have ever imagined."

"How are things between you and Grace?"

"Better," he answered, rapping the steering wheel a little. "Ella had a turn in her sleeping habits. Nothing like shared worry and strife to unite people. It tore my guts out to hear her cry like that, but it's changed things between Grace and me. I know Grace is feeling it too. It's a struggle, but I'm trying to be patient."

In spite of their mutual fatigue, he'd caught her watching him with guarded appreciation in her eyes the other morning. He hadn't been wearing anything special—just a shirt and shorts—but Grace had always liked that look most of all. And he'd let his stubble grow because he knew it drove her wild. He knew attraction wouldn't be enough to encourage her to give their relationship another try, but it couldn't hurt matters.

"Patience is good," Blake said. "I'm not sure I've heard you use that word often, but it's promising."

No, his natural impulse was to rush in and make things happen. "I want Grace back, but I'm afraid that if I don't show her I've changed—that she and Ella are as important as football—it will hurt my relationship with both of them in the long run."

"You mean Grace might stop being your neighbor," Blake said and sighed deeply. "You're wise to keep that in mind, Jordan. Grace will pull back if she feels pushed. It took guts to move into that house, if you ask me."

Yeah, he knew that. And while she'd had a constant look of nostalgia on her face for the first few days, she'd never said anything about the yellow house's twin. "It's like walking a tightrope sometimes between the past and now, but I know she'll give me a sign if and when she's ready." He hoped it was more a question of when than if.

"Maybe let her give you a couple of signs before you act," Blake told him. "That way you'll know you're not just seeing what you want to see."

"Have I done that?" he asked with a snort.

"Frequently. I believe Coach Garretty repeatedly said that in camp about you and football. I won't comment on your personal life."

There was undoubtedly some truth in that, but Jordan knew that his imagination and ability to visualize a situation from all sides helped him on the field. "I'll take your advice. Look, I'm almost home. I need to send the nanny off."

"Nanny," Blake said wryly. "Who would have imagined you would be the first one to use those words."

"Not me, that's for sure, but it's working for me. Being a daddy is the best thing ever. Maybe even better than winning a Super Bowl, although it's kind of neck-and-neck for me."

"Hearing you say that gives me hope, Dean," Blake said. "The guys and I were pretty worried about you when you told us Grace was pregnant. But from where I'm sitting, you couldn't have handled it better. Say hi to Grace for us, and plan on a big get-together when the season finishes."

During the season, no one had the luxury of a Once Upon a Dare weekend, let alone a quick visit—not even to celebrate a new baby.

"Maybe you and Natalie can come to one of my games and see my daughter," Jordan said. "I'd love at least one of you guys to meet her before she starts walking."

"I'd like that. Now, go kiss your kid and have a night of it," Blake said.

"Tell Natalie hi for me," he said, pulling into the garage. "Talk to you soon."

"Later, Dean."

When Jordan exited the car, he headed straight for the gate separating the two houses. Every time he opened it, he felt lighter inside, knowing what awaited him. Just the thought of seeing Ella made him grin, and now that things were easier between him and Grace, he was excited to see her too. His two women.

They were everything.

***

Grace reveled in the one dinner shift she worked since becoming a mommy. The lunch shift was okay, but the dinner shift was where the action was, and every good chef knew it.

"You were on top of your game tonight," Tony said as she washed down the stainless steel prep area. "You must be getting a little more sleep than last week. I didn't see you drinking as many espressos."

"Or closing your eyes while beating the ricotta for the fish sauce," Victor said from across the way, grill brush in hand.

Had she closed her eyes while making the sauce? This sleep deprived, she pretty much didn't remember anything, which was why she'd had to post the menu by her station. Usually she knew it by heart, but she wasn't taking any chances. The last thing she wanted was to ruin a dish by leaving an ingredient or two out.

"Thanks for trusting me when I'm this tired," she said to Tony.

He nudged her gently. "We were keeping an eye on you."

"I know," she said, grinning at him. "I haven't stayed for an after-shift drink since before Ella was born. I could probably have half a glass of red wine."

Her restaurant family had been supporting her for so many months now. It was time for some normalcy to return to their relationship. Jordan wouldn't mind if she stayed an extra hour. She only had to text him. Besides, it wasn't too late yet. She would likely be home before one.

"Beer is better for nursing mothers," Tony said. Grace caught the shocked look on Victor's face before he went back to scrubbing the grill.

"How do you know that?" she asked.

"I know things," he said with his usual mystique. "Come join me at the bar after you finish up. I'll pour you a special sour beer I think you might like."

Grace would have rolled her eyes if he weren't so sweet.

"Tony looking out for your milk?" Ricardo said, holding his head. "That man truly was a dairy farmer in another life."

"Ah," Victor cried out. "Now I know why he can always tell which whole milk is better. He's an expert."

Her cheeks flared. "Cut it out, guys. Don't make me get out the meat cleaver."

Carlo put his hands to his chest as if he had boobs. "Don't hurt these babies."

She glared at them, but part of her was delighted that her co-workers' days of treating her with kid gloves were over. The kind of talk dished out in the back of the house could be brutal, and while she'd appreciated their overprotectiveness, she'd missed their teasing.

"Carlo, you *wish* you had these babies." She cupped her own breasts before stripping off her apron and following Tony out to the bar. The guys were still hooting behind her, making her smile.

There was only one table left. The black book was splayed open, as if the diners had already paid but were lingering. One of the two men saw her and immediately stood. Grace didn't know what he was doing, so she continued toward the bar. He intercepted her, an exuberant smile on his handsome face.

"Are you the chef who made my dinner?" he asked, unbuttoning his navy suit jacket. "Because I have to tell you, it's one of the best sea bass dishes I've ever had in my life."

Her guard lowered. "I'm one of the chefs here, yes. I'm happy you enjoyed it. I love everything on the menu, but I have to confess the sea bass with the ricotta sauce is one of my favorites."

He leaned in conspiratorially. "I love hearing about a chef's favorite dish. Did you create it?"

"I did." She finally took his measure. He was tall, well built, and had a nice head of brown hair. She caught him taking her measure as well, and for a moment it felt weird. No one had really checked her out in a long time, and here she was standing in her plain white chef's outfit, smelling of a dozen different dishes.

"Then you're as talented as you are beautiful," he said, gazing at her. "I'm Aaron, by the way."

"Grace," she said, holding out her hand and shaking his.

He continued to hold it with gentle pressure, and she saw Alfonso step out from behind the bar. It had been a while since a man had made a move on her in the restaurant, but it had happened.

"I know this a little crazy," Aaron said, "but my friend and I clearly need to leave since you guys are closing down. Would you consider going out to dinner with me sometime?"

Grace blinked. "Well...ah." Somehow being asked outright threw her off balance. "I don't know." And she didn't. He was handsome and seemed nice, but no one really did it for her but Jordan. Apparently that was still the case since she didn't feel so much as a ping for this handsome guy.

"I promise I'm the kind of guy who would bring you flowers without expecting anything at the end of the night if that's what worries you," he said, squeezing her hand again.

She laughed. "Goodness, you're direct."

His grin deepened. "Maybe we can text a little, and if you don't find me completely repulsive, I can pick you up and take you out to dinner on your next night off?"

"Repulsive, huh?" she said, chuckling softly. "You don't seem very repulsive."

"I'm glad we agree on that," he said. "I try really hard not to be. I even shower."

Her lips twitched. He was funny. She had to give him that. Maybe she should give it a try. It might quell her on-again, off-again feelings for Jordan. "And you managed to scrounge up a jacket tonight in keeping with our dress policy for men."

"I can read too," he said in a hushed voice, like they were sharing a secret.

Okay, that did it. "All right," she said. "The reading and the showering convinced me."

"You'll go out with me?" he asked, and he sounded like he'd won the lottery.

He must *really* like her. It was a little heavy-handed, sure, but it was flattering. "Yes."

"Awesome," he said and dropped her hand so he could pull his cell phone out of his pocket. "Great! What's your number?"

She repeated the numbers and watched him dial in her name as well.

"I live close to you, so I can just pop over and pick you up."

A chill skittered down her spine. "Wait! How do you know where I live?"

But even as she said it, she knew. She started backing away. His smile died, and he reached for her hand again.

"You must have said it," he told her, but his eyes betrayed him.

She shook her head as Alfonso headed in their direction. "You'd better go. Alfonso and the rest of the staff don't take kindly to people messing with me."

He looked around and held up his hands. "Look, do I know you're Jordan Dean's baby mama? Sure. Am I a huge Rebel fan? Yeah. But I like you, and you're prettier in person. What's wrong with hoping I might meet him if things...clicked between us?"

Her ears started buzzing, and the whole room seemed to fill with water. Aaron was trying to talk to her, but she could no longer hear him. She turned around and walked smack dab into Tony. Then she fled to the kitchen.

The minute the doors swung shut behind her, she started shaking.

"Grace!" someone shouted, and soon Victor, Carlo, and Ricardo swooped in around her like a bunch of protective hens.

"Give her some space," Tony shouted, making her jump.

She wrapped her hands around her body. "He knew." How could she have been so stupid? "He knew who I was."

"He's gone," Tony said, "and he won't be allowed back inside the restaurant."

That wasn't the point. "I thought this was all behind me. I'm not even safe here."

Tony put his hands on his hips and stared her down. "Yes, you are, Grace. This is why you shouldn't talk to the patrons."

"So I'm never supposed to talk to anyone?" she asked, feeling her heart beating out of control in her chest. "What kind of a life is that? I don't want to hide in the kitchen just because of Jordan." Suddenly she was so incensed by the injustice of it all that she wanted to throw something.

She wanted her life back. The old life. She had walked through the world anonymously before Jordan had become famous and tethered her to his stardom.

She took deep breaths, watching as Tony made a gesture to the staff to clear the kitchen. Even though she knew she was in the grip of a panic attack, she couldn't stop it.

Tony helped her over to the chairs one of the guys had brought over. He sat beside her as she put her head between her legs, but she could only focus on breathing.

"I can't do this again," she said after the worst had passed.

"You don't seem to have a choice," Tony said. "It is your life now, Grace. Maybe we can come up with some positives to focus on?"

"Like what?" she asked. "Are we talking about all the money and the perks? Tony, I don't care about any of those."

"I know you don't. I was thinking about charities and helping people." He shook his head. "Perhaps it's time to accept things have changed and do your best to follow the new lines defining your road. I'm sorry."

He patted her back and left her alone.

CHAPTER 17

Jordan was pacing in front of the windows, bursting with news for Grace. Ella had done something pretty spectacular, and he couldn't wait to tell her about. Where was she? Ella had rolled over. His daughter had rolled onto her back. She was a genius!

He hated that Grace hadn't been there. It was like walking for the first time, right? But he'd done his best to encourage Ella to do it again by dangling a toy within her reach, and darn it all if she was the smartest girl in the world. She'd done it again, and he'd gotten it on video for Grace that time. Being a dad totally rocked.

But Grace hadn't answered any of his texts. He hadn't wanted to call. Maybe they had a late table, but Tony usually sent her home by midnight. Right now, it was just shy of thirty minutes past one. If he didn't hear from her in another thirty minutes, he was going to call Tony.

Fifteen minutes later, the security guard alerted him that Grace was at the gate. Except she was in Tony's car, not hers.

Something had happened.

He opened the front door and was waiting in the driveway when Tony pulled to a halt. When Grace left the car moments later, the set of her shoulders was all the confirmation he needed.

"Grace," he said as she came forward.

"Not now, Jordan," she crisply replied, heading past him into the house.

He strode over to the driver's side and rapped on the glass. When it lowered, he noted the tension in Tony's face.

"What happened?" he asked.

"A customer asked Grace out after her shift, and from what she told me, the man knew who she was."

His stomach sunk. "Shit."

"The *testa di cazzo* gave himself away by saying he didn't live too far from her, and then everything untangled. He was a huge fan. Grace freaked out."

Jordan pushed away from the car and let out a stream of cuss words, wanting to punch something. "How could this happen?" he asked Tony when he stalked back to the Porsche. "Dammit! You and I talked about everyone keeping an extra eye out for her."

"We are, and we did, Jordan," Tony said in a curt tone. "The man complimented her about the meal, and Grace waved off Alfonso so she could talk to him. Everything seemed to be fine...and then it wasn't. Trust me, that man is never going to return to my place."

He took some cleansing breaths. Taking his anger out on an already pissed off Tony wasn't the way. "But the damage is done."

"Yes," Tony said, tapping the steering wheel. "I insisted on driving her home because she had a panic attack and wasn't steady enough to drive. I'll have one of the guys bring her car back in the morning."

"I can arrange that," Jordan said, already thinking of his next move.

"I can fucking handle it," Tony said with edge. "It's late. I'm going home to sharpen my knives. Goodnight, Jordan."

Jordan empathized with the need to do something physical. Rather than head into the house, he walked down the drive.

Of all the things Jordan had feared, he'd never thought about some Rebel fan asking Grace out to get to him. Maybe since he'd never considered the possibility of Grace dating someone else period. Had she wanted to go out with this guy before she'd found out the truth? Tony seemed to think so.

That knowledge sliced him to the core. Maybe she didn't want him, after all. Maybe Blake was right, and he had a dangerous habit of seeing what he wanted to see.

Well, he'd broken this. It was his responsibility to fix it. He would save his hurt feelings for later.

He let himself back into the house. Her bedroom door was open when he reached the upstairs, but when he looked inside, she wasn't there. Jordan padded silently to the nursery. Soft light spilled out into the hallway. He peered into the room. Grace was in the rocking chair nursing Ella, her eyes pinched shut like she was fighting her own demons.

He almost hated to alert her to his presence because she hadn't thrown a blanket over Ella, which meant she hadn't expected him to follow her. Even though he knew he should announce himself, he couldn't look away.

She'd kicked her shoes off carelessly, and they lay haphazardly on the rug. The rocker moved in a slow rhythm as she pushed off the floor. Ella's little fist rested against her mouth as she nursed. He could tell his daughter was mostly asleep.

He leaned against the doorjamb and fell into the moment. Seeing them like this... It was simply the most beautiful thing he'd ever witnessed.

Grace was so still that Jordan thought she might be asleep too. But then she opened her eyes and saw him in the doorway. Jordan didn't move. When she reached for the blanket hanging on the side of the rocker, he uncoiled from the door.

Bending on one knee in front of her, he stopped her hand. "Don't."

Ella stirred and opened her eyes, turning her head to look at him. She reached for him with her little hand, so he took that precious link. He breathed a sigh of relief when Grace let the blanket fall to the side.

Jordan looked down at his daughter, her face so dear to him. Then he shifted his gaze to Grace.

"She rolled over tonight," he told her, watching her expression change from anger to shock.

"She did?"

"Yeah," he said quietly, hoping this would help reestablish the ground they'd made over the past weeks. "I coaxed her with a toy to do it again and caught it on video for you. I'm sorry you weren't here for it, but maybe when she walks..."

"I can't wait to see it," she replied, soothing Ella's little curls. "It was a...horrible evening."

"Tony told me," he said, feeling Ella's hand go slack in his. "I'm sorry, Grace."

Her eyes clenched shut briefly again as she shook her head. "Me too."

"I think she's asleep," he said, gently placing Ella's hand on her tummy.

"Give it a couple of minutes," Grace said. "She sometimes starts nursing out of the blue."

Sure enough, Grace was right. Her little mouth

started sucking again, and Grace rolled her eyes. "It's gotta be instinct. Usually I wait until her whole body gets heavy, but even then, it's no guarantee."

"I fed her a bottle before bed," he said. "I'm surprised she was hungry."

Grace looked down and fingered Ella's nightgown. "I wanted to feed her."

He didn't say anything, but he'd read how some women nursed to savor the connection with their child—even if they weren't hungry.

"She was clearly a little hungry," he said, going along with her. If Grace had needed comfort or connection from their daughter, he was glad she'd sought it out.

He stayed on the floor and watched them. The moment was simple—two parents sharing a private moment with their baby—but it felt like a revelation. Jordan hadn't expected the intensity of it, but in this moment, the past fell away. Love swept over him like an intense wind.

He reached forward to touch Grace's cheek. "I've never seen you more beautiful than you are in this moment. Thanks for letting me see both of you like this."

She lifted a shoulder, but didn't respond. Pretty soon, even Jordan could see Ella was sound asleep. Her mouth finally fell away from Grace's breast, and from the tension in Grace's shoulders, he could see her embarrassment.

"Here, let me take her," he whispered and carefully scooped Ella up, stepping away to pat her on the back to bring up any burps.

There weren't any, and he rocked with her until he felt it was time to put her in the crib. When he turned around, Grace wasn't in the room any longer. He tucked the blanket around Ella and then went off in search of her. Again, she wasn't in her bedroom, but down in the kitchen, making herself a cup of tea.

"You didn't send the video," she said.

She was waiting for him, which lit an ember in his chest, but she still had her work clothes on, which meant she hadn't felt comfortable enough to change into her pajamas while he was burping Ella. Her guards were back up.

"I thought it would be more fun if we could watch it together," he said honestly. "I didn't want you to feel bad for not being here, especially when you were working."

She took the steaming mug of tea over to the kitchen table. He grabbed his phone out of his jeans pocket and took a chair next to her. She grew very still, and he feared all of her earlier tension had returned.

When he hit play, he watched her face—not the video, which he'd already seen tons of times. The stiff muscles in her shoulders dissolved, and a radiant smile flew across her face.

"Oh, look at her! She did it!"

"Yeah," he said, taking in the quiet force of her beauty. "She's a genius."

"And she knows it too," Grace said, playing the video again. "Look at her smile at the end after she grabbed the toy from you."

"She knew what the game was," Jordan said, puffing his chest out.

"Oh, I wish I'd been here."

"Me too," Jordan said. "Every time she does something, it's like a miracle, you know?"

She gave him a beaming smile. "I know. She's the miracle."

"She is at that," he said, and then watched Grace play the video three more times, giving a play by play with each viewing. "You'd make a great sports announcer."

And just like that, the smile disappeared from her face.

"Tell me what happened tonight, Grace," he said, seeing no reason to delay it.

Her green eyes blazed like holy fire when she looked at him again. "Didn't Tony tell you?"

"I want to hear it from you," he said, not reaching for his phone when she slid it his way.

"One of our patrons flattered me, which then turned into a dinner invitation." She gripped the handle of her mug. "I agreed, but then he gave himself away by saying he knew where I lived. I lost it, and while he tried to assure me that he liked me and that I was prettier in person even though he was a huge fan of yours, it made me pretty upset."

Prettier in person? He wanted to beat the man into a bloody pulp.

"What can I say to make this better, Grace?" She was so tightly wound, a gentle touch might shatter her.

"There's nothing. Tony was right. It was my fault for talking to one of the customers."

He reached for her hand. "I know that breaks your heart because you like to talk to people."

"I don't want to have to live my life always on guard, Jordan."

He stroked the back of her hand. "I don't like it either, Grace. Sometimes, I hate having to look at the person in front of me and wonder if they're being nice to me because they're nice or because I'm Jordan Dean."

"I thought you stopped caring about that a long time ago," she said, watching him with narrowed eyes.

"I'm not sure that ever goes away," he said with complete honesty. "When my dad left, and I found out all the bad things he'd done, I wondered if he'd been..."

"What?" she asked softly. The tenderness in her voice gave him the strength to continue.

"I wondered if he'd been pretending to like me the

whole time. Otherwise, why would he have done those things and then up and left us? He lied about so many things, maybe he lied about caring about me."

She squeezed his hand. "Oh, Jordan. I'm so sorry. Whatever your dad did, I'm sure he loved you. You were his son."

And yet he'd left without a word. "I've always wanted people to like me—really like me—because..." Oh shit, if he was going to be honest, he might as well go all the way. "Because then they won't leave."

Her eyes closed for a minute, and she looked down. "That's gotta hurt—being worried about that."

It sucked. Big time. "Sometimes, it's in the back of my head that even the people closest to me don't really like me. That's why I pretend not to care about the haters. It's my way of protecting myself."

She was silent for a long time. "This helps me understand you. I'm glad you finally told me you feel that way."

His chest wasn't as tight now. "I'm glad I did too."

"I wish I didn't care so much what people said," she said, putting her free hand to her forehead and rubbing it like she had a headache.

"It's one of the things that made me fall in love with you," he said, feeling the jolt in her hand as the words shot through her body. "Even when you left Deadwood for the big city, you never stopped treating people like we were living in a small town."

"People deserve to be treated with respect and dignity," she said simply, letting go of his hand and standing up.

"Not the ones who use you to get to me," he said, rising from his chair as well and gazing at her steadily. "Not the ones who say you're prettier in person. Grace, how could any man look at you and not see how beautiful you are? How your smile lights up a room? How your very voice both calms and excites? How your hands are sheer perfection, whether they're holding a butcher knife or your newborn daughter? But mostly, how could any man look at you and not see how sweet and kind you are?"

Her chest rose with a deep breath.

"A man like that isn't worth an ounce of your energy," he said, crossing to her. "Do you believe that, Grace?"

He watched her eyes, making out the gold and browns around her irises. She, in turn, searched his gaze. "I want to, Jordan."

He took a step closer, and when she didn't back away, he took it as a sign.

"Then believe it," he said, "if you've never believed anything else I've ever said to you."

Her gaze was steady, and he could see the pulse pound in her neck. But he remembered Blake's advice and stayed where he was, waiting for another sign from her.

"I'm afraid no one else is going to see it besides you," she whispered.

Part of him wanted to shout to the rafters at that admission, but he knew it could pitch them either way: into the past or into the future.

"We couldn't make it," she said again, putting her hand tentatively on his chest.

It was another sign, but she'd had a tough night, and he didn't want to press his advantage. "We didn't let go of each other because we stopped loving each other."

He heard her audible inhale and waited. One, two, three, he counted.

"No," she said, shaking her head. "We didn't."

Then she leaned her head against his chest, and since he didn't know how else to soothe the agony in her voice, he put his arms around her.

CHAPTER 18

Grace knew letting Jordan hold her was a bad idea.

Being in his arms again reminded her of how long it had been since they'd touched each other except in relation to Ella. She'd missed it down to her bones.

When he'd told her all of the things that had made him fall in love with her, she could hear what he wasn't saying—they were all still true for him.

Jordan wasn't any less in love with her than she was with him.

Tonight she didn't want to fight that any longer— even if she had no solution for what had torn them apart the first time. She let her hand trail up his chest to rest on his heart. Then she pressed back and gazed into those amazing blue eyes of his. She'd seen desire in them thousands of times, but somehow it all felt new again.

"Gracie," he said in a deep voice. "Be sure."

She wasn't sure beyond this moment, but she was okay with that. She was tired of fighting what she wanted. Over these last few months, she'd fallen in love with a new side of Jordan, the doting, big-hearted father.

"Be with me," she whispered, stroking his cheek with her other hand. "I want this. I want you."

Jordan lowered his mouth to hers, keeping his eyes on her the whole time. When he kissed her, there was a new gentleness tempering the passion, love, and intention that were so deliciously familiar.

Grace opened her mouth to take the kiss deeper, but Jordan kept his pace slow. Grace felt the emotion boiling inside him. She could also feel his determination not to mess up, and somehow that soothed her tension. They were both in uncharted territory.

The natural fragrance of his skin, as beloved as it was familiar, had her hands caressing the defined muscles of his back. What had been a gentle kiss changed into something deeper, more urgent. Grace ran her tongue over his bottom lip and teased the seam of his mouth.

He gave a soft grunt of pleasure, and Grace pressed her tongue to his. He answered in timeless moves they'd perfected over years of kissing each other, and just like that, they fell back into the perfect ebb and flow of loving each other.

As the kiss built, Jordan slowly sucked on her tongue. When she gave a soft moan, he nipped her bottom lip at the corner. It was something that had never failed to make Grace groan.

He ended the kiss slowly, his heated blue eyes gazing at her steadily, gauging her mood, her passion. Even in the harsh light of the kitchen, she could see the flush of desire on his face.

He smoothed a hand over her cheek. "Are you sure, Grace? I...need you to be sure."

He'd asked her that before, and it touched her that he would ask again. After his earlier revelations about protecting himself, she knew he was asking for him too.

"I'm sure."

He kissed her again on the mouth. "You have three minutes. Five minutes tops. I'll be right back."

Then she watched him walk out of the kitchen. She'd thought he was kidding, but when he didn't immediately return, she went to the front door. Sure enough, he was running for the gate between their houses.

What in the world was he doing?

She gave a huff and headed upstairs to check on Ella one last time. If he'd said he was coming back, he was coming back. After ensuring their daughter was sleeping peacefully, she headed to her bedroom and took off her shoes from her perch on the bed. Her bedside clock said they were nearing three o'clock, and while she wanted Jordan, she was tuckered out. If he didn't come back soon, she was going to end up asleep. She heard footsteps in the hallway and turned. He stood in the doorway, breathing hard.

"I think that was the fastest I've ever run," he rasped out. "Tell me you're still sure."

Sue her, but he was even more attractive to her when he was slightly sweaty. "Why in the world did you take off like that?" she asked in exasperation.

He held up a packet of condoms. "I assumed you weren't on the Pill, and while I love Ella, I didn't think you'd be up for Irish twins."

Good Lord. "Birth control."

"Yeah," he said, still not moving from the doorway. "I need you to say the words one more time, Grace."

"I want you, Jordan," she said and held out her hand to him.

"Thank God," he said and strode forward with purpose toward the bed.

He joined her there and followed her down to the mattress, kissing her with increasing intensity. Oh yeah, this was the focused, intense lover she'd missed.

She gripped his back as their tongues dueled, wanting an anchor in this emotional storm buffeting them both. They'd come together after being apart before—when she'd gone to Italy for training or when he'd been away at training camp—but this homecoming was different.

She ran her hands under his T-shirt finally, needing to feel his bare skin, and on cue, he rose over her and stripped it off. All the saliva dried up in her mouth. Jordan was breathtaking with all his hard, taut muscles and six-pack abs. Reaching for the T-shirt she wore under her chef jacket, he nudged her hands aside and helped her remove it. Then, before she could blink, he unsnapped her bra. He'd always had mad skills that way.

He stopped and looked down at her breasts. "You have no idea how much I've missed these. How much I've wanted to see how they've changed."

Her cheeks immediately flushed. "I...ah...they aren't like they used to be. Jordan, I'm pretty self-conscious about this, but my breasts...ah...crap...they leak sometimes. I have no idea what they're going to do...if you keep touching them."

His gaze was all business now. "I've read about breastfeeding and sex."

That was a shock. "What?"

"Before you go thinking I had ideas, first, I'm a guy, and second, I was curious. I want you to be comfortable, Grace. But you don't need to worry about them leaking or squirting or doing whatever they want to do."

Now she really wanted to squirm. *"Jordan."*

"You love having me touch your breasts," he said, caressing the sides of them with his fingertips. "I want this to be good for you. So good."

She arched her spine in response to his touch, which she did love. "Promise you won't laugh, and if it gets too weird, I'll cover them back up."

"I won't get weird," he said, "but I promise to honor your wishes if you get uncomfortable."

He leaned closer and kissed the curve of her breast, moving slowly but with determination. He caressed them, and when he tugged, she gasped.

"They're pretty sensitive, and not in a comfortable way," she said, and he fell back to kissing the sides again.

Watching her intently for cues, he grew adept in deciding where and how to stroke her. Pretty soon, he was kissing her mouth while caressing her breasts. Arousal pooled in her center, and she relaxed into it all.

"I've missed you, Gracie," he whispered.

Grace looked at his face, so beloved to her. Those piercing blue eyes, the straight nose, the strong, stubbled jaw. There had never been really anyone for her but Jordan. The tie that held her to him both humbled and enraged her. But it was there.

It moved her, the slowness and care he was taking with her. Their last lovemaking had possessed none of this deliberateness.

"I've missed you too."

He lowered his mouth slowly. Their tongues danced, and Grace caressed his jaw, her fingers tingling from his sexy stubble.

Not wanting to rush the moment, they kissed and kissed and kissed. Every now and then his hands would venture down to caress her breasts with careful intent while hers traced the defined muscles of his chest.

When he kissed his way down her neck to her belly, she let her eyes flutter shut. God, she was ready for him. But he paused, and she opened her eyes when he traced her Caesarean scar.

"I wish I could have endured this for you," he said quietly.

Her heart seemed to expand like an over-filled

balloon. "We got Ella out of the deal. That's all that matters."

"Thank you for her," he said, meeting her eyes. "I can't imagine my life with her—or you."

Oh, the way he was weaving words tonight. She could barely soak it all in, so she only gave him a brilliant smile. He slid his hands to her hips and kissed her right below the line of the scar.

She flushed with passion. "I can't wait," she breathed out, lifting her hips so he could slide her pants off.

"You don't have to."

Like a pro, he tugged both her pants and panties off in one motion, pausing only to take off her socks and kiss the soles of her feet before nudging her legs apart.

He pressed a kiss to the core of her, and her loud groan filled the room.

He touched her slowly. "Tell me if this is all right. I know they say to wait six weeks, but I don't want to hurt you."

"Jordan, it's been fourteen weeks," she said, arching into his touch, "but you're sweet to be concerned."

"I would never want to give you another moment of pain after everything you went through with Ella."

There it was again, the sensitivity and vulnerability she hadn't seen in Jordan since he was a young boy, the emotions being a father was bringing to the surface.

"I'll be fine," she told him to assure him, "but I'll let you know if there's anything to be concerned about."

Mostly she was still worried about her breasts. They were downright unpredictable.

He nudged her legs open wider with his shoulders, and Grace nearly moaned in anticipation. He looked up and smiled—he knew what this did to her. He kissed her inner thighs, turning playful.

"*Jordan.*"

"All right," he said in a teasing voice, "let's give you what you really want."

Grace jolted when he slid his tongue into her. Short strokes later, her hips were jerking against his mouth, and she shattered. Jordan continued to caress her, taking her even higher.

With her eyes closed, she could only focus on the pressure of his mouth and the glorious pleasure coursing through her body. She finally tugged on his hair to get his attention.

"I want you inside me," she whispered, aching for him. "Now."

His eyes were slits when he raised his head. His pulse beat visibly in his neck.

Awash in sensation, she slid her bare leg along his spine, which she knew drove him wild.

He uncoiled like a spring so he could finish undressing. When he stretched out naked against her, she kissed him deeply and ran her hand down his chest. He caught her before she could touch him.

"Not yet, Gracie," he said hoarsely. "I won't be able to stop."

"Who says you have to?" she asked, in the thrall of her own empowerment and desire. It was a heady mix for a woman who rarely thought beyond the baby's next feeding and her role at the restaurant.

She stroked him, watching his face. She knew exactly where to touch him to make his head fall forward. They'd gotten good at knowing how to pleasure each other.

"That's enough," he ground out.

He grabbed a condom and handed it to her. She delighted in slowly putting it on him.

"You're killing me, Gracie."

His teeth clenched, and Grace smiled. Oh, yes, she'd missed driving him wild like this.

Jordan must have caught her look because he slid his hand between her legs and caressed her.

"Oh, God," she said, her head pressing into the pillows. "Just like that."

Her eyes closed again, and she felt Jordan ease between her legs and slowly enter her.

He took his time, and for a moment she wondered if he was still worried about hurting her. But when he was finally buried deep inside her, all she could do was arch her back to bring him in a little deeper.

At his groan, she opened her eyes. He was watching her, his lips slightly parted.

They were filled with desire, yes, but there was so much love there.

***

Seeing Grace under him, feeling her skin, being inside her again, filled Jordan with a sense of awe. She was back with him. They were together again. And he was going to savor every moment.

He started a slow rhythm, and she responded by moaning and locking her legs around him. He caught her hands in his, wanting the connection.

Desire raged and swept them into a more frantic pace. Thrusting into her with longer, harder strokes, he watched her head thrash back and forth. She was moaning brokenly now, and Jordan felt his own body flush with sweat. He put a strong forearm under Grace's hips, changing the angle, and she flew over the edge, her body pulling him over with her.

He lowered himself to Grace, resting on his elbows so as not to crush her. She'd always liked his weight on her, especially after they made love. He worried he weighed too much, but she would wrap herself around him as if she didn't want to let him go—just like she was doing tonight.

He pressed his forehead to her shoulder and concentrated on taking deep breaths, filling his lungs with her scent, muskier now from their joining. Even though he was in tip-top shape, his heartbeat was pounding in his ears. Jordan couldn't remember a time when their lovemaking had been this powerful. Their first time had been fraught with nerves, but good, really good. This, though? They'd reached a whole new level. He kissed the top of her head. The shorter curls still looked different than her old hair, and part of him missed weaving his hands into her hair when he kissed her.

He felt something wet on his chest and then heard her utter a sharp gasp. That made him smile, and he pushed off her and handed over his T-shirt for her to clean up. When she left his shirt over her breasts, Jordan decided not to tug it away. She was a little flustered now, beyond the flush of orgasm.

"No big deal," he said, stooping to kiss her neck. He put his hand over the T-shirt covering her breasts and caressed them in the hopes of helping her past her embarrassment.

To his relief, she snuggled close instead of pulling away. He pulled her onto his chest after dispensing with the condom. After a moment, he raised himself up to look down at her. Her lips were swollen, her face flushed. The green eyes gazing at him were calm and filled with a joy he hadn't seen for a long while. His heart squeezed painfully in response.

"Grace," he said simply.

She leaned in to kiss him, and he let her. Slowly. Deeply. That kiss forged a new bond between them, one even stronger than their lovemaking. When she pressed away, she fitted herself against his side again, stroking his chest.

His body grew heavy, poised for sleep, but he could

feel the tension return to her muscles. He could hear the wheels starting to turn in her head and wished he had a fork to grind them to a halt.

"It'll be okay, Grace. We'll figure it out. Together."

She fell asleep in his arms a short time later while he caressed her, and only then did he allow his eyes to close.

He awakened to Ella fussing on the monitor, and it took him a moment to remember where he was. Then he smiled at the sensation of Grace's slim, warm body pressed next to his. He looked over at her. She was snoring softly, something she never did, and had plastered herself all over him in her sleep.

Carefully withdrawing her arms, he rolled out of bed, hoping she wouldn't wake. Good Lord, it was seven o'clock. Ella had given them both a treat by sleeping a little later than normal. Perhaps it was the extra feeding Grace had given her after coming home. He shut off the monitor in the bedroom and walked naked down the hall because he could. Because last night had changed things.

Ella lay on her back, squirming like a helpless little bug, whimpering.

"Hey, sweet pea," he said, and she thrust her hands up in the air and gave a demanding cry. "Did you miss me? I missed you."

Jordan picked her up, and she immediately started rooting around against his chest.

"You just had to be hungry," he said with a sigh. "Do we go for a bottle or your mama?"

He didn't want to wake Grace—God knew she needed the rest—but he carried Ella back to bed because he didn't want to keep their family apart for another moment.

The low lamplight made her look even more at

peace. Grace was lying on her side, so he pulled his shirt away from her and arranged Ella close to her body. He guided her little mouth to Grace's breast, and Ella rooted around until she clamped on the nipple. Grace lifted a hand to cuddle Ella closer, but her eyes remained shut as the baby drank noisily.

Grace seemed to fall back asleep, and Jordan stayed where he was, one hand on Ella's back to support her while she nursed. There was beauty here, and he savored every minute as he watched the two most important women in his life.

When Ella started to fuss after letting go of Grace's nipple, Grace shook herself and half-sat up. "You're fine, baby. Let's switch sides."

And then her eyes opened all the way, and she blinked at Jordan.

"Oh," she said in a sleep-roughened voice. "Hello."

He couldn't stop himself from smiling. "Forget I was here?"

"I was...out. God, what time is it?"

When she turned to look at the clock, Jordan could tell she was fighting some morning discomfort.

"A little after seven." He ran his hand over Ella's head. "I love watching you nurse her."

She curled back into the covers and guided their daughter to the other side. "That's easy for you to say. You don't have to pump every day and wear pads in your bra."

He saw her point, but it didn't change how he felt. "I know it's not perfect, but it's beautiful, Grace. It's like being a dad. There are the dirty diapers and the spitting up. And then she falls asleep on my chest, and it nearly stops my heart."

"You've surprised me these last few months," she told him.

"I've surprised myself," he answered honestly.

She leaned forward and lightly kissed him on the lips.

He felt there was a message in that kiss, but couldn't decipher it. "What was that for?"

"I never thanked you for giving her to me," she said, and then she smiled.

They lay there as a family, enjoying each other. When she finished nursing, Jordan encouraged Ella to roll over. Grace reminded him that she'd only spit up. He smiled as Ella looked back and forth between him and Grace. It was like she was wondering what had changed.

When Ella fell back asleep, he took her back to her crib. His heart grew in his chest as he stood in the doorway to Grace's bedroom. She hadn't made a move to the shower. She lay there curled up on her side, waiting for him.

When she held out a hand, he let her pull him onto the bed.

CHAPTER 19

When Grace awoke again, she couldn't ignore the warm male body curled up behind her. If his light snoring was any indication, Jordan was still sleeping. She could hardly blame him. Between the lack of sleep, emotions, and love play, she was exhausted, but she had to face the full consequences of her actions.

She'd slept with Jordan. Twice.

Her resistance had been waning ever since she'd told him about Ella, if she were being honest. But was she really ready to try again with him or was last night...just last night? She could not admit to herself that she'd gone to bed with him without fully thinking things through. That made her feel like crap. She knew better—for him and for herself. Plus there was Ella to consider.

She opened her eyes finally, hearing Ella grunt and coo on the monitor. When she eased out from under Jordan's arm, he mumbled and then grabbed a pillow to his chest. Turning off the monitor, she closed the bedroom door and went to get Ella. Her daughter was lying on her back, doing her best impression of singing for a three-month-old. When she saw Grace, she kicked her feet excitedly and gave a toothless grin.

"Hey, baby girl," she sing-songed. "You look happy. Thanks for going back to bed earlier and sleeping better last night."

She picked her up and hugged her tight. Oh, the love. Every morning, she was in awe of this precious little being. The knowledge that Jordan felt the same way had enhanced her feelings for him.

She'd fallen in love with the hard-working man who had big dreams. Now, she'd fallen in love with the family man and wasn't so sure she could stay away. Being in this house together made her feel like they really could be a family. Jordan showed every sign of wanting that. Could she trust it?

After giving Ella a quick bath and dressing her, she took her downstairs to feed her. The morning sunlight was especially lovely in the family room at this time of day, and since it was her day off, she planned on taking it slow.

She was nursing Ella when Jordan came down. His hair was wet from the shower, and he'd changed into one of the spare outfits he kept in the guest room.

Ella stopped nursing and turned her head on the yellow nursing pillow, cooing.

"Hey, princess," he called out, crossing the room to join them. "Are you having breakfast?"

After a moment of tension, Grace relaxed. She wouldn't try to cover up—not after what they'd shared last night.

"Hey," he said to her, stroking Ella's head when she resumed nursing. "Sorry I slept through her second wake up. You should have poked me or something."

"You were snoring," she said, feeling a little shaky.

"Charming," he said, rolling his eyes. "Ah...would it be weird if I kiss you good morning? I...kinda want to."

She straightened against the sofa cushions, surprised he would be so direct. Ella stopped nursing and turned her head to stare at him, giving him an eyeful of nipple. Grace felt another twinge of embarrassment. She cupped Ella's head and guided her back to nurse.

"Ah...no, it wouldn't be weird," she said, her voice cracking.

Well, that sounded convincing.

He exhaled sharply. "Great." Leaning over her, he gave her a soft kiss. "You look beautiful. I'm...happy this morning in a way I haven't been for a long time."

"I'm glad," she said awkwardly because she could hear the subtext behind his words: *we should do this more often, like every morning.* The Jordan who focused on what he wanted and didn't stop until he had it was back in force. She felt unsure in the face of it.

Ella let go of her nipple again and gave him a toothy grin that sent milk running down the side of her face. Grace reached for a burp rag. "You're distracting her from her breakfast," she finally said, giving him a look.

He held up his hands. "Sorry. Have you eaten yet?"

"No," she said. "Ella always gets first dibs."

"Is it okay if I make you some eggs and share them?" he asked, rocking on his heels. "I have some time before I need to head to the stadium."

Lovemaking and breakfast too? He'd hardly ever cooked for her in the past, always preferring to take her out. Yeah, he was focused. "Sure. There's some bacon, chives, and cheddar cheese in the refrigerator."

"Cool," he said, heading over to the kitchen. "Do you want more tea?"

So he was going to wait on her too? "I could have another cup."

For the next ten minutes, he brewed her more tea and made them both eggs. When Ella finished nursing, he took her and burped her while he sat next to Grace. He absently picked at his food and drank the espresso he'd made in between wrangling their increasing wiggly daughter.

"The eggs are good," she said, also picking at them, her stomach nervous from all his attention.

"They're not yours, but I didn't want you to have to cook when you do so much else around here," he said, giving her a full-watt smile.

He was impossible to resist when he was like this, and part of him knew it.

"She's becoming more active, isn't she?" He dropped his fork when Ella turned sharply in his arms.

"Yes. I don't miss the old days when all she did was eat, sleep, and poop. This is more fun."

"You can see her personality starting to develop," he said, tapping her nose playfully. "When you moved your plate back from her little hands, I swear I saw her brow wrinkle. It was like you'd ticked her off."

She chuckled. "Jordan, I don't think you can tick off a three-month-old."

He nuzzled their daughter's neck, making her belly laugh. "I'm not so sure."

His eyes tracked to the clock to the right of the sink, and she knew he was marking off time. Soon he would have to leave. He had already stayed later than he normally did.

"What are you beautiful ladies going to do while I'm at work today?" he asked, and Grace could feel him weaving the ribbons of being a family around them.

"Take lots of naps," she said. "I don't know. Maybe play on the blanket outside or go for a walk. The leaves are finally starting to turn and show their fall colors."

"That sounds fun," he said, rocking Ella when she cuddled against his chest. "I wish I didn't have to go in and be tortured by... What do you call them? Fat guys in tights?"

"I might have used that term," she said, and there it was, the gentle teasing between them.

"I'd rather stay here with you guys," he said, giving Ella a smacking kiss on her cheek, making the baby laugh.

Grace joined in, and as she did, the nerves in her stomach loosened. Hadn't her mom told Ella she and Jordan had stopped laughing? It seemed that was back.

Jordan glanced at the clock again while tickling Ella. There was no postposing the inevitable.

"I know you need to leave," she said softly.

His artic blue eyes met hers, and the uncertainty in them touched her soul. "We haven't talked yet."

"No," she answered.

He took a deep breath, holding Ella easily in place with one hand. "Will you...can we talk after I get home tonight? Once Ella goes down, of course. We need... some time."

"That would be fine," she said, sounding a little prim—even to her own ears.

He stretched his neck from side to side, like it had grown tense during their exchange, and Ella laughed at the motion. "Great. I'll see you then."

Grace took Ella from him after he kissed her on the cheek and said his goodbyes. He stood over her for a moment before cupping the back of her neck in his damp palm and leaning in to kiss her briefly on the mouth.

"Talk to you later," he said and left.

Later wasn't too far away. Grace had some thinking to do.

She was puttering around with Ella, putting away

her clothes and restocking the diaper table when Tony called.

"I'm on my way over with your car," he said. "Some fresh parmesan arrived, and after we broke the seal this morning, I thought you should have a piece for the house. I'll be there in five."

When he knocked on the front door, she picked up Ella—who hated to be alone even if it was only for a minute—and answered it.

"Hi there," she said to Tony, who stood unsmiling in his Italian leather jacket and jeans.

"Buon giorno," he said, kissing her on both cheeks before studying her and then stroking Ella's cheek.

"You didn't come by just to drop off my car and bring me parmesan," she said frankly as Ella reached for Tony.

He played with the baby's little fingers. "I was worried. We all were. Being Italian, I brought you a little treat."

They detoured into the kitchen, and Grace placed Ella down on one of her soft receiving blankets. She kicked her feet, cooing, as Tony sank onto the floor beside her. He handed the parmesan up to Grace, and she put it away.

"Do you want an espresso?" she asked.

"Not right now. Some Pellegrino would be great."

After pouring them both some sparkling water, she sank onto the floor beside them. "I'm fine." At his incredulous look, she shrugged. "I'm better. Well...I don't really know what I'm feeling right now. Things got...confused last night."

Tony tickled Ella's belly, making her giggle. "You got back together with Jordan," he said, stating it as a fact and not a question.

"How in the world could you know that?" she asked, blinking.

Ella turned her head as if sensing the change in her voice. She gave the little girl a smile, and her heart melted when Ella returned it.

"I've known you both since New York," he said dryly. "Give me some credit. I was also...unsure how Jordan would handle the news. I knew he would feel responsible, but it's natural that he would also feel threatened. Any man would when another man asks out the woman he loves."

"Huh," she said, sitting back on her haunches. "I hadn't thought of that." Jordan always seemed so strong, so sure of himself. But hadn't he told her last night that he still felt threatened? That he sometimes worried the people who said they liked him were only pretending? Did he believe that of her?

"How did you leave things with Jordan?" Tony asked.

Tracing Ella's blanket, she let out a deep breath. "We haven't talked yet. We're going to tonight. I'm...not sure what to do. I'm not completely certain the reasons we broke up have changed."

"I suppose the question is: have you?" Tony asked, grabbing Ella's giraffe toy and squeezing it so it would squeak.

"Have I?" she asked. "What do you mean?"

"It's obvious you two haven't stopped loving each other," Tony said, setting the giraffe on Ella's tummy so she could flail her arms at it. "Now you have Ella."

"You think I should get back together with him to give Ella a father?" she asked, rubbing the tightness in her diaphragm.

"I'm not saying you should do anything," he said, gazing at her steadily. "I'm only saying Jordan has surprised you by how he's acted with Ella. He's stopped putting you and your family on hold for his career. Isn't that worth something?"

It was worth everything, but that didn't mean the rest of their problems would just go away. "What do I do about the media or guys like the one last night?"

"If Ella wasn't here, I would use harsher language," he said with a wry smile. "The clean version is to stop caring what they say. I'd hate to see you give up on something you want because of fear, Grace. You don't do it in your professional life. You can kill a lobster with a knife between its eyes. You can go off to Italy to work in another famous chef's kitchen. You're a mystery to me sometimes."

She was like Jordan that way, she supposed. She focused on what she wanted professionally and didn't take no for an answer. It was on the personal front she had trouble finding her voice.

"You're right. I know you are. But Tony, it's hard to explain how exposed that kind of media attention makes me feel."

"Then you have to decide if what you two have together, and with Ella, is worth facing it."

Ella cooed and thrust out her little hand, which Grace took. "I want her to have everything," Grace said softly. "I want her to have...oh, God...I want her to have a home with two parents who love her. I've always wanted that. Heck, I'm living in the replica of the home I've always dreamed about. But I also want her to be safe. I don't want anyone to ever make her feel like she's not good enough."

"You and Jordan will handle things as best you can," Tony said. "He's already gone to great lengths to keep this compound guarded."

"But he can't protect us outside our home," she said. "Last night proved that."

He frowned. "I know, and for that I am deeply sorry, but it also helped me understand Jordan's frustration. I was awake half the night, angry it had happened in my place. It was sobering, let me tell you... It was hard for me to conclude that none of us can shield you from the world's interest, Grace—not even at the restaurant."

Hearing that made her heart beat faster. The restaurant was her home, her family, which was why the incident had shaken her to the core.

"But I finally fell asleep like a baby when I figured out a different way to look at it," he told her, tickling Ella's little feet. "Can I share it with you?"

She nodded, feeling her throat thicken at the softness in his voice. He was being so gentle with her. She was so lucky to have him for a friend.

"So what if that guy asked you out because he wanted to see Jordan?" Tony said. "You were never really unsafe in the restaurant. We were all there. And if you'd actually gone out with him? The truth would have been discovered sooner rather than later. As soon as you discover a person's not genuine, all you have to do is leave."

She thought about it for a moment before answering. "Okay, I'll concede I wasn't in mortal danger, but it felt so invasive. How am I supposed to know if people are just using me? It's an awful feeling. Tony, I don't want to go through life constantly questioning the people I meet. And not everyone is that benign. The press especially."

"You can't live your life tucked away or in fear of being hurt," Tony said. "In the end, you have to decide how you want to live and let life rise to support that. I left Italy with a vision for my life, and it's worked out pretty well for me."

"You barely spoke English. I sometimes forget that."

He gave an expressive shrug. "My desire to explore life's possibilities was stronger than my fear of not being successful. I started my first restaurant in New York because I wanted to be in one of the world's biggest food capitals and show I had something to share. Jordan is in the so-called football arena because he has something to share too. He's accepted the other crap as part of being there. Perhaps you need to as well, if you're to be with him."

She thought about her discussion with Jordan last night. He was more affected by the so-called haters than she'd thought, but he'd found a way to cope with it. Could she accept that her life would be composed of invasive photos and questions? And that Ella's might be as well? Could she do that? Did she want to?

"You've given me a lot to think about," she said, giving him a pointed look.

"It *is* your day off," he said, stroking Ella's cheek and then rising. "I need to get back. Let me know if you need anything. Otherwise, I'll see you tomorrow."

She stood and kissed him on both cheeks, adding a third kiss for extra affection, which made him laugh.

"Thank you, Tony," she said, putting her hand on his arm.

"Later, *bella,*" he said with once last glance. "I'll see myself out."

After he left, she sat cross-legged beside Ella. "Your Uncle Tony is pretty great, isn't he?"

Ella cooed, drooling as she smiled. Then suddenly she turned to the right and rolled onto her tummy.

"Oh, my goodness!" Grace said, tears popping into her eyes. "Look at you. You did it again, sweet girl."

Her daughter's head rose, and she laughed out loud. Grace found herself joining in, wiping the tears streaming down her face. She needed to text Jordan and tell him. Rising, she grabbed her phone off the counter only to discover he'd already texted her.

Hey! I forgot to text you the video of Ella rolling

over. Hopefully she'll wow you on her own today. Thanks again for giving her to us, and thanks for making my life so happy. I'll see you tonight.

There it was again. That word. Happy. He'd added a heart emoticon at the end, which touched her deeply. Sure, it was a silly cartoon symbol, but Jordan didn't use such things lightly.

She texted him back.

Hey! She just rolled over for me, and I'm in awe. She's the most talented little girl ever. I couldn't be more delighted. See you soon.

And because he had opened himself to her, she added a heart at the end of her message too.

CHAPTER 20

By the time Jordan arrived home, he'd gone from focused to frazzled. The team was set to take on its toughest opponent to date this Sunday, but the prospect of talking about last night with Grace was more daunting. Despite the encouraging text she'd sent him earlier.

He let himself out of his car and stared at the door to his own house. If he were honest, he hated this house now. Before, he'd told himself its sleek modernity better suited his tastes. But the yellow house across the way with the traditional front porch was home now. Grace had been right to call it her dream house. When he looked at it, it seemed to hold everything he'd ever wanted.

Please don't let me lose that tonight.

Postponing his talk with Grace wasn't going to help anything—besides, he was eager to see her and Ella before she went to bed.

He detoured into his house and picked up Grace's favorite wine, which he'd kept around because...he just had. He'd thought about getting her flowers on the way home, but the gesture had seemed too overt. The last thing he wanted was for her to feel he was hurrying things, even though he wanted to. But he'd texted her to let her know that he was on his way.

When he let himself in the house, he called out to her like usual. "Hey!"

"Up here," she called back from the stairs.

He set the wine on the counter in the kitchen and headed to the second floor. They were playing on the floor when he found them in Ella's nursery. Their daughter's hair was damp from her bath, and she cooed when she saw him, kicking her feet wildly.

"Hey, baby girl." He plopped down on all fours and started kissing her belly.

She giggled and wiggled her little body, making him laugh. Then he nuzzled her neck before he could summon up the courage to look at Grace. She was smiling, but there was wariness in her gaze.

"Hi," he said, deciding to go ahead and kiss her cheek without asking.

She tensed up a little and let out an audible breath. "Sorry," she said, giving his shoulder a mere brush with her fingers.

All right, so they might not be easy touching each other yet, but she was trying too. This was progress, and he managed to suck in a deep breath.

"How was your day?" he asked.

"Good," she said quickly. "We both napped. Went for a walk. And ate some fresh-off-the-boat parmesan from Parma. You're welcome to have some."

Sharing Tony's special parmesan with him was more than an olive branch. It was an overture. They'd eaten it together on more than one occasion, paired with a bottle of wine, and made love afterward.

"We must be on the same wavelength. I brought over a bottle of Barolo Montfortino."

"You did?" she asked, blinking. "How did you…"

He gave her what he hoped was an easy smile. "I had a few bottles in the cellar for special occasions. Like when Ella took her first steps." That was true, but not entirely so. This was no time for him to hold back, so he forced himself to say, "It's also your favorite wine."

"Well," she simply said. Some inscrutable emotion passed through her eyes, but she returned her gaze to Ella before he could interpret it.

He did the same, noticing the baby's eyes were drooping. She gave him a drool-filled smile as he ran a finger over her feather-soft brow. "Someone's sleepy."

"Yeah," Grace said, holding one of the baby's little feet in her hand. "Do you want to put her down or did you have a tough day? I forgot to ask."

Another encouraging sign. "It was mostly good. Practice is going well this week. I think we've come up with a good game plan."

"It's a big game this weekend," she said with a slight hesitation in her voice. "Two undefeated teams coming together."

"I didn't know you kept up with the team," he made himself say.

Of course, he had wondered. Before they'd broken up, she'd stopped attending his games, saying the press was beating on her. Which was true. It had hurt him more than he'd cared to admit. Football was so much of who he was, what he loved. It had been hard not to share it with her.

She lowered her eyes. "I thought Ella would like to know what you're up to."

"Ah." Not quite the answer he was hoping for, but he let his hand cover hers briefly. "Go on down and chill. I'll be there in a bit. She won't last long."

He picked Ella up, and they both stood.

"I'll open the wine and set the cheese out," Grace said. "Did you eat?"

"I grabbed something before I left." He started patting Ella on the back and bouncing on his heels.

Grace gave him one last half-smile and then turned off the light on her way out. Ella raised her head from his shoulder at the change and then snuggled back against him. Already her body was growing heavy. He rocked her to sleep, humming to her, as he contemplated the woman waiting for him downstairs. Grace might be guarded, but she wasn't closed off. He let hope fill his heart as their daughter's warmth spread through him.

When he finally made his way downstairs, Grace was waiting for him at the kitchen table. The open bottle of wine presided over two crystal red wine glasses. A plate of parm and grapes sat beside it. He grabbed a chair as Grace poured the wine and handed him a glass.

He extended it until their rims touched. "To the most beautiful and amazing daughter in the world and to the woman who gave her to me."

Her green eyes warmed, and the corners of her mouth rose in a brief smile before she drank.

They watched each other as they drank, the silence of the room wrapping around them. The whispers of Ella's sound machine could be heard over the baby monitor. Jordan finally set his glass aside since he didn't drink much during the season—something Grace knew—and reached for the cheese knife. Without ceremony, he cut a slice of the parmesan and plopped it into his mouth.

"This," he said, groaning, letting the texture and taste wash over his tongue: smooth and buttery with a slight tang. "What in the world did we put on spaghetti as kids?"

"Sawdust?" She laughed. "Certainly not this."

He cut her a slice and handed it to her. Their fingers

brushed when she took it from him. Their eyes met, and suddenly all he could think of was making love with her again. Like they used to. She seemed to sense it because she broke eye contact and fiddled with the grapes.

Dancing around the subject wasn't going to get them anywhere, but he wasn't exactly eager to jump into it either. "It was nice of Tony to bring this by," he said to be conversational.

She took a drink of her wine before speaking. "He mentioned he found himself sympathizing with you after last night."

"He did?" he asked quickly.

"Yes," she said. "He realized how frustrating it must be that you can't keep people from bothering me because of you."

Shit. He set the half-eaten slice of parmesan on the table. "Frustrated is a mild term. Pissed off is closer, but since you dislike me using dirty words, it will have to do. But the anger's not the worst of it. It makes me feel powerless. And since it's part of the reason I lost you—besides my own actions, which I take complete responsibility for—it also makes me feel really sad. I hate that most of all."

Her glass bobbled when she set it aside with shaky fingers. Unlike she'd begun believing, Jordan wasn't invincible after all. Just like her, he battled feelings of helplessness and sadness.

"I didn't really understand that fully until Tony told me. I'm sorry."

It cut him deep that Tony was the one who'd made her understand something that had been bothering him for a while now. "I wonder why you couldn't hear it from me."

"Maybe I was too wrapped up in my own fears," she said, gesturing awkwardly with her hands. "Or maybe it was what I blamed our problems on."

"I know I've said it before, but I'm sorry I stopped putting you first, sorry I stopped making you happy. I've hoped...to show you that I've changed."

She put her hand on the table, and he covered it with his own. Her green eyes met his.

"I want to try again, Grace," he said, clearing his throat when it clogged. "I want you and me and Ella to be a family, but when it comes right down to it, I just want you."

She sat there quietly, holding herself together. "I want us to be a family too. I never wanted it to be this way."

Encouraging words, but not the ones he needed her to say. "But what about me, Grace? I'm still a football player. I can't give you your dream yellow house in Deadwood and work with your dad. I can't keep the media from saying anything about you. But I'm here with you and Ella because I want to be."

She scooted her chair close to him until their knees touched, keeping their hands connected. "Seeing you these past few months, it's like you're *you* again—but different. More open. Do you understand?"

He could feel the tightness in his chest intensify. "I know you're scared I'll lose myself again and forget about you and Ella, but I won't. Okay? I promise you that, Grace."

Her quiet reserve unsettled him.

"Now that I'm where I want to be, I can scale back to what's vital. You and Ella are so much more important to me."

She looked down, and he scooted his chair even closer to her since the slight contact of their knees wasn't enough of a connection right now.

"I don't know if you've realized it," he continued, "but I haven't been partying as much or doing all that extra stuff. I don't miss it really. When I leave the field, all I want to do is come home to you and Ella."

She bit her lip and turned her head away.

"Are you crying?" he asked, hoping it meant he'd finally reached her—and not that she was about to turn away.

"A little," she said, sniffing. "Jordan, I want to believe you. I want to believe we can make this work."

He gripped her hand harder to bring her attention back to him. "If we want this to work, then it will. We decide, Grace. I'm not going to let anyone else interfere, including me or the media or assholes like that guy at the restaurant last night. Is that something you're willing to do?"

Despite all he'd said, she had to make the choice. He held his breath.

She leaned forward, and from the warm glow in her green eyes, he knew her answer before she spoke the words.

"I want it too," she said in the sweetest voice he'd ever heard. "I've been thinking about it all day—heck, since that moment when we went baby shopping. I'm happier with you. And so is Ella."

He closed his eyes briefly. "Thank God."

Then he felt her shift in her chair. Her mouth covered his, and they tumbled into the deepest, most mind-blowing kiss they'd ever shared. Suddenly, the world was theirs again, and everything was possible. They were soaring through the evening sky like a kite.

He pulled her onto his lap, groaning as she curled into him. Sliding his hand around her nape, he brought their mouths together with greater intensity, changing the angle, kissing the corner of her lips before making sensual passes with his tongue.

She moaned too, offering herself up to him. Any final

walls between them seemed to crumble, and he broke the kiss so he could look straight into her eyes. She paused, panting.

"I love you," he uttered harshly. "I never stopped. I'll never stop."

Her brows drew in as she fought tears. "I love you too. I always have."

Their mouths met again, and he scooped her more securely into his arms and carried her upstairs.

When they entered her bedroom, he laid her on the bed and proceeded to show her all the words he held in his heart for her.

CHAPTER 21

Since Grace and Jordan both worked unconventional hours, they'd always favored morning sex. Ella's presence in their life was changing that, and while Grace loved her daughter to pieces, it couldn't help but make her a little cranky.

"We're going to have to set an alarm or something," Jordan mumbled, rubbing his eyes as she fed their daughter. "I knew she got up early sometimes, but it's not even light out yet. I was hoping to have a little time together before she woke up."

Grace wasn't any less tired than he was. Their reconciliation had lasted well into the night. "Let's just pray she falls back to sleep."

He folded his hands prayer-like on his chest. She was too tired to laugh.

Ella let go and turned her head to smile at her daddy, drooling madly. God, how could she be so wide awake? There was no way she was falling back to sleep.

"Do you think she's wondering why I'm here like

this?" Jordan asked. "I made sure to read what the experts say about being naked in front of your kids without it being weird. We have a few years."

This time the laugh bubbled out despite her exhaustion. "Jordan strut-his-stuff-on-and-off-the-field Dean is worrying about being naked?"

He shot her a look. "Hey! I'm trying to be a good father here."

That shut her up. "I know. I'm sorry I laughed."

"It *is* kinda funny," he admitted, cupping Ella's head. "If only my Once Upon a Dare guys could hear this conversation."

"They wouldn't believe it," she said, stroking the soft curls on her daughter's head. "Ella, let's finish eating."

Her daughter turned at her name, smiled, and went back to nursing.

"She's not going back to sleep, is she?" Jordan asked.

"No," she answered, watching their daughter kick her feet. "She'll probably go down for a nap around ten."

"Oh, well," he said with a sigh. "Everyone says this is natural. We'll just have to carve out some extra time for us. And not just for sex—although I love that—but to... well...to be together. Maybe have a date night. I...want you to feel special to me again."

Oh, Good Lord. This was the sweet and considerate Jordan she'd missed. "I'd like that." Then she thought about what it would mean to go on a date in public with him and tensed. Ella stopped nursing again and looked up at her.

Jordan laid his hand on her arm. "We'll find somewhere private, Grace. Trust me on this."

Everyone would know they'd reconciled if they were seen in public without Ella. Was she ready for that? Was she ready to face another round of mean-spirited comments about her looks, about how Jordan Dean was settling? She decided this wasn't the time to bring it up.

"Okay."

He frowned a moment before taking a breath and smiling. It was his way of shaking things off.

"I'd also like to bring over some more things if that's okay," he said haltingly. "I'm not saying we need to talk about anything else yet, but I'd...like to keep some things here in your bedroom and bath."

'Anything else' meant marriage. That thought made her heart beat faster. Surely that was where this would lead. It was what she'd always wanted, and he knew that. But it wasn't going to be a simple, normal people kind of marriage like she'd imagined. Part of her went cold with fear at the thought of the media always being in their lives.

"Breathe, Grace," he said, rubbing her arm briskly. "I know you're freaking out. We can go as slow as you want. I don't mean to rush you."

Rush her? She hadn't been the one dithering. "Of course you can keep some things in here. I want you to feel comfortable." She couldn't say yet: *I want you to feel at home.*

"Great," he replied, tickling Ella's little feet. "I'll bring some things over after I get home tonight. I'll text you when I'm on my way. You have the lunch shift today, right?"

She nodded.

"I can burp her and get her bathed and dressed while you shower," he offered.

Amy usually did that for her, but since Ella had awoken at the crack of dawn, there was no reason to wait. "That would be great. Then you can hop in after me."

He leaned over and kissed her. "Take your time."

"Jordan, we have a three-month-old. Taking our time is a thing of the past for a while."

"Has she finished nursing yet?"

Ella turned her head again and gave him a toothless grin.

"You're distracting her," Grace said, but their daughter deserved to share in their happy reunion. After all, she was one of the reasons it had happened.

Jordan pulled up the sheet and covered his head. "Is this better?"

Sensing a game, Ella cooed and started kicking her feet wildly.

"Okay," Grace said, "I think you're finished, missy."

As she laid Ella down on the bed, Jordan lowered the sheet and said, "Boo."

Their daughter laughed, and Grace caressed her soft cheek.

"She's all yours."

He lifted her onto his chest. "Good, because that's what she is. All mine. All right. Show Daddy how you burp."

Grace's heart felt aglow as she slipped into the shower, listening to the mingled sounds of her daughter's cooing and Jordan's laughter. She and Jordan might not have made love again this morning, but they'd had family time. Right now, that felt equally as precious.

Even though she was bone tired, Grace found herself humming under the hot spray. Jordan had been so in tune with her last night, and as she washed her body, she couldn't help but think of everywhere he'd touched her. Goodness, she'd missed being with him. When she left the shower, her cheeks were flushed from more than the hot water.

Maybe Ella had fallen back asleep.

But when she got out to dry off, she heard her daughter laughing along with Jordan's baritone rumble. No such luck. She dressed quickly for work and joined them.

"You left the bathroom door open," Jordan said when she returned.

"Yeah, I did," she said, looking back at him curiously.

Ella was lying on the bed beside him with a rattle he must have snagged from the nursery.

"Good...I wasn't sure you would...never mind. Here, take this little sweetie pie. It won't take me long to get ready."

"Really?" Jordan always took his time, saying appearances must be observed like a character plucked out of *The Great Gatsby.*

"Yes, *really,*" he said, scooping Ella up and carrying her over to Grace. "I can change. I can grow."

"You can indeed," she said, fighting laughter.

"I am not that vain," he said, giving her a decided frown.

"Of course not," she said, mostly teasing.

"You'll see," Jordan said, handing her the baby. "Set your watch and prepare to be amazed."

Ella cuddled against Grace's chest and then pulled away to watch her daddy walk into the bathroom, as if she too wanted to time him.

"I'm also leaving the door open," he called out as if it were a proclamation. "Oh, I'll need to use your razor to shave."

Man, he was going to hate that. Her razor always left him with a trio of nicks on his chin. "Why don't you shave at your house?"

"I want to spend as much time with my girls as I can."

She left the bedroom with a spring in her step, delighting Ella, who liked the motion.

When he jogged down the steps not too much later, his hair was damp and finger-combed. Sure enough, there were some nicks on his chin. But he was smiling as he pointed to her. "You made coffee. And eggs? You didn't need to do that."

He wasn't the only one who wanted to spend more time together. "We both needed to eat. Go sit at the table. Everything is ready."

"Did you time me?" he asked, picking Ella up from the receiving blanket. He put her in her carrier and set it on the table so she could better see.

"It looks like you took fifteen minutes," she said, which was a record for sure since it normally took him at least forty minutes.

"Thirteen," he said with a wink. "I can shave off a few more minutes when I have my own razor here."

"Jordan Dean talking about getting ready in less than thirteen minutes?" she teased. "I don't know who you are right now."

He went silent and turned his back. She'd intended it as a joke, but the words had clearly dug deep. Walking over to him, she hugged him from behind.

"I'm sorry if I hurt your feelings."

His chest rose and fell with a deep breath. "I'm trying really hard here, Gracie."

She turned him to face her. "I know, and I appreciate it. I'll be more careful with my words."

He hugged her to him. "Good. I'll be careful too. Come on, let's eat."

They sat down together, and Ella's wide blue eyes tracked between them while they ate. Whenever she caught Jordan or Grace looking at her, she'd grin. The reality of the situation washed over Grace. When they'd broken up before, it had only impacted the two of them. With Ella, everything had changed. They *had* to make this work.

"Hey," Jordan called, setting his espresso aside. "It's okay. We're going to be okay."

She gave him her best smile, and he took her hand and kissed it. After he finished his breakfast, he rose and kissed Ella, playing with her little feet and talking baby talk with her, which always amused Grace. Then he crossed to her and pulled her against him.

"I won't tell you not to worry because I'm doing it too," he said, "but let's be honest about what we're going through. Coach Garretty always used to say it's easier to carry your fears when you share them."

"You've told me a million words of wisdom from that man," she whispered against his chest. "But not that one."

"Because I...wasn't sure I could do it," he said softly.

She edged back. "Why didn't you think you could?"

He shrugged. "I don't know." But his eyes said otherwise.

"Yes, you do. Tell me."

There was a moment of silence before he said, "I was afraid it would only make you worry more if you knew about my fears. You worry a lot, Grace. I...don't know how to help you with that. It's...you worried about the media and things like money so much, it got...it was a lot to handle sometimes. The more I tried to reassure you or help, the more upset you got. I...crap...I felt pretty damn helpless sometimes."

She swallowed thickly. "I'm sorry. I'll try to work on that."

He gripped her more securely. "I didn't tell you to make you feel bad. I just wish...you'd be able to let some of your fears go. It's like you hold onto them. That's not how I function."

No, he'd told her he still had fears. Just not what he did about them. "What do you do?" Her voice sounded small.

"I think about them," he said. "I face them. And then I drop kick them out of my... don't laugh. My private stadium."

"I wouldn't laugh about that," she told him. He had made himself vulnerable to her again, and that was worth honoring. "Maybe I need a private stadium or something. Wait. I know. My own private kitchen." She and the other chefs at Marcellos were scrupulous about keeping their kitchen clean and in order. Fear was rather like a bunch of rotten vegetables, now that she thought about it. Who would willingly leave those in the fridge?

"I like it," he said and glanced off quickly. "Look, I have to run, but I'll be home as early as I can."

She heard the hesitation in his voice. It was obvious he was feeling the stress of the big game this weekend. "I'll see you when I see you. Have a good day."

"You too," he said. Catching her eyes, he lowered his mouth to hers and gave her a slow, soft kiss filled with a thousand promises. "I love you."

"I love you too," she said, still getting used to both saying and hearing the words again.

He gave Ella another kiss and jogged out.

Grace looked at her daughter. "It's all going to be okay."

After Amy arrived to take care of Ella, Grace left for work. Without exactly intending to, she found herself calling her mom on the way to the restaurant.

"Hi, honey," her mom said when she answered. "How's your day so far?"

"Pretty good," she told her. Gripping the steering wheel, she let the words come out in a rush. "Mom, Jordan and I decided to get back together."

"Oh, Grace," she said, the words filled with love. "I'm so happy for you both. This is what I'd hoped for."

"Me too," she admitted, "but I'm still a little scared. I want this to work so badly. For me and for Ella."

"Then make it so," her mom told her. "Half of any good marriage is choosing to be in it every day. The other half is remembering the love that made you decide to be there in the first place."

She gripped the steering wheel. "Mom, Jordan and I haven't talked about marriage yet." This time, she had to believe he really wanted to marry *her*—now—and not because Ella had entered their lives.

"But you will," her mom said, her tone no-nonsense. "Why do you think I used the word? This way you can freak out on your own before Jordan brings it up. Because he will, Grace. He might have dithered about it in the past, God knows, but things have changed. You have a child together. You're living on the same property. This is the next step."

"You always use a two-by-four to drive your point home," Grace said.

"Grace, you love that man, and he loves you. And you have Ella to boot. Talk with each other about why you broke up. Get to the bottom of things. Once you do, let yourself love that man with everything you are. I know that's the way you love, Gracie, because it's the way I love too. All you have to do is do it. Don't let your pride get in the way. I know you waited seven years for him before, but it might be wise to let that go."

"You make it sound so easy," she said, taking the interstate exit to the restaurant.

"It is, Gracie. I know you have your fears. We all do. But as your father and I have told you all your life, the best course is not to wallow in them. It's why you left Deadwood to go to culinary school. It's why you went to Italy even after you discovered you were pregnant. It's why you agreed to live in your dream house in Atlanta next door to Jordan to provide a home for Ella. All that took courage. Remember your grit, Gracie, and when you forget, you call me. Okay, honey?"

Tears popped into her eyes, and she blinked furiously

to clear them as she pulled into Marcellos' parking lot. "Mom, you're the best. You know that, right?"

"I've put in a lot more years than you, is all," she said. "It's my job to share with you what I know and what I see in you. You'll do the same with Ella and any other children you and Jordan have."

More children? Her stomach quivered. Her mother sounded so sure of herself. "You really believe Jordan and I can do this?"

She snorted. "Grace Elizabeth Kincaid. The same blood that brought my great-great-grandparents out West in that wagon train runs through your veins. Of course, I believe that. Besides, I've been on this earth long enough to know true love when I see it. And I see it when I look at you and Jordan. He might have lost himself for a while, but he's realized what's important. That man will be true to you until the day he dies—and with all the temptations around him as a football player, that's saying something."

How many times had her mother used the wagon train story? But somehow, being reminded of her roots helped. She was also happy to hear her mom thought Jordan had changed. It helped to have another person confirm it. After turning her car off, she let her hands fall to her lap.

"If there's one thing I trust, it's that Jordan would never cheat on me. He might be a little tempted on and off, but he wouldn't do it."

"Hard not to be tempted as a man when a bunch of hot women are always sticking their boobs and butts into his face."

"Mother!"

Her mom gave a gusty laugh. "Grace, how many times have we talked about those parties you used to attend with Jordan? I recall you talking about miles of surgically-enhanced cleavage and butt implants."

She had regaled her mom with those stories, and they'd laughed together. It had been a coping mechanism of sorts. But she'd lost the ability to find humor in it after the breakup.

"Point taken," she said, pocketing her keys in her purse. "I'm at the restaurant. Thanks for talking things through with me, Mom."

"Anytime, Gracie. It's one of my greatest blessings. Love you."

"Love you too," she said and ended the call.

She hadn't intended to tell anyone else about her reunion with Jordan. Not until she was more certain of them. But she felt more grounded as she walked into the restaurant, more certain of what they were doing. She realized that keeping their relationship a secret would be a mistake. It was counter to the openness they'd need to show to each other to make it work.

When she walked into the kitchen, she put her hands on her hips. Tony looked up from slicing the skin off a halibut. Victor and the others stopped what they were doing.

"Jordan and I are back together," she said, firming her legs to stand tall. "I wanted to let you know."

Tony gave a slow smile. *"Congratulazioni."*

Everyone else joined in, and Tony walked over and embraced her.

"I'm happy for you, Grace," he told her, kissing her cheeks Italian-style. "And for Jordan and Ella."

"Way to go, Grace," Victor said, lifting his butcher knife in a salute. "If the media messes with you anymore, you let us know."

"Yeah, we'll take care of them," Carlo said. He was smiling, but Grace knew they weren't completely joking.

The other kitchen staff nodded, and she put her hand

on her heart. "Thank you. Now let's get back to work."

Tony snorted. "We've already started. Feel free to join the party."

She gave him a pointed look, knowing he was teasing her for being a little late. "Happy to."

CHAPTER 22

Jordan pulled back onto the interstate after being given a warning for speeding. The police officer had clocked him at eighty-eight miles per hour. Too fast, he knew, but he was eager to see Grace and Ella. The past two weeks had been some of the sweetest of his life.

Reining himself in, he decided to call Sam as a distraction. They were in the same time zone, so he figured he might catch him on his way home from practice.

"Hey," Sam answered. "I'm just heading out from the stadium. You got lucky."

"I was hoping to," Jordan answered. "You ready for Brody this weekend? He wants to kick your ass."

"And I want to kick his," Sam replied good-naturedly. "I don't like playing one of my brothers, but when I do, it's not personal. I want Brody to have his best game. I plan on having mine. The rest will be decided on the field."

"I'm glad my game is at the same time. That way

I won't be tempted to peek at the score." He hated watching his brothers square off against each other. It meant he couldn't root for either team—just for his friends to play good games.

"It's the biggest game of the season for you so far on Sunday," Sam said. "You ready?"

"Yeah," Jordan replied, tapping the steering wheel in eagerness. "As much as possible. You know how it is."

"I do," Sam responded. "How's the little one? Ella gets cuter with every picture you send. Are you the one putting those colorful little bows in her hair?"

"No," Jordan replied, shuddering. "I'm still a little terrified to stick a metal object into her hair, although Grace continues to assure me it's fine." He didn't plan on changing his stance until Ella personally asked him to fix her hair.

"You're saying her name differently," Sam commented.

"Who? Ella?"

"No, Grace," Sam replied. "Something's changed, hasn't it?"

Only Sam would pick up on a little detail like that. "We're back together. I haven't told anyone else yet."

Truth was, he was still getting used to the idea. They were doing great so far. She'd even cleared out a couple shelves in the bathroom vanity and her closet to make space for him.

"You're worried she'll back out again?" Sam asked.

"Yeah. Maybe. I realized today what was bothering me. Why I haven't told anyone. I haven't asked her to come to one of my games. I've been afraid to."

"And Sunday's is even bigger than the one against Baltimore," Sam said, sighing. "I can see your conundrum. She could sit in the owner's box, I suppose."

"She never really felt comfortable with everyone

there," Jordan said, "and she's never made friends with any of the players' wives." Grace said they didn't have much in common, and she wasn't far off. Many of the wives and girlfriends didn't work outside the home, and some were airheads and gold diggers, but deep down Jordan suspected she hadn't tried very hard to connect.

"If it's important to you, you need to ask her," Sam said. "People who love each other support each other. Do you want her there?"

"Yeah," he answered honestly. "And I want Ella there too, but part of me wonders if I'm asking too much. I mean, Ella is still really little. We still haven't even shared a picture of her with the press, and the media's put out a bounty for the first picture. This would take that off the table." But he hadn't told Grace. He was afraid she'd freak—because he didn't much like the thought of it either. He didn't have an answer, and that frustrated him to no end.

"Not an easy place to be in, Jordan. She's a little girl. Any mother would want to protect her child from the kind of media scrutiny Grace has endured. Maybe give Grace a pass on bringing her until she's older. It's a lot of people, and heck, the noise makes me half deaf after the game. Hard to imagine the effect it would have on Ella."

Talking it through with Sam was helping. Why hadn't he thought about all the people and the noise? He wanted to kick himself. "Am I just stressing about this because I want Grace to prove to me she's serious about us? I trust it when we're behind closed doors—"

"But the public thing has been one of the biggest problems between you two," Sam finished. "You're going to have to talk about it sometime. Best do it early in case..."

"Things revert back to the way they were." God, the thought depressed him, but Sam was right. The worry was festering inside him. "I'll find a way to talk about the game with her." It was too early to mention the bounty. He wondered if she'd heard about it, but surely she would have mentioned it. He felt completely helpless. He didn't want to give in to the jackals and release a picture of their daughter. It was like negotiating with terrorists, if you asked him.

"She'll listen to you," Sam said. "Grace has a good heart, and if she wants to give things another shot, it's because she loves you. Try and remember that."

"You're the best," Jordan said.

"Nah. I've just racked up a few more years than you have. Good luck talking to Grace and with the game this weekend. Call me if you need anything."

"Thanks, Sam," he said, feeling a smile tip up the corners of his mouth. "Here's to playing your best game this weekend."

"From your lips to God's ears," Sam said.

"Tell your mom hi."

"I will. She loves seeing pictures of Ella too. It's like pre-grandma fever."

"Good thing she doesn't pressure you to settle down," Jordan said, chuckling softly.

"She knows me too well. I like to do things my own way and in my own time."

Jordan took the exit that would bring him home. "I don't know anyone who would make a better family man than you."

Sam snorted. "On that note, I'll sign off. Later, man."

"Later," he responded as the call ended.

When he entered the gates of their property, he drove down the lane to Grace's house. Since their reconciliation, he'd taken to parking his car in her driveway rather than his garage. So far, she hadn't said anything.

In fact, he hadn't gone through the yellow gate between their two houses since they'd gotten back together. He hoped there would never be a need.

Tonight he was about to find out how far they'd come.

**

Grace looked at the garage door button, but she bounced on her heels a little before opening it. Ella grinned at her and cooed as it rose.

"Thanks for the encouragement," she told her daughter as she carried her down the three steps leading to the driveway.

Jordan's car was cruising toward them, but she'd known he was coming. At her request, the guards at the gate had texted her an alert. He pulled to a stop, and the passenger window lowered.

"Park in the garage," she told him. "It's going to rain."

She turned around and headed back inside quickly, not waiting for him. Waiting would mean allowing him to park in the garage was a big deal. She didn't want to make it a big deal. But her palms were undeniably a little sweaty as she headed back to the kitchen to the pan of boiling water she'd started for pasta. It might be a late dinner, but they could still be civilized about it.

On the platter sitting on the counter, she'd arranged some seasonal meats and cheeses. Freshly sliced red pepper and tomato rested on a bed of buffalo mozzarella lightly dressed with olive oil and shredded fresh basil, topped off with some Celtic salt Grace favored for its rich sea flavor.

Two veal cutlets sat on a plate, coated with the Italian bread crumbs she'd made at the restaurant. A bottle of Nebbiolo was breathing.

"Whoa! She's still awake," Jordan said when he came through the mud room door.

"Yes," Grace replied as Ella cooed and bounced in her arms, clearly happy to see her daddy.

"What do we have here?" he asked, nodding to the kitchen.

"I decided to cook something special," she said as he came toward her.

"After you cooked most of the day?" he asked, suspicion in his voice.

He knew she rarely cooked for herself—well, them—on the days she worked in the restaurant.

"I wanted to," she said, trying not to downplay the gesture.

He stopped in front of her. As his gaze slid down her body, she couldn't help but do the same. His outfit—a white T-shirt under a leather bomber jacket, paired with fitted jeans—sent a flare of lust through her. He was hers again. Hers for the taking. Whenever she wanted.

Except when Ella was awake. Like now.

His eyes heated when she met his gaze again. "Hi," he said, giving her a soft, slow kiss on the mouth.

Ella reached for him, cooing like crazy. He took her from Grace.

"Hi," she responded, slightly breathy.

"Hey, princess," he said, and Ella uttered a squeal loud enough to make them both wince. "How's my little girl?"

She patted his leather jacket and became fixated with the brass buttons. When she leaned forward, he made a face and held her away from his body.

"Let's not chew on Daddy's Italian leather jacket," he said.

Grace couldn't help but laugh. "I thought you'd decided not to wear anything super nice around her after the demise of your shirt."

He gave her a saucy wink. "I wanted to look my best

for you. Shorts and a shirt weren't going to work."

That surprised her. "You know I don't care about that."

"I do, and you might not have looked at me like that just now if I'd dressed differently," he said. Ella shrieked again. "Okay, now, sweetheart. I know you don't like being thwarted about my jacket, but give Daddy's eardrums a break. Mommy's too."

After setting Ella down on the blanket on the floor, he shrugged off his jacket and tossed it on the couch. Grace couldn't help but sigh. Jordan wasn't exactly the tidiest person, and his stuff used to be scattered everywhere across her old apartment. More than once, she'd asked him to pick up after himself, but somehow he'd always managed to get out of it.

"I'll hang it up when I'm finished playing with her," he told her. "I promise."

She nodded and spun around to pour them some wine, needing another minute to compose herself.

"I told you I'm trying," he said softly.

When she turned around to look at him, she saw the intensity on his face. He meant it. "I am too."

"I know," he said, reaching absently for Ella's little foot, but still watching her. "Thanks for letting me park in the garage. I didn't know it was supposed to rain."

She cleared her throat. "It's not a high percentage, but you know Atlanta weather. Things change suddenly." She was so full of it.

Rather than call her on it, he turned his full attention toward playing with Ella on the floor. When her eyes started to droop *finally,* Jordan picked her up, rocking her.

"What can I do to help with the meal while you nurse her?" he asked, bringing the baby over to her.

"Nothing. If you'd like some wine, I set out a glass for

you. But you don't have to drink. I know it's the season and all."

"I'll have a little with our dinner," he said as she sat down with Ella, arranging her against her chest.

"How was your day?" he asked, resting his hand casually on her knee under the nursing pillow.

"Good. Lunch was a bit zany. Tony announced we're booked out with reservations for six weeks now. It's a record."

"Wow! That's huge. Congratulations. Maybe we should pop some champagne."

"I'm allowing myself a little wine while I'm nursing, but we'll have to save the champagne for later." Every mother had different feelings about alcohol and nursing, but Grace had chosen to adopt the Italian way, which meant not denying herself the occasional enjoyment of one of the great pleasures in life. Vino.

"It's a date," he said, taking hold of Ella's little foot, which of course made her turn her head for a moment before resuming her feeding.

"How was your day?" she asked him.

He rolled his shoulders as if he'd suddenly grown tense. "Good. We're ready for Sunday."

Now she knew why he was tense. Was he going to ask her to go to the game? She'd been wondering about this. She'd expected it. She wasn't sure she was ready for it.

"That's great to hear," she said, switching Ella to the other side.

He rose and picked up his jacket from the couch. "I'll hang this up."

When he left the room, she frowned, feeling that wall rise between them again. This wasn't what she wanted. She had promised him—and herself—that she would try.

"Do you want me to go to the game?" she made herself ask when he came back in.

He froze in the doorway. "I don't think that's the question."

Her heart started beating faster. "Okay. What is?"

"Do you ever think you'll want to see me play in person again?" he asked.

Ella stopped nursing and stared at her. Grace saw a flash of light in her daughter's eyes, and it was like the baby was telling her that this was something she needed to do.

"Would it be possible for me to bring a friend?" she asked. "Carlo has become quite the football fan since moving here from Rome last year."

Jordan came over and sat beside her. "Of course you can bring a friend. I know you don't feel comfortable in the owner's box alone, but that's the safest bet."

Safe. Yes, that was important to her. "Okay."

He ran his hand down her arm as if gauging her reaction. "I also know it would be a public declaration that we're back together. I haven't said anything to anyone except Sam."

She'd wondered. "I told everyone at the restaurant the day after it happened. And my mom."

"You did?" he asked, falling back against the cushions. "Well..."

"I needed to."

"I'm glad," he said, scooting closer until their sides brushed. "I didn't know how you felt about telling people."

"We're together," she said simply. "I told you I want this to work. If you can arrange for me and Carlo to come to your game this Sunday, I'll go."

He put a hand on her knee. "Do you want to go? Be honest, Grace. I can take it."

She took a breath. "Do you remember how it used to be when you played in high school? Or the couple of games I visited for in college? I could just sit in the stands and watch you. No one cared who I was. I miss that." More than she wanted to admit.

"I don't blame you," he said. "Things were...simpler then."

"I won't lie," she continued. "I love watching you play. I love hearing your deep voice call out plays and watching you drop back to pass the ball. I love seeing you...don't laugh...chest bump the other guys after a touchdown and the grin on your face after a win."

His blue eyes stared back at her, and for a moment she thought he was getting teary-eyed. She felt a stab of guilt realizing she'd stopped sharing what he loved. It had obviously hurt him more than she'd guessed.

He swallowed thickly. "You have no idea how much that means to me, you saying that."

"Jordan, I love being at the game. It's different than watching at home, but going now...with you being so... huge... It's become a thing. I used to have to talk myself up for it, and then with the media, I got...I decided it wasn't worth going anymore."

His fingers rubbed the outside of her knee like he was soothing her. "I have to talk myself up for it sometimes too. I remember the first time I played Monday Night Football. The audience...it blew my mind. And the President watched me play in the Super Bowl. Trust me, I know it's become a thing. Sometimes I feel like a human pressure cooker."

He'd never shared these thoughts with her, but she was glad to hear them now.

"I wish I could tuck you into an awesome seat on the forty-yard line and pretend no one was going to recognize you," he said. "But we can't lie to ourselves, Grace. The owner's box is safer, and I want you to feel safe. I also plan to entertain the heck out of you."

"Then I'll go," she told him, aware that Ella had stopped nursing completely to watch them. "Just don't ask me to meet you after the press conference. I'm...not ready to face the media yet." She knew pictures would be taken of her even there. She was sure Farley would salivate over her being back in his camera's crosshairs.

"I wouldn't ask that of you. I'll arrange everything with the front office."

"Let me talk to Tony about Carlo taking off for the game," she said, hoping it would work out. They would have to shift some things around for the dinner shift, but it might be okay. Sunday wasn't as busy a day when the Atlanta Rebels were playing.

"I could fly your parents or your brothers in for the day if you wanted," he said, giving her a half smile.

Given how strained their last visit had been, his offer made her chest tighten. She shook her head. "That's too much. I'll work it out. I also need to make sure Amy is available."

"If we need to find someone else to look after Ella, we will," he said, "but I don't want you to stress. I didn't give you a lot of notice about the game. It's okay if it doesn't work out."

He meant what he said, but something told her she had to be up in those stands on Sunday. "We'll make it work. I was thinking it would be wise for us to have a backup sitter anyway. For last-minute things."

"Agreed," he said, giving her a hesitant smile. "I'll contact the service tomorrow and ask for some more candidates. Grace, having you there means the world to me. I hope you know how much."

She did, which was why she was holding her fears in check in front of him. When she put Ella down to sleep for the night, she could sink into the rocking chair and have a freakout before coming back downstairs.

After she finished nursing Ella, Jordan surprised her by volunteering to put her down. Even though Grace needed to turn the water back on high to boil again for the pasta, she couldn't make her legs work.

She had her freakout right there on the couch.

CHAPTER 23

After agreeing to attend the game, Grace had pretty much walked around in a cloud of anxiety for two days. Jordan had bitten his tongue more than once to stop himself from telling her to back out of going, especially when he'd seen her bring home a shopping bag from an upscale Atlanta boutique. He knew she didn't usually buy her clothes at those places.

That was when his light-bulb moment had come. Scoring four last-minute tickets wouldn't ruffle anyone's feathers in the front office. He was the Rebels' quarterback, after all. Hopefully, his gesture would help.

On Saturday morning, Jordan snuck downstairs before either Grace or Ella awakened—pretty much at the butt-crack of dawn—and let in the caterer he'd hired through Tony. The older, no-nonsense woman turned on the oven for the strata she'd made and unpacked the fruit and muffin trays he'd ordered.

When he heard Ella cry, he told the caterer to let herself out when she was finished and rushed upstairs.

His daughter was emitting little squeaks—what he'd coined her fake cry—and kicking her feet. Turning off the monitor in the hopes of giving Grace a few more Zs, he picked Ella up. Her diaper was a soggy mess like usual, but she gave him a toothless grin and darted her head forward, doing her best to head butt his chest.

"Hey missy, go easy on yourself," he said gently. "You're still learning your strength."

Her motor skills were changing all the time. Right now, her head was bobbing forward along with her body. It was like she was trying to propel herself through the air.

"Are you ready for Mommy's surprise?" he asked and dug out his phone to send a text to the people who were a part of it.

Then he changed Ella and woke Grace up to feed her. Ella wasn't known to wait long in the morning for her breakfast.

Grace came awake with a start—something he'd come to realize was a mommy thing. It was like she was instinctively wired to hear the slightest sound and jump to answer it.

"Oh, hi," she said, rubbing her eyes. The pillow crease marking her right cheek was so adorable he had to reach out and touch it. "Has she been up long?"

Given that he was already dressed, it was a reasonable conclusion. He had to be at the stadium around ten o'clock, and it was only eight right now. "Not long. How about you feed her? I'll come back when she's finished so you can shower. I can bathe and dress her today." He kissed her good morning.

"Sounds good," she said, taking Ella from him and fitting her to her breast. Almost immediately her eyes closed again as they snuggled in the bed. He let himself out.

The caterer was gone when he came back down the stairs. He scanned the kitchen table. Everything was ready, so he texted his surprise guests to come up to the house.

Rubbing his hands in delight, he waited to be called back upstairs. When Grace hollered for him, he took the stairs two at a time. He could barely contain his excitement as he got their daughter ready.

"We're wearing something extra special that Daddy had made," he told her, dressing her in the pink baby Rebels jersey with lucky number seven on it—his number. He had set out a second one out on her changing table for game day. He thought about writing a note to say he hoped Grace would put Ella in it tomorrow, but that felt unnecessary. She knew how important it was to him.

Once he left today, he wouldn't see Grace or Ella until after the game tomorrow night. Even though it was a home game, the team stayed at a hotel downtown. That way, everyone would be accounted for by curfew. Every NFL team did it, but this was one time Jordan wished he could come home.

"I'm taking Ella downstairs," he called out to Grace.

"Okay," she hollered back. "I'll be down shortly."

He gave Ella a conspiratorial grin, which she responded to with a delighted coo. "Mommy's going to be so surprised."

Carrying the baby downstairs, he went to the front door and opened it to find his surprise waiting. Blake was sitting on the front porch with his wife, Natalie.

"My goodness," Natalie exclaimed, hopping out of her chair. "Is that Ella? Oh, Jordan, she's the sweetest little girl ever!"

Blake stood to greet them. "She sure is. And she's wearing her Daddy's number too."

Ella cuddled close to Jordan as his friends gathered closer. "Give her a little time to get used to you."

"Being a daddy looks good on you, Jordan," Natalie said, giving him a half hug. "Hey, sweet pea. I love your jersey. Are you planning on rooting your Daddy to victory tomorrow?"

Ella gave her a grin and held out her little hand.

"She's a charmer," Blake said, giving him a nod. "You did good."

"It's all her." He raised her up and gave her belly a zorbert. She squealed in glee. "She's the best."

"She sure is," Natalie said in between making sweet faces at Ella.

Blake put his arm around her shoulders. "We want one of these, don't we, babe?"

"We're doing our darndest to have one," she told Jordan. "It's just taking a little longer than I'd hoped."

"You'll get there," he said, trying not to make light of her frustration.

He and the rest of the guys had all been thrilled about Blake and Natalie's reconciliation. They seemed stronger and happier than ever after their brief divorce. The main reason he'd arranged for them to come was to set Grace at ease. She'd always gotten along with Natalie since they were both in the food industry and called things like they saw them. He was also hoping that seeing their friends so happy together might make Grace more open to marriage. He hadn't bought a ring yet, but he'd been doing his research.

After making her wait for seven years, he wanted to go all out. He needed her to understand he wanted to marry her for her—not just because they had a child. Though a part of him was still scared of messing things up, he was learning that balance and communication were the key. They certainly had the love.

"Come on in, but try and be quiet," Jordan said. "Grace should be down pretty soon. She's going to be so happy to have you guys at the game with her. Thanks for coming last minute."

Once they were all inside, Jordan led them into the den and kitchen area.

"Oh, look at the spread," Natalie said.

"Please make yourselves at home," he told them. "Let's see if she wants to go to you now." But Ella gripped his shirt in her little fists. "Okay, sweetheart. No rush. You'll get there when you're ready."

Blake gave him a hard pat on the back. "It's great to see you like this, man. I can't say it enough."

Ella suddenly turned her head and squealed, and Jordan knew Grace had arrived unsuspected. He locked gazes with her when he turned around.

"I thought it might be nice for you to have a bigger group of friends at the game," he said simply.

"Natalie! Blake!" She put a hand to her mouth as tears filled her eyes. "This is..."

"We know it's a total shock," Natalie said in her no-nonsense voice, crossing the room and hugging Grace. "But I hope you're cool with us flanking you as you walk into the dreaded owner's box and shake hands with all the 'important' people. It's so good to see you, Grace. It's been too long."

"Yes, it has," Grace said, smiling when they released each other. "I was so happy to hear you and Blake got back together."

"Me too," Blake said, hugging her as well. "Congratulations on the most beautiful baby in the world."

"Thank you," she said and then turned to him. "And thank you, Jordan."

The vulnerability in her green eyes undid him, and he found himself unable to even smile. "I wanted you to be accompanied by the best people I could think of. No one is a better protector than Natalie."

His lame attempt at a joke had the woman snorting. "It's terrible we even need protecting. Right, Grace?"

She nodded, still looking at Jordan.

"I remember what it was like to go to this guy's games," Natalie said, jerking her thumb at Blake. "I'd gussy up and hope I was presentable, but there would always be some awkward photo of me where it looked like I was picking my nose. It was like the press was going out of their way to make me look ugly."

"Are you regretting this plan yet?" Blake asked Jordan.

No, this was exactly the kind of solidarity he'd hoped Natalie would have with Grace.

"And then there's all the women in the box," Natalie continued, looking up as if beseeching heaven. "Sure, some of them are nice and normal and have real breasts like you and me, but some of them... I used to have the urge to bring some scarves to drape over their ample chests."

"Tell me you didn't bring any scarves," Blake said. "I can see the video footage on the local news now."

"You know what I mean," Natalie said with a frown. "Anyway, we'll go to the game with you tomorrow and eat lots of awesome food because usually they don't scrimp on that at least. And we'll root for Jordan. After which, you can come home to this beautiful little girl you have, and I can sit back and thank God yet again that Blake retired from professional football."

"Babe, please don't hold back on how you feel," Blake said with a groan.

She sidled up to him and gave him a kiss on the cheek. "You know I love you, but you also know what I'm talking about. The women who love you guys deserve a special badge of honor."

A special badge of honor? Was it really that bad?

Then Jordan remembered everything Grace had gone through in the press—from the cruel stabs about her looks to the mob scene that had surrounded them after baby furniture shopping.

"You're absolutely right, Natalie," Jordan said, giving Grace an encouraging smile. "We're lucky you put up with us."

"Amen," Natalie responded with enthusiasm, putting her hands on her hips. "I'm glad you realize it. Jordan, I think whatever you have in the oven is done."

Grace rushed over and opened the door. "Yeah, I can smell it too. Oh, strata! Jordan, where did you get all this food?"

"I captured an Italian food fairy," he said with a laugh.

Blake gave a snort, his shoulders shaking.

"Fine, don't tell me," Grace said, taking the pan out of the oven. "Let's eat."

Jordan didn't stuff himself like the others did since he had practice. But he did feel more settled now that he had their friends around, like he and Grace were back to old times with them.

They fell into comfortable conversation, and Grace and Natalie were catching up about Marcellos and Natalie's job as the head caterer and right-hand of celebrity chef Terrance Waters at The Grand Mountain Hotel in Colorado.

By the time Jordan finally rose to head to the stadium, Ella was sitting on Natalie's lap and cooing at her. Grace was laughing as Natalie droned on about professional football players' fascination with fake breasts and butts. Blake was smiling indulgently, his arm slung over the back of his wife's chair.

"I need to go," he said, giving Grace a kiss on the cheek. "Love you."

"Have a great game tomorrow since I won't see you," she said, putting her hand on his arm. "Love you too."

Jordan sank down until he was eye-level with Ella, who was leaning back against Natalie's chest. "And you, sweetheart. You root especially hard for Daddy tomorrow."

Blake shook his hand, and they shared a look that spoke of mutual understanding.

"Play your game," Blake said, echoing the words of Coach Garretty.

***

When Jordan called in reinforcements, he didn't scrimp. Grace had always enjoyed his Once Upon a Dare brothers, and Natalie was a gift from heaven. Her wisecracks about the hype around professional football were enough to put a stitch in Grace's side—and they made her feel like she wasn't the only one the press had picked on.

On the drive to the game the next day, Natalie told her story after story about the myriad ways in which the press had made her life difficult, and Grace knew she was doing it to make her feel better. It still worked.

They picked up Carlo on the way to the game, and by the time they all made their way up to the owner's box, Grace felt some of that Midwestern grit her mother had reminded her she had. Jordan had gone to great trouble to support her, and his efforts helped fortify her courage all the more.

Of course, Carlo's promise that he'd grab one of the knives from the buffet and filet anyone who so much as made a wrong move toward her bolstered her spirits too, especially when Natalie said she would join him. Her colleague and Natalie had hit it off, talking about foodie stuff, and it felt good to see her world and Jordan's unite in this new way.

"You're going to do fine, Grace," Blake said as they walked into the box. "If you need any of us to step in, just say the word. I wouldn't mind kicking someone's butt on national TV."

Natalie threaded their arms together. "Smile and remember: the people in this box know they need to be nice to you. You're Jordan's, and they want to keep him happy."

Right. She just hated that their reception of her was more based on Jordan than on any interest in her.

"Grace!" she heard a man call out, and looked over to see the Rebels' owner himself, Chaz Hallowfield, parting the crowd to reach them. "And you brought friends. Blake Cunningham. Good to have a great quarterback in our midst. And Natalie. Jordan has said wonderful things about you."

"I'll bet," Natalie said dryly.

Chaz laughed, the wrinkles around his eyes growing more pronounced. "And Carlo Medzioni," Chaz continued, surprising Grace with how well he'd memorized the names Jordan must have given him. "I'm a big fan of Marcellos."

As Grace recalled, Chaz was over fifty and had inherited his money from a family fortune in oil and real estate. Married more than once, he was an unapologetic Southerner who could be both charming and ruthless. She'd never trusted him.

"How is that beautiful little girl of yours and Jordan's?" he asked, showing her his dentist-white teeth. "My wife and I keep hoping we'll get the chance to meet her and welcome her into the Rebels' family. Everyone is so eager to share in your good fortune. Including the fans."

Grace didn't believe he was the least bit sincere, and neither did Natalie from the way she locked their arms together even more securely.

"Our daughter is still pretty young," Grace replied. "There will be plenty enough time for that."

Grace had a feeling that if the owner thought it would make Jordan happy, he'd host a lavish first birthday party for Ella when the time came. No way was she allowing this man to get his hands on her daughter for PR.

"I'm sure she's the sweetest thing," Chaz said, "but none of us have seen so much as a photo of your daughter. Jordan has been incredibly tight-lipped about her despite how much the Rebels' fans want to celebrate with him."

There it was again. From her earlier interactions with Chaz, she remembered him circling back to points when they hadn't originally gone his way.

"Since we all know Jordan isn't usually tight-lipped," Blake said with what Grace thought was an equally fake smile, "we should respect his wishes. He's got good instincts about things. So does Grace, by the way."

She gave him a smile. "Thanks."

Chaz raised his hand in the air. "Of course Jordan does. He came to Atlanta, after all, and he chose Grace here. Any man could see he has good taste. I'm sure Grace has good instincts too. She's a successful chef in her own right."

The man's pandering was going to drive Grace crazy. "Perhaps you could tell us where we're sitting, Chaz. I'd like to make sure we're settled before the game starts."

"Goodness me," Chaz said with extra Southern charm. "Get some grub first. Jordan asked me to put y'all in the back, as far away from the press as possible. Of course, it would be lovely if you would show your face a little, Grace. Especially since you and Jordan are back together." There was a feral gleam in his eye as he said it.

"I'm here to support Jordan," she told him pointedly.

"Not to give the press a story."

"Coming here to support Jordan after you broke up with him and had his baby is a heck of a story, honey," Chaz said, his tone patronizing enough to put Grace's teeth on edge. "Don't kid yourself."

Blake put his hand on Grace's back. "I'm not used to being in the box during a game or enjoying all the food and drink you guys supply. Since Grace is the accomplished chef here, I hope you don't mind if I borrow her so she can help me pick the right things to try."

As a retreat, Blake's play was a smart one, and from the way Chaz smiled at him, the owner seemed to know it.

"Try the lobster, Blake," Chaz said, gesturing to the buffet. "It's delicious today. I found a new chef. You might know him, Grace. Simon Querald."

Was he trying to remind her that her kind of people made the food for shindigs like this? "I don't think Simon and I have crossed paths."

"There are a lot of chefs out there, Mr. Hallowfield," Carlo said.

"I know you have many demands on your attention, Chaz," Blake said. "If we don't have a chance to chat with you again, I hope you enjoy the game."

He cocked his brow. "Y'all as well. Make yourselves at home and holler if you need anything."

Natalie steered Grace toward the bar. "Please tell me you're drinking at least a little while you're nursing. I'll need a Manhattan after that exchange. Good heavens is he full of himself."

"Red wine," Grace said, wanting to crack the tension in her neck. "And yes, he's a pill. Always has been."

"Good job," Blake said as they approached the bar. "You held up. That's all anyone could ask."

"Some of the owners act like they're gods," Natalie

said, ordering Grace a glass of red from the bartender. "Chaz is clearly one of them. I'm glad Mr. Farnsworth isn't like that. He's the owner of Blake's former team, the Denver Raiders."

"That guy is a jackass," Blake said, patting her on the back.

"A *testa di cazzo*," Carlo agreed.

"I hope it doesn't offend you if I say how much I adore hearing you speak," Natalie purred, waggling her eyebrows at Blake. "Sue me."

"But Chaz knows how to run an organization," Blake said, waggling his eye brows right back at her, "which is why he's well regarded. Let's set him aside. Grace, are you okay?"

She took her wine and drank. Then she drank again. "I'm handling it."

"Good," Blake said, taking the bourbon he'd ordered from the bartender. "Let's settle in and do what we came to do. Watch Jordan win a heck of a game between two undefeateds. He's already knocked Baltimore down. I'm ready to see him do it again with this team."

They found their seats in the box. When Jordan ran onto the field with the team, Grace's heart swelled at the sight of him in his red jersey. He looked up at the box and blew a kiss.

This was why she was here.

CHAPTER 24

Losing sucked.

Jordan hated it when his team lost a game, but he especially hated it when *he* was the one who had blown it. How had he not seen the defensive lineman waiting for him to pass the ball to his wide receiver? He'd thrown an interception, which had resulted in a touchdown for the other team. That score had put the competition ahead of the Rebels with less than a minute remaining on the clock. He hadn't been able to pull a rabbit out of the hat and score before the seconds ran out.

He wanted to throw things. He wanted to curse. Instead he apologized to the team, and they all responded by slapping him on the back and telling him it was okay. But it wasn't. They were no longer undefeated anymore.

It was even suckier that Grace had been in attendance for the first time in more than a year—along with Blake and Natalie. He hated losing in front of his family.

He needed to go home and close himself off. Watch the play again and try to understand how he hadn't seen it. He wasn't making that mistake again. Coach said they'd deal with it in practice in the morning, and they would. He and the offensive coordinators would break down everything. It was a bitch having your every mistake picked apart, but that's what made it football. He'd chosen to play a game where someone lost and someone won, where someone was perfect and someone wasn't.

He hadn't been perfect today.

The after-game interviews were a bitch, with everyone asking him how he felt now that the Rebels were no longer undefeated. The reporters were morons sometimes. How did they *think* he felt? But he got through the interviews and said all the right things, that it was his fault and he'd do better in the next game.

By the time he drove home, he was at once pissed and weary.

He parked at his old house after deciding to give himself some extra time before heading down to Grace's. She never knew how to approach him after a loss. He didn't see that changing. Usually he slept on the couch after watching his mistakes.

But he wanted to say goodnight to Ella—even if she was already asleep. And he still needed to talk to Blake and Natalie, especially since they were leaving in the morning.

He walked into his old house and found Blake drinking a beer in the kitchen. Natalie was nowhere in sight. It was obvious his buddy had been waiting for him.

"Hey," he said heavily. "Sorry you came all this way to see me blow an undefeated season."

Blake crossed his arms. "I didn't see it coming either. I would have thrown that pass. A few of the guys texted me and said the same. I won't tell you not to beat yourself up, but that lineman just made a sweet-ass play. I'll bet he makes it into the Pro Bowl this year."

Yeah, DeThomas was one of the top defensive linemen in the league, but still...

"Thanks for saying that. I fucking hate to lose." He kicked the kitchen island for good measure.

"Good thing you don't make a habit of it," Blake said, coming over and smacking him on the back. "Let the loss make the team stronger. You know how Coach Garretty always said losses can be blessings in disguise."

"Yeah, I know that too," Jordan said, hanging his head. "I always hated it when Coach said that."

"But it's true," Blake said, rubbing Jordan's shoulder, which was aching from all the passes he'd thrown in the game—a record number. "You just need to punch something and work it out. You can wallow with Brody. Sam kicked his butt today."

Sucked for Brody. "I didn't see the score. What was it?"

"Pretty big margin after all the hype," Blake said. "31-17."

"Ouch." Brody would be throwing things for sure. "At least he wasn't the one to lose the game."

Blake cringed. "He had three interceptions, Jordan. Washington's defense shredded him."

Okay, that *really* sucked. "On to better topics. How did things go with Grace?"

His friend shrugged. "Chaz is a piece of work, but she stood her ground. He was pushing her about releasing a picture of Ella to the press. She deflected things well, but she's still not super comfortable with all the stares and interest. We pretty much stayed in our seats the whole time. Once the game started, she relaxed a little. Halftime sucked since there was mingling. You know how it is."

"Yeah," he said, wondering how she was faring now.

"She was super upset at the end of the game when

you...you know," Blake said. "There might have been some hair pulling—not that she has much anymore."

It was nice to hear that Grace had gotten into it. She did like football. She just didn't like what it entailed for him now. "Did anyone rag her about my interception after the game?"

Blake's frown was colossal, and Jordan narrowed his eyes at his friend. "Please tell me no one suggested I threw that interception because she was in attendance for the first time this season."

"You know how it is. People want to blame someone."

"Fucking great!" he said, crossing to the Sub-Zero and pulling out a sparkling water. "I'm trying to build up our family, and everyone outside of it is doing their damn best to undermine it."

"She loves you, man," Blake said with a sigh. "Give her time. That sort of thing takes a lot out of a person. She's too nice sometimes, and that's what makes her so special. But she's an easy target because she doesn't fight back. Natalie has sharper teeth."

Yeah, and he didn't know how to stop that. "Speaking of your wife, where is she?"

"Over at Grace's place," Blake said. "Natalie knows what it's like to deal with one of us after a loss. She wanted to give you a little space."

Yeah, that's usually what he needed, but now there was Ella to consider. He wasn't going to miss saying goodnight to his little girl just because he had a really shitty game. Even if she was asleep already.

"Head on down to see Grace and Ella," Blake said. "I don't want to see you back here tonight—even if you're pissed. I'll see you before Natalie and I take off in the morning."

After another man-hug with Blake, Jordan headed to Grace's house. When he reached the yellow gate, he realized it was the first time he'd used it since their reconciliation. He hoped he wouldn't be using it much longer. In fact, he wanted to tear it off the hinges right about now.

Since he respected girl time, he opened the front door and called out softly, "Man approaching." Walking slowly to the den, he peeked around the corner. "Everyone decent?"

"Like I'd be waiting in something scandalous for you," Natalie said, rising from her place beside Grace on the couch. "Sorry about the loss, Jordan. That was tough. DeThomas came out of nowhere."

His eyes locked with Grace's. "Yeah, tough. I know Ella's out, but I'm going up to see her."

"I'm going to head back to my hubby," Natalie said. "I'll see you two in the morning." She walked over and gave Jordan a bear hug. "I hope you shake it off."

Grace still hadn't said a word, so after giving her another long look, he headed up the stairs. Ella was sleeping peacefully when he went into the nursery. He watched her for a while, struggling to repress the image of his opponent scoring the game-winning touchdown. Realizing he was gripping the rungs of the crib, he detoured back downstairs.

Grace was still sitting on the sofa with her hands clenched. "I'm sorry about the loss, Jordan."

He remained where he was—near the edge of the room. "Me too."

"I was just telling Natalie I never know what to say to you to help after you lose a game." She bit her lip. "She told me she used to feel the same way whenever Blake lost."

Did she really want to talk right now? He wanted to either punch something or spend the whole night watching replays. Anything to ensure it didn't happen again. "There's really nothing to say. I threw a pick. I cost us the game. I might have cost us the Super Bowl."

Looking down in her lap, she nodded. "Do you want space tonight? I can go on up if you want."

Shit. He could all but hear the resignation in her voice. Their old patterns were emerging right before his eyes. "How do you feel when I shut myself off and sleep on the couch?"

Her head shot up, and from the widening of her eyes, he could tell he'd shocked her. "I feel...pretty darn awful. I wish you'd let me help you."

Help him? He'd just lost the biggest game of the season. "You can't change what happened."

"No," she said, releasing a long breath. "But I would like you to let me comfort you. When you're like this...I feel like you want space from me."

"It's not you." Great, now he really felt like shit. "I don't want to be around *anyone*. It's hard for someone who doesn't play to understand."

"You assume that I don't know what it's like to feel disappointment because I haven't lost a game?" she asked, standing.

"This isn't disappointment, Grace. This is...agony. I lost us *the game*. Don't you understand?"

She fisted her hands at her sides. "It's hard for me to understand because you don't talk to me about it. You always make me feel like I'm doing something wrong when you're like this."

He sucked in a breath. Well, points to her for directness. "I don't mean for you to feel that way. Look, this is why I don't talk to you or pretty much anyone after a loss. I'm a jerk. I need to deal with it on my own."

She stormed toward him. "Fine. Do it on your own. I was only hoping that since I bucked up and went to your game, you might change your routine for once and let me comfort you. Guess I was wrong."

He listened to her footsteps up the stairs and uttered a dirty curse word he wouldn't have dared in her presence. Great, she was as mad as he was. This was not what he'd intended. He sank into the couch and wove his hands through his hair, thinking about what she'd said. Comfort him? He didn't deserve comfort. He'd messed everything up.

Then he realized he hadn't asked her how she'd felt going to the game. He'd asked Blake, but not her. Was he so wrapped up in his own loss that he couldn't support her?

That didn't sit well with him. No, not one bit. It hadn't worked for them in the past, and it wouldn't work for them now.

He headed upstairs. Her door was closed, a telltale sign. He rapped on the frame and opened the door a crack. She was putting lotion on her legs in bed.

"Can I come in?" he asked in response to her glare. "Grace, I don't want us repeating old patterns either."

She nodded, her body stiff as she put the lotion back on her bedside table. She had on a serious mommy don't-touch-me nightgown that fell below her collar. He sat on the bed and pulled his clothes off. Once he was nude, he slid under the covers.

She lay back against the pillows as well, her body rigid beside him. "I don't know what to say."

"Why don't you start by telling me how you felt going to the game?" he said, steepling his hands behind his head. "I'm sorry I didn't ask you. I asked Blake for his perspective, but…I didn't ask you. That was inconsiderate of me, and I'm sorry."

She rolled onto her side, and he did the same. "I was glad I had friends with me. There were a lot of eyes on me. I didn't talk to too many people. I hope that's okay."

"I don't want you to feel like you have to talk to

anyone you don't want to," he said, reaching a hand out to her across the small distance separating them.

She grabbed it. "I still don't like Chaz. He's a slime ball."

He laughed. "Slime ball? I don't think I've heard you use that since third grade."

"I haven't felt like using it since then," she said, tucking her other hand under her pillow. "I really am sorry you lost."

The inner raging was quieter now than it had been a few hours before. He no longer wanted to storm through the house and watch replays until his eyes burned. Now he simply felt resigned...and sad. "That makes two of us. I'm sorry you didn't have a better time."

She scooted a little closer. "Once the game started, I had a good time. It was...great to see you play again in person. Watching on TV is different. The fans...I'd forgotten how much they love you."

"Until I lose," he said, sighing deeply. "I know the team is behind me, but the fans are a fickle lot. You should have heard talk radio."

"Blake said he didn't see that lineman coming," she said softly. "Can't you take a little comfort in that?"

He wished he could, but when it came down to it, he was the one who'd made the split-second decision to throw that pass. The guys might say the same thing would have happened to them, but who knows? "Not really."

"Well, at least that's honest."

She scooted a little closer to him and let go of his hand, only to caress his face. His eyes met hers, and she gave him a soft smile. "Win or lose, I still love you. Ella does too."

Of all the things she could have said, that moved him more than he could have imagined. In fact, all the breath suddenly crushed out of his lungs. "Thanks for that. It means more than you know."

Her hand lowered. "I'm trying to understand what it must be like," she said in a soft voice. "I'd feel pretty low if I messed up a meal for the people from Michelin."

"And blew your star for the restaurant," he said. "That would be more like losing the Super Bowl."

"Yeah, the Michelin star is like our Super Bowl." She gave a humming sound. "I sure would be upset about."

"Grace, I don't want to shut you out after a loss," he said, deciding it was time for a new tack. "I can't promise I'm going to be at my best, but I don't want to make you feel bad or sleep on the couch anymore."

"Sometimes you wouldn't come over at all after a game when we lived apart," she finished for him, shadows under her eyes. "That's when I really worried about you."

He opened his arm to her. "Come here."

She slid next to him and cradled her head against his chest. They stayed that way for a while. She caressed his skin gently while he ran his hand up and down her nape.

Finally she rose over him. "Why don't we try this too?" she asked, and then she lowered her mouth to his.

The feel of her lips was soothing and arousing all at once, and he surrendered to the pull. She was soft, and when she parted her lips, he slid his tongue in and kissed her long and slow. Cupping his face, she straddled him.

He tugged her nightgown off. "Not that it doesn't have its charm..."

She was still a little cautious of her breasts when they made love, but he slid his hands under them and caressed their weight the way she liked. Her head fell back, and she moaned.

Soon she was joining their mouths again, everything about her suddenly hot and lush. She broke the kiss to slide down his body, putting her mouth to his skin and making him tighten with arousal. And when she took him into her mouth, he fell back into the most beautiful, generous gift she could give him. When it became too much, he tugged her up and over him. Now that she was back on birth control, there weren't any barriers between them. She slid onto him in one fluid line.

Rocking, always rocking, she joined their hands and urged them toward release. He kept his gaze on hers as he lifted his hips to hers in a tantalizing rhythm. Even when his body was screaming for release and all he wanted to do was roll her under him, he bit his lip and held back, letting her give. And give and give until there was nothing between them but a hundred moans and a thousand sighs.

When she fell to his chest and laid her cheek against his, he whispered, "I love you."

"I love you," she whispered back, and the lingering agony of the loss fell away, leaving nothing but peace in its wake.

CHAPTER 25

Agreeing to go out on a public date with Jordan felt like an even bigger step than attending his game. He hadn't been with her in the stands, so the press hadn't zeroed in on her presence the whole time. But they would when he was next to her. They always did.

She told herself the date was the right move. Jordan had let her in after his huge loss a few weeks ago, and it had deepened their connection. Putting it off any longer would have hurt their relationship. Before their breakup, he'd stopped sharing his frustrations about things that came up in practice. He'd associated football with the problems between them, and so he'd shut her out. Because he'd stopped talking about work, so had she, and the air between them had started to dance with all the things left unsaid.

Now they were pretty much sharing everything, and she felt more included in his life than ever before—this crazy life packed with so much pressure and attention.

Last week, she'd switched one of her two days off to

Tuesday, which had enabled them to spend more time together, even though he went to the stadium for longer than she might have wished. Jordan didn't always make it home before Ella fell asleep, but he tried to, unless he was staying at the hotel with the team the night before a home game or traveling for an away game. Their life together no longer seemed like the soft peaks of egg whites, but solid, sturdy baked meringue. She realized they were living together—something she'd always resisted—and told herself he would surely ask her to marry him someday soon. Integrating herself more into his life and facing her fears seemed an integral part of the process, and she was willing to play her role. Jordan was playing his, after all.

Grace had chosen Bacchanalia, one of Atlanta's top restaurants, for their date. Jordan had suggested a few places, leaving the final decision up to her. Marcellos hadn't been on the list. Before the breakup, they used to hang out there because it provided Grace with a buffer from the press and made her comfortable, but tonight couldn't be like that.

She had to step out with him.

In the past, she'd worn black to subdue her presence and deflect attention. But not tonight. Because she knew their date was special, she had splurged on a fiery red designer dress that fit her curves and made a statement. Her nails and toes were painted the same fiery color, and as she put on her make-up, she made her eyes smokier and more exotic than usual. After finishing with a touch of matching red lipstick, she surveyed herself in the mirror. She looked like a woman on a mission—and maybe she was.

Grace planned to reclaim her power by acting—and looking—like the kind of woman who wouldn't mind being photographed with a gorgeous, successful man.

She was going to fake it until she made it, like the experts said.

When she came down the stairs, Jordan was sprawled on the floor with Ella, tickling her belly. She was laughing out loud, and from his side profile, she could tell he was grinning. He had on gray slacks and a white shirt with an Italian belt and shoes. His cheeks looked freshly shaved, and even from across the room, he smelled delicious.

Ella turned her head and screeched, kicking her legs as she caught sight of her. Grace smiled.

"Who's having fun with Daddy?" she asked and walked forward.

Jordan gave her his full attention, his eyes trailing from the top of her head to the tips of her toes. "Whoa," he uttered in a baritone voice shades deeper than his usual.

Grace tried not to fidget. As far as she could remember, she'd never worn a red dress before. T-shirts, sure, but they both knew this was different.

"I've never..." He cleared his throat as he pushed off the floor. "You look stunning, Grace. Beautiful is too tame a word. Wow. That's all I keep hearing in my head. Just wow."

His hand reached out and traced her bare collarbone. Their eyes locked, and she could see the heat in them.

"You're making me reconsider going out," he said, his voice still rough as gravel.

She decided to be bold. "That was the idea. I want you to be thinking about bringing me home tonight while we're out."

His brows rose. "Be assured I will be." He leaned in and kissed her gently on the lips.

She put her hand on his chest, feeling the soft cotton of his Italian shirt and the heat of his skin. He tugged on her bottom lip, and she wanted to moan.

"If Ella weren't here," he whispered against her lips, "I'd take you right now before we left."

And he would. He had before. She missed that.

She couldn't help but smile as she edged back. "If Ella weren't here, I'd take you right back."

He ran his hand down the small of her back until it curved over her behind. "Amy will be here shortly. Come have some wine before we go."

She had some wine while he looked on and some more in the back of the town car he'd arranged to drive them to the restaurant. The driver was likely going to double as a security guard, she expected, but she didn't ask. This was an important night for them, so she tried to stay in the moment and enjoy holding his hand on their first night out together since the breakup.

When they arrived at the restaurant, they were greeted with special attention by the staff. It was impossible not to feel the stir their presence caused amongst the patrons, even in a restaurant as high-end as this one. Heads turned. People gasped and lurched for their phones. The hand Jordan had placed on the small of her back pressed into her skin with a little more pressure, as if offering his support. She inhaled deeply, keeping calm as camera flashes punctuated the restaurant.

Their driver was right behind them, she realized, and the male members of the wait staff seemed more alert now.

He kissed her cheek. "I'm going to take care of things. Give me a sec."

After stepping away from her, he planted his feet and surveyed the crowd. The cameras continued to flash, but the noise level dropped.

"Hey, everyone," Jordan said, flashing that killer smile of his. "Hope you're having a great meal. I just wanted to let any fans know that I won't be signing autographs or taking pictures with anyone tonight. This is the first night out Grace and I have had since having a baby, and for those of you that are parents, you know what a big deal that is. I'd really appreciate you helping make this night special. Thanks."

She blinked, shocked he would handle things so directly, but then he crossed the room to rejoin her and took her hand. The hostess escorted them to their table in the corner. Their driver positioned himself off to the side with his arms crossed, keeping his eyes on the crowd.

After helping her into her seat, which had her back to the restaurant, Jordan took his own seat across from her. "See. That wasn't so bad. What would you like to drink?"

Parts of her were still shaking, but she gave him an encouraging smile. "It's been a while since I've been here. I'd like to see a wine list."

Jordan arranged that with their server, and after looking it over, she selected an earthy bottle of Burgundy that she knew they both enjoyed. She made herself ignore the price. The restaurant might comp them on the wine or the meal. Jordan often received favors, but the chef also knew Grace.

"Most people have to make reservations three months in advance to get in here," she said, putting her napkin on her lap.

"You knew that when I suggested it, and yet you still chose it." He gave her a wicked grin. "I was proud of you."

"It felt a little naughty, but I decided to go all out," she confessed. "I talked it over with Tony to assuage my guilt. They could always have said no."

He laughed. "Like they would have. They might

put up with me, but they like you. The chef insisted on making something special for us."

"Chefs always do that for other chefs," she said, looking forward to seeing what he had created for them. "It's out of respect and competition."

He waggled his brows. "And that's what I benefit from when I go out with you. People are always going to serve us their best food."

She hadn't thought of that. "Happy to bring something to the table."

He took her hand and rubbed the back of it with his thumb. "You bring a lot to the table. And you look ravishing tonight. I've never seen you more beautiful." Then he shook his head. "No, that's not right. You're this beautiful when you're nursing Ella. And when you held her for the first time."

"That's a mother thing," she said, fighting the urge to tug at her bodice.

"No, that's a *woman* thing," he said, continuing that lazy stroking. "But this is another side to you...one I haven't seen before. I like it. You're hot."

She immediately lowered her gaze. "No, I'm not." Although she wanted to be. For her and him, but also to stick it to everyone who had ever said she was "Too Dull for Dean."

He squeezed her hand. "Yes, you are. And it does things to me. Ones I'm not going to get into here. But when we get home...don't agree to a drink with the chef after dessert, okay? I'm really going to want to go home."

The heat between her thighs made her want to shift in her chair. Given his reaction, she might be a little hot, she supposed. It was a victory she'd take. "Okay, I won't. But it will be rude."

"Tough. Take a rain check. We can always come back."

That knowledge set her back in her chair. She supposed they could return for dinner. Tonight was the beginning of other nights out. Funny, how she'd only focused on this one—as if it were some challenge to be bested.

"This is going to be fun, Grace," he said, squeezing her hand again. "I promise."

"And you made sure my back was to the restaurant."

He gave her a look. "Of course. I told you I would do my best to take care of you."

"You always sign autographs for the fans," she commented, raising her brow.

His shrug was half-hearted. "Not tonight, and perhaps not as much anymore when we're out. I'm making adjustments too."

The middle of her chest expanded with so much love for him, she leaned across the table. "I love you. I just... needed to say it right now."

He leaned in and caressed her face. "And I love you. Thanks for going out with me tonight."

She found her mouth transforming into an easy smile. "Thanks for asking me."

"Expect more invitations," he said with a sexy wink and then let go of her hand as the server brought the bottle of wine.

The Burgundy was excellent, and so was the food. Chef had outdone himself with a collection of perfectly paired plates—everything from the shell of an artichoke holding poached lobster shavings that melted in the mouth to the dramatic finish of a lavender-infused chocolate ganache layered over a passionfruit panna cotta.

Sure enough, Chef came out at the end of the meal. She felt a little bad about asking for a rain check when he invited her to have a drink with him in the wine cellar, but it wasn't as hard as she'd expected, especially since Jordan grabbed her hand and told Chef they were new parents and needed to get home to check on the baby.

A couple of the remaining patrons took photos of them when they walked to the front of the restaurant. Sated from a delicious wine and meal, Grace found it easier to smile, tucked up against Jordan's side. She'd had fun tonight—and it had been wonderful to recall they could enjoy each other out in public like this.

When they reached the door, he gripped her a little tighter. "The driver told me there are some photographers outside. The car is only a few steps away. I have you."

He nodded to the driver who was standing at the door, waiting on them. And so they moved forward. Once the door opened, Grace could see why he'd warned her. There was a huge crowd of photographers outside.

"Do you trust me?" Jordan whispered into her ear.

She nodded.

"Okay, everyone," he said, holding up his hand to get their attention. "I know you're looking for some pictures, so we're going to make this easy on you. We're going to stand here for a few moments while you do your job. And then you're going to back up and let us get to the car easily. I don't have to tell you how upset I was when some of you cornered Grace and me while we were baby shopping. Let's be civilized this time."

The rapid-fire camera flashes made Grace see spots in her vision, but she focused on the solidness of Jordan's presence next to her and the firmness of his hand around her waist.

"All right," Jordan said, waving his hand in the air. "Thanks, everybody."

He led her through the crowd, which didn't press into them as they had before.

"How's your daughter?" someone called out. "When are we going to get a picture of the little tyke?"

Grace immediately tensed at the sound of Farley's country drawl, but Jordan continued to lead her toward the back passenger door. The driver was standing beside it—his solid presence comforting.

"She'd cry if she saw your face, Farley," Jordan said tersely. "Good night, everyone."

He helped Grace into the car and slid in after her. It didn't matter that he was sitting on the fabric of her skirt. She was too relieved to care.

"That wasn't too bad," he said, lifting up her skirt and tucking it around her. "Are you okay?"

She was still shaking a little, but she nodded. "Great," she said, partly to reassure herself. They'd had a lovely meal together. She'd gotten through the photographs.

He lay back against the leather seats and brought her against his chest. "I plan on making you feel even greater once we're home."

Arousal shimmered inside her, forcing the lingering tremors away. "I like that plan."

"Take a nap," he suggested, rubbing her back slowly. "We're going to be awake for a while."

She let her eyes close, relaxing in the knowledge that she was safe.

And thinking about how she wanted this night to end.

***

When they returned home, Jordan walked to the nursery with Grace after saying goodbye to Amy. Ella was sleeping soundly, her little tummy rising with each breath. Grace tucked her blanket closer around her while Jordan caressed her little brow.

As they stepped away from the crib, he reached for Grace's hand and then drew her into the hallway. She tugged free and walked a few steps in front of him before looking over her shoulder at him. There was desire in her eyes as she unzipped her gown and let it fall to the floor.

Shock and arousal slammed into him.

He had wondered what Grace had on under that sexy red dress of hers, but his imagination had not done her justice. Her black and lacy negligee did things to him. His eyes traveled down to her legs. Sheer black stockings were secured by garters. She popped one of them with her fingers as she walked off to the bedroom.

Kicking off his shoes, he followed her in and closed the door behind them.

She stepped in front of him, standing just out of reach.

"I want you to do two things for me to start. Take your clothes off." The low, seductive pitch of her voice almost unmanned him.

He was already unbuttoning his shirt. "What's the second?"

"Let me lead."

She looked like a siren before him in the soft lamplight. Her green eyes were enormous in her face, the lashes framing them long and black. The spicy perfume she wore wove around him.

Jordan nodded his acquiescence and stood there, rooted to the ground.

She walked behind him and helped ease his shirt open. When he shrugged out of the sleeves, she threw it across the room. Her hands came around him, and he felt soft fabric brush his stomach as they wandered up his chest.

"You're mine tonight. And you're going to let me do whatever I want to you." She slowly unveiled a black silk tie. "I bought this for you when I bought my dress. I'm going to put this over your eyes. Is that okay?"

Was she kidding? "You can do whatever you want to me. You know I trust you."

This woman—the one in the red dress who had smiled in front of the cameras—was powerful and sexy, and he liked seeing this new side of his Grace. Usually he was the aggressor in bed. It was nice to have the tables turned.

"One other rule," she said in that same hot-siren voice. "No touching me."

Sweat broke out across his skin.

"At least until I tell you to."

His mouth went dry as she placed the tie over his eyes and secured it. The darkness made his other senses kick in stronger. She was breathing hard, but then again, so was he. And she smelled delicious. Her hands reached around again and brushed his stomach as they undid his pants. He shucked them and his briefs to the floor, then quickly stooped to deal with his socks.

"Someone's clearly ready." She boldly stroked him, and unable to anticipate her moves because of the tie, he quivered with uncertainty. The full length of her body pressed into his back, and he groaned at the contact.

She was going to destroy him tonight, and he couldn't help but grin. "I love where you're going with this."

"It's just us tonight," she said, kissing his back. "I want you to feel how much I want you."

She traced his body as she walked around him.

"I'm going to own you tonight," she said, caressing his chest now. "And make you feel everything you've always made me feel."

Jordan's breathing hitched in his chest. He didn't know this Grace, but even with the tie over his eyes and her seductive commands, he felt the intense emotions arcing between them.

He gave himself over to her.

Her hands were suddenly curled around his thighs and then her mouth...

She loved him thoroughly until he sank to the floor after his release. His heart was beating like crazy, and he was struggling to breathe, but with her head resting on his stomach, it didn't matter. Every moment of surrender had been worth it.

"Can I take this off finally?" he asked, caressing the nape of her neck. "I really want to see you."

She traced his thigh with a fingernail. "If you want," she said hoarsely, rolling onto her side next to him.

Jordan tugged the tie off and looked at the woman before him. Her black lingerie was striking against her pale skin. Her pulse beat strongly in her neck, and there was a slight sheen of sweat on her skin. He could all but taste the desire racing through her veins.

"Come here," he said, fitting her over him until she straddled him.

He pulled her forward until her body rested on top of his, then took her mouth in a slow, wet kiss. It was filled with promise, longing, and heat.

"Bed or floor?" he asked.

She pulled back, breathing shallowly. "Floor."

"Good decision," he whispered before she pressed her lips to his.

She ran her hands down his body, and his arousal peaked again. Jordan lifted his hands to her breasts, caressing their softness through the negligee. He felt the stays in the garment and reached around to take it off.

Her hands stopped him. "No, it stays on tonight."

Jordan wasn't sure about the rule, but he wanted to give her what she wanted.

When her mouth cruised to his jaw, he reached his hands down her bottom and caressed her through the black cloth there. She stilled and moaned brokenly.

"Oh, God," she whispered.

He pressed deep as her head fell back and her thighs

opened to him. Wanting to be with her all the way this time, he levered them up to a sitting position. Her legs wrapped around his waist, the heels of the shoes she still had on biting into his back.

She looked up at him, her face flushed.

"Tell me this thing unsnaps," he said, his voice almost pleading.

"It does," she said with a smile.

"Grace Kincaid, I pretty much love the heck out of you right now." He found the seam and gently unsnapped the tiny buttons there. She quivered as his hand brushed her core.

"I pretty much love the heck out of *me* right now," she told him, pressing into his hand. "I talked myself out of buying this in the store. I got to the stoplight a block away and had to go back for it."

"There's nothing wrong with some hot lingerie," he told her, well aware of the conventions both of them had been raised to follow. "In fact, there's nothing wrong with the tie either."

And then instead of sliding into her, he eased her onto her back before him, wanting to take her to new heights tonight—just as she had done with him. "Do you trust me?"

She gulped and then slowly nodded. "More than ever."

The thought of how far they'd come made his heart expand even more in his chest. "Do you have any idea how much I love you? How much I've always loved you?"

And then he ran his hands over her core. He pushed the black lace to her waist and touched her. When she was finally moaning, totally under his spell, he rose onto his knees and placed his mouth on her. She exploded under him, and he coaxed her through her release until her eyes opened and held his.

"Come into me," she said, holding out her hand.

He stretched out over her and slid into her body slowly, pausing to kiss her deeply before resting his forehead against hers. Her breath warmed his face as he reached for his control. He wanted this to last, and even though he was sated, his desire was white hot.

Grace's lipstick had worn off, and her cheeks were flushed red. The green eyes that held his seemed to reach into his soul. He pressed to the hilt, and she moaned, her lids falling shut again.

"No," he whispered, "don't close your eyes."

And she didn't. She held his gaze the entire time he loved her. Fully. Completely. Bracing himself with his arms, he thrust into her with an easy, sensuous rhythm until his control finally snapped. His strokes grew more powerful, and she responded by locking her legs around his waist and gripping him hard.

He wanted to possess her in that moment, and from the feel of her nails digging into his back, so did she. He gave in to it. When her body coiled and shattered around him, he let himself go, eyes still locked with hers.

Spent, he rolled them onto their sides, lifting her leg over his hip to keep them joined. Her breath feathered his chest, and suddenly Jordan knew they weren't finished yet. He didn't want them to be finished.

"I need this negligee thing off now, Grace," he said and slid his hand down her back in a caress. "I want to feel your skin against mine."

She pulled back and together they took it off. Jordan threw it across the room and filled his hands with her breasts. He caressed them and kissed the undersides until her eyes closed and her breath grew choppy again. And then he took off her stockings and shoes like a man unwrapping the hottest, sexiest gift ever. When she lay totally bare before him, he loved her again.

Afterwards, she rested on top of him, her body slick and warm. He traced her spine and waited for his heart and breath to return to normal. Man, they hadn't made love like this since they'd first started dating. How had he missed this assertive, carnal side of Grace? Part of him wanted to kick himself for not encouraging her to buy lingerie sooner, but perhaps this was a step she'd needed to take on her own.

"I need water," she said hoarsely, and he laughed.

"I'll get some," he said and picked her up and carried her to bed. "Be right back."

Kissing her lightly on the lips, he tugged the covers up and over her. She snuggled into the pillow and smiled back at him. "Hurry."

He ran downstairs and pulled out half a dozen bottles of water. Catching his reflection in the mirror in the den on the way back, he couldn't help but shake his head. His hair was stuck to his head from sweat and sticking up in other places. Boy, they'd had a bout.

When he returned to the bedroom, Grace was lying on her side, her hand tucked under the pillow. Her eyes opened, and she reached for the bottle of water he held out.

"Do I look as wild as you do?" she asked, propping herself up to drink.

He drained half the bottle before answering. "Wild looks good on you."

She let out a breathy laugh. "It feels rather good. I started wondering why we hadn't done something like this before, but I already knew the answer. Me."

He drained the rest of the water and then lay back, bringing her against his chest. "I was just thinking about that too. But it's no one's fault. I'm just glad you opened up like this with me. Grace, you might not want to hear this, and maybe I don't have the right to say it, but I'm proud of you. I know tonight wasn't easy."

"No, it wasn't," she said, putting her hand on his stomach. "But I decided I needed to be bold and stand in my power, so to speak. If I want to be a good role model for Ella, I need to stop backing away from the things that scare me. You know? I told myself that after she was born, but I haven't been as consistent as I'd like. I'm still growing, I guess."

"It takes time to get used to the media," he told her. "It took me some time and some coaching, and I still have my moments. You're doing great!"

She traced his thigh. "I want to be more empowered with you too. There have been things I've wanted to do with you in bed, but I was...too scared to ask."

"You never need to be scared about that," he said, looking down at her. "I want you to have what you want. Always."

Her face turned a delightful pink. "All right. There are some more things I've been wanting to try."

"Let me grab you a notepad so we can write them all down."

He received a half-hearted punch in the gut. "I'm serious."

"I know," he said, rolling them onto their sides so they could face each other. "But you can always be honest with me, even when it doesn't feel completely comfortable. I want us to be completely open with each other."

She looked down and sighed deeply.

"What?" he asked.

"Nothing," she said half-heartedly.

He cupped her cheek and made her look at him. "Tell me." When she still hesitated, his belly grew tight with nerves. *"Grace."*

She took a deep breath and blew it out slowly. "I've been trying not to think about it, and I know it's none of my business since we were broken up, but..."

His stomach dropped. "You want to know about the women I was with while we were apart." Sweet Christ, why hadn't he expected she would think about that? "All right, ask me what you want, and I'll be as honest as I can with you."

"I feel like it's my fault," she said in a hushed voice. "I know you agreed to the breakup, but deep down I know it really was my choice. I can't help but wish they hadn't happened now that we're back together again."

Jesus Christ. The casual dalliances had meant so little to him, and he'd hoped they would never resurface. "Oh, Gracie. Come here."

He held her gaze, stroking her spine as he gathered his control.

"Part of me doesn't want to talk about this," she said, "but I just can't let it go."

"Is that what tonight was about?" he asked, his heart breaking at the thought.

"No," she said softly. "I only decided that if I could do all this, then I could tell you it was bothering me. That it has been for months."

"A night for courage, eh?" he asked. "When you decide to go all the way, you never stint. I remember seeing you have moments like this when you decided to go to culinary school in New York City and not closer to home. No one was going to stop you. Grace, if this has been on your mind, we need to deal with it."

"Okay," she mumbled.

Jordan kept his face neutral. "Yes, I slept with other women while we were apart. But not nearly as many as you may imagine from the media coverage, and none of them made me feel even a fraction of what I feel when I'm with you. I need you to believe that, Grace. More than anything." He hoped she wouldn't ask for details because he didn't want to share them. They didn't matter.

"I was afraid it was only confirmation that I was too dull for you," she said, crushing him. "Or not pretty enough."

Pain flashed through his chest. "Oh, Grace! I never thought that! Ever! You're beautiful and funny and... pretty much everything to me."

She studied him for a long moment, making him feel totally exposed.

"I believe you," she finally said.

He stopped holding his breath. "Thank you."

She gave him a hesitant smile. "I know it won't surprise you, but I didn't sleep with anyone. There was an Italian man who pursued me while I was in Rome after our breakup, but I just couldn't do it. I...still loved you too much, and it wouldn't have been kind to him."

He wasn't surprised other men had wanted her, but he felt kind of glad there hadn't been anyone, which also made him feel like a heel. "Thank you for telling me."

"Jordan, I still have moments of worry that I might not be enough for you," Grace said, her green eyes direct. "There are so many gorgeous women around you all the time. I know you wouldn't cheat on me, but I...crap...if we're sharing, I might as well go all the way. I don't want you to get bored with me, and being a new mom...well, I've worried about that too, Jordan."

To give himself a little time to find his words, he stroked her cheek. "Grace, since the first day I kissed you, I've been scared of how much you make me feel. Before she died, my mom used to say, 'that Grace is such a good girl, Jordan.' You *were* a good girl growing up. You still are." His mom had been over the moon when they'd started dating, but she'd died shortly afterward. It still saddened him she hadn't seen how far they'd come, and it especially hurt that she'd never meet her grandchild.

"Good isn't a compliment." She made a face.

"It's not something to be embarrassed about," he told her, eager to make her understand. "When we first got together, you told me there had only been one guy in college, but you know I...wasn't so discriminating."

Plenty of girls had made crazy overtures because he was a football player. He hadn't resisted some of them. He'd fallen into the same pattern when he and Grace had split.

"So let me be clear, while I completely and physically enjoyed your seduction scene tonight, it's not something I expect—or need. I want you to share with me what you want to share. I'm glad you did tonight. But if you're worried about being enough for me, you're crazy. It's the Grace that I know and love that I want to make *love* to. Okay?"

She smiled hesitantly. "I'm glad."

His chest felt ten times lighter now. "I'm not scared of football, Grace, but I am scared of what I feel for you sometimes. I don't ever want to lose you again, so you just keep telling me what you feel, and I'll do the same. I'm in this all the way. I hope you know that."

She sat up higher until she was lying on his chest, supported by her elbows. "The same thing that scares you scares me. Even if you had a normal body or a paunch, you'd still be it for me."

He was oddly touched. "That's good to know, I guess. I won't be playing forever, and it would be devastating to find out after retirement that you were only in it for my hot body."

Her laughter soothed his vulnerable heart. "You are pretty hot."

"So are you," he said, running his finger along her jaw. "I wish you knew what you do to me. Just by being you."

She smoothed his hair off his forehead. "Even in my flannel nightgown and the missionary position?" she asked, a smile touching her lips.

He started laughing. "Even that. You do like your flannel."

"Hey," she said, narrowing her eyes at him. "It reminds me of South Dakota."

He bit his lip to stop from making a Laura Ingalls Wilder joke. It was one of her favorite book series and a touchy subject. "Are we good now?"

"Oh, I hope so. If not, you'll just have to tie a blindfold around me and do some more convincing."

He blinked. "Seriously? You know I can pretty much go all night, Grace, but that would be pushing it." In a flash, he had her on her back. "Just kidding."

She rolled her eyes. "I was worried for a moment. You calling uncle? But let's wait until tomorrow night. Ella is going to wake up at her normal time, so we should get a little sleep while we can."

He gave her a soft kiss on the lips before turning and tucking her back against his body. "Tomorrow night then. Love you."

She laid her hand over the arm he had wrapped around her. "Love you too."

Right before Jordan fell asleep, he realized they were one step closer to him asking her to marry him.

Chapter 26

Grace was pretty pleased with herself: she had attended another game with Carlo in the owner's box and managed to make nice with a few of the people in attendance. Chaz had asked again about when everyone was going to see a picture of their daughter, and Grace had finally told him flat out that it wouldn't happen until Ella was older.

When she told Jordan how she'd handled Chaz's question, he gave her his full support. His knotted brow told her he was a little anxious about the whole thing, but so was she, and it relaxed her to feel they were on the same page.

Their sex life blossomed despite the changes Ella had made to their schedule. Late evenings together were filled with lots of laughter and more pleasure than she expected a new mother to experience. Her heart was happy, and her body felt languid. She decided to grow her hair out when Jordan hesitantly shared he missed running his hands through it and feeling it brush his chest.

They asked each other questions. Listened. And shared their deepest thoughts and feelings—something they'd stopped doing before. Each day she fell more in love with him as a man. And then there was their daughter...

Ella continued to grow before their eyes. She started to babble, and Jordan loved to babble right back at her, which always made the baby laugh. When she popped her first tooth, Jordan raised her hands in the air like a champion. Family time became as special to them as the time she and Jordan spent alone, and that made her happiest of all. They had finally settled into a good groove.

They came to a mutual decision to spend Thanksgiving in Atlanta by themselves. Grace had to work that Friday and Saturday and Jordan had a game that Sunday. But Grace invited her mother to fly in for Jordan's final game of the season the weekend after Thanksgiving. FaceTime was great, but Meg wanted to see her grandbaby again, and truth be told, Grace missed her.

When her mom arrived at the house the Saturday afternoon before the game, she held two brightly colored gift bags, one with a giraffe and the other a violet bow.

"Is that my Ella?" she asked, grinning from ear to ear. The baby babbled and leaned toward her with outstretched arms. "Yeah, you remember Grandma, don't you, sweet girl? And Grace...you look good."

"It's so great to see you, Mom," she said, holding a squirming Ella. "Jordan is sorry he couldn't be here."

She hugged Grace and Ella holding both bags. "I know he's busy with the game tomorrow. Let's go inside so you can open your presents, and I can hold this precious little baby."

When they reached the den, they hunkered down on the floor. Grace pulled out the gift paper and tossed it out of reach so Ella wouldn't put it in her mouth. She was sticking everything she could find in it these days, and since she could roll over like a pro, she could travel a bigger area.

"Oh, look," Grace called out as she opened Ella's present. "It's a doll! Mom, did you sew this? It looks like the one you made me when I was little."

"I was a little rusty, but after making two of them, I caught back on." She laughed. "Your dad got weirded out by the first couple, so I put one of them under his pillow. I love keeping that man on his toes."

Grace laughed with her, imagining her father's startled reaction. Ella got a good grip on the doll and tugged it toward her, so Grace lowered her and the doll to the receiving blanket.

"Goodness," her mom said. "It's hard to believe she's going on five months old already. Time flies."

"It sure does," Grace said, watching her daughter gum the doll's brown hair, which her mom had made out of yarn. She waited for Ella to make a face at the taste and then shook her own head. "Yuck, yuck."

"Her one tooth is so cute," her mom said. "Any more of them?"

"Not yet," Grace commented. "And I'm okay with that. I don't want her to be without teeth, but it's not so fun when I nurse her."

Her mom gave a belly laugh. "I don't miss those days. Nope, not one bit. All right, missy. Time to open your present."

"You didn't have to get me anything, Mom," she said, pulling it onto her lap.

"Mother's prerogative," she said, patting Grace's leg. "You're my little girl too, even if you are a woman now."

"Ah, Mom," Grace said when she pulled out the small copper pot she recognized from her childhood. "This was Grandma's saucepan!" Grandma had splurged on the pan on a long-ago visit to Chicago, and for a time, she'd been the only woman in all of Deadwood to own one. It was a treasured family possession that had been passed down to Grace's mom ten years ago, upon Grandma's death.

"I don't use it much anymore," her mom said, tracing the wooden handle. "I thought you might like it. Maybe you can give it to Ella one day if she takes to cooking like you and I did."

Grace liked to think about all of the women in the family being connected by her grandma's special copper saucepan. They leaned closer to hug one another again. This time, they held onto each other while Ella babbled in the background.

"You don't have to tell me how happy you are," her mom said, squeezing her tight. "I remember how miserable you looked when I came here when you were pregnant. My, how things have changed. Gracie, I'm glad everything is good between you and Jordan."

"It is," she said, smiling. "We've been close before, but we're more in sync with each other than ever. When we're together, we're just together. You know? No TV or movies. We just talk and..." She broke off, appalled at what she'd almost said.

Her mother laughed in her ear and pushed back. "I know what a man and woman do, Grace. I'm so happy for you guys."

"Me too," she said, feeling her cheeks flush.

"Any talk of marriage yet?" her mom asked with a sly smile.

Her mom never beat around the bush. "Not officially, but we both feel like this is forever. I'm sure we'll get there." She was feeling more certain Jordan wanted her and her alone. He was stripping away all of her past worries—layer after layer of them.

"I'm sure you will too," her mom said. "I'm happy to

take care of Ella if you and Jordan want to get away for a few days or so once the season ends. Might be easier once you've weaned her, but it's not impossible. You can pump."

Getting away would be nice. Maybe they could go to Italy again and walk in Piazza San Marco in Venice, one of their favorite places in common. "I'll keep that in mind. Thanks, Mom. I love Amy and all, but—"

"I'm your mom," she said, leaning back on her elbows to recline beside Ella, who was kicking her feet with the doll against her chest.

"I'm feeling more confident about going to the games," Grace said. "I'm not used to all the cameras yet, but I'm getting better about it. Jordan and I went out last Tuesday night and had a blast, but the reporters are never far away, including Farley. Or his fans."

This time, he'd signed a few autographs while she'd waited for him at their table. She'd told him not to deny himself the connection with his fans, which meant the world to him. The chef had outdone himself on the meal, and afterwards, Jordan had used the leftover chocolate ganache he'd asked to take home all over her body. She wasn't sure she was ever going to be able to make another chocolate dessert at Marcellos without blushing to her roots.

Of course, Farley's comment in the paper the next morning that she hadn't yet lost all her baby fat had dimmed her joy a bit. Jordan had called him a liar and a jerk and threatened to sue him. That had soothed her some.

Her mom looked over her shoulder. "Well, it's six o'clock. I should get dinner started. I was going to make your favorite."

Fried chicken. Yum. "Mom, you don't have to do that. Really. I was going to put together an antipasti tray and make some shrimp scampi with linguini."

"No," she said with a determined shake of her head. "You worked today. You're not cooking twice. Do you have chicken in the freezer?"

Grace rose after tickling Ella's tummy. "No, Jordan has been eating more beef. And we're out of milk for the gravy. Let's just make what I had in mind."

Her mom rolled her eyes. "I'll just go to the store."

"You know Atlanta traffic. How about delivery?"

"Grace." Her mom held her gaze. "I'm making fried chicken."

Her mother was immoveable when she was like this. Usually Grace ordered what she needed for the house at the restaurant and brought it home with her. Could she ask Jordan's driver to go to the store for her? She hated to impose on him.

"What's the problem here?" her mother asked, cocking her head. "I can handle the city traffic. I did when you were on bed rest."

"But there was a local market around the corner," she explained. "The grocery store is twenty minutes away down a major thoroughfare." She hesitated mentioning that her mother grew flustered driving in the big city.

"Then you drive. Come on, Ella. Let's go. Granny has chicken to fry."

Grace realized she was wringing her hands. "Mom, I don't usually take Ella out of the house."

Her mother looked up sharply. "Ever?"

Her chest seemed to squeeze shut. "Well...Amy comes here, you know. I've taken Ella to the restaurant a couple of times, but she's still pretty little."

"Grace," her mom said softly. "Are you telling me you haven't left the house with Ella except to go to Marcellos?"

"The baby books say it's not uncommon for a new mother to wait until her baby is a little older to take her on errands," she said, her hackles rising. "I'm doing my best here."

Her mom rose and wrapped her in a hug. "I'm not saying you aren't. But Grace. She's five months old. I know it's a little intimidating to think about going out in public with her—not just because she's little, but because of Jordan. Maybe I can help with that. We can go together for the first time."

"Mom," she said, her muscles tightening at the very thought. "I don't...I don't want to go out in public with her yet. I'm afraid something might happen."

Her mom put her hands on her shoulders. "Gracie, it's just the grocery store. It'll be fine. We'll be in and out before you know it. No one will be the wiser. Besides, you love going to the grocery store."

"Not on a Saturday night," she said, crossing her arms. "It's a zoo."

"Come on," her mother said, giving her a playful shake. "It will be an adventure." She picked up Ella. "Are you ready for your first trip to the grocery store, sweet girl? I wonder if you'll like to cook like your mommy and your granny. Let's get you in your carrier."

Before she knew it, her mom had Ella buckled in and was carrying her to the garage. Grace's legs moved like they were made of clay.

"Come on, Grace," her mom called, opening the car door. "You don't have to go. I can take her with me. I've got GPS on my phone."

"No, I'm coming," she said, grabbing her purse.

After securing Ella, they drove off. Grace's hands were locked around the steering wheel.

"Breathe, Grace," her mom said as they drove through the gates, her mom waving at the guards. "We're just getting chicken and milk. Unless you need anything else."

She shook her head. All she wanted to do was get in and out. "Nope, that's it."

Focusing on driving, she crawled along with the traffic on the main road.

"Goodness me," her mother said after they waited through three green lights to turn left. "You weren't kidding about the traffic."

No, Mother, she wanted to say, but bit her tongue. It took them thirty minutes to get to the store, and Grace was strung out by the time she parked in the crowded lot. There were cars everywhere.

"I'm going to carry her inside," her mom said, lifting Ella out of her carrier. "Be easier than hauling this thing. Pretty cool, huh, sweetheart? Welcome to your first grocery store."

Ella's eyes were wide as she took everything in. When a Honda honked at a SUV for backing up without looking, she babbled wildly, drool rolling down her chin.

"See," Grace's mom said with a proud smile. "She's eager to take in this new world. Come on, Grace. Let's pop in and get what we came for. Won't take but five minutes."

But her mom was wrong this time as well. The aisles were packed with people shopping for dinner, and Grace's nerves grew tauter when a few people stopped and stared at her, as if trying to place her. She told herself she was being paranoid—that no one would recognize her without Jordan—but her body felt like a tightly strung guitar.

"Why don't you find the chicken while I grab the milk?" Grace suggested. "I can meet you at the checkout."

Her mom narrowed her eyes. "Won't be any faster, and Ella is enjoying looking around. Let's stay together."

As if to prove her grandmother right, the little girl babbled again and reached out to the balloons floating in the florist area.

"Fine," she said tersely. "But let's not dawdle."

She increased her speed down the aisle, and her mom matched her. Ella continued to babble and take everything in. At least the baby didn't seem anywhere near a meltdown. That would have been too much for Grace to handle.

Since they were there, she grabbed some sour cream in addition to the milk and followed her mom to the meat aisle. After looking over the choices, her mom pointed to a fryer.

"I'll cut it up when we get home," she told Grace.

Grace wrapped the fryer in a meat bag and twisted the top. "All right, let's blow this joint."

They wove around carts and screaming kids, whom Ella regarded with wide eyes since she hadn't been around other children yet. Grace fought her impatience as she joined the line at the express aisle behind six other people.

"Not so express, is it?" her mom whispered.

Grace gave her a tight smile. "I told you this was a busy time."

Her mom shrugged. "Oh, well. We're together, and that's what counts. At least Ella is too little to want candy. I swear, getting you and your brothers to drop the gum and chocolate bars you'd picked up was a pain in the you know what."

Grace tapped her foot. The checker was moving slowly, unconcerned with the customers' growing frustration.

"Hey!" A man tapped her on the shoulder. "Aren't you Jordan Dean's girlfriend?"

Every muscle locked in place. "No," she finally said, staring straight ahead.

Her mom gave her a sharp look before glancing back at the man behind her.

The guy leaned closer, and Grace saw his head appear in her peripheral vision as he studied her. "You sure do look like her. Wait! Is that Dean's kid? Holy crap! The tabloids have been begging for a picture of her. It's worth a thousand bucks."

A thousand dollars? No, they wouldn't have done that. But then she remembered what jackals they were.

Lots of people were staring now. A man further up in line nudged his friend, whispered something, and they both turned to look at her. Grace felt her mother grab her arm.

"Is Jordan here?" the guy behind her asked, tapping her on the shoulder again.

"Do you see Jordan anywhere?" Grace's mom asked, giving him a pointed look. "Now, how about you stop bothering my daughter and let us check out in peace."

"So she is Dean's baby mama!" the guy said, slapping his hand to his forehead. "Wow. Can I get a picture of you and the baby? I could really use the money."

Grace shook her head. "No, you can't."

The guy tapped her on the shoulder again, and Grace swung around with the groceries in her arms. "Stop touching me. I said you can't take a picture, and I expect you to respect that."

"Shit!" someone else cried. "It's Jordan Dean's baby mama with the kid. Hurry! Get my phone. There's money in it for the first baby pic."

Grace's heart rate spiked, and suddenly there were a few people gathered around them with their camera phones outstretched. Her mom bumped into her, and she heard Ella start to cry. She looked over. The baby's face was red, her eyes were wide with terror, and tears were rolling down her little cheeks.

"Stop it!" she called out. "You're upsetting her. She's just a baby."

Someone pushed Grace's shoulder again, and she slammed into her mom. Ella let out a high-pitched scream—a sound Grace had never heard her utter before. She dropped the groceries and grabbed her baby from her mother, pressing Ella's little body to her chest and shielding her head.

"Shhh," she said to her wailing daughter. "It's okay. I've got you."

She swung around to face the guy behind her, who had his phone in her face, taking pictures.

"Get out of my way," she growled at him.

He tried to step back, but there were more people crowding in behind him now. They were snapping pictures too.

"Please let us out!" she cried. "Can't you see? My daughter's scared."

A large man in overalls·four people back met her gaze. "Let them out!" he bellowed in a decided Southern accent. "Y'all should be ashamed of yourselves, frightening a child like that, and over money too. Come on, little lady. I'll help you. Move back, everyone."

He made a motion with his hands and managed to herd everyone out of the checkout line to let them out.

"I'm right behind you, honey," her mom said, pressing a hand to Grace's back.

A crowd had gathered. Several people stood around with their shopping carts, gawking and taking pictures with their phones. Ella continued to wail, her little body shaking against Grace's chest.

"Let me help you to your car, ma'am," the large man said, his brow knit with concern.

"Thank you," she managed to say. He took charge of the crowd like the hero he was, leading them through the crowd. Since all the lines were full, they had no choice but to go back to the side and out the main door.

"Oh, baby," Grace whispered to Ella, who was crying as through her heart was broken. "I'm so sorry."

More people paused as they came into the grocery store, sensing something wasn't right. When they broke through the revolving doors, Grace increased her pace, jogging to the car. The man who'd helped them leave the store jogged beside them, and when they reached the vehicle, Grace's mom dug her hands into her purse.

"I need the key, Grace," she said, rubbing her back. "Oh, sweet girl, it's okay now."

Grace shifted Ella in her arms. The little girl was clinging so hard her fingernails were digging into her skin.

Her mom finally found the key and unlocked the car. A couple of people were running out of the store, as if news had spread and they were eager for a look at them. Or maybe a picture to sell to the tabloids.

Her fear spiked anew.

"Best get into the car, ma'am," the older man said. "People just suck, don't they?"

Putting Ella into the carrier was a Herculean act with her daughter screaming and clutching her, but she managed.

"Get in the back with her, Grace," her mom said, taking charge. "I'll drive."

Grace hopped inside, doing her best to soothe the baby. The older man shut the door gently and tipped his finger to his head at her.

Her mom opened the driver's side and jumped in. "Let's get out of here."

She backed out of the slot and then drove out of the parking lot. Grace stroked Ella's face as she looked over her shoulder and watched the older man stride off toward his car.

"I didn't even thank him," she said, fighting tears.

"I did," her mom said in a hard voice. "That man was an angel, for sure. Grace, I'm so sorry. I'm just...I'm sorry." Her voice broke.

And that broke Grace the rest of the way. She pressed her cheek to Ella's soft hair, unable to stop her own grief.

Her mom pulled the car to a stop in a remote part of a furniture store parking lot and got into the back with them. She put her arms around them tightly, stroking Grace's hair.

"You're okay," her mom said, trembling like Grace was. "You're both okay."

Grace took the baby out of the car seat and rocked her until Ella's sobs finally slowed. She continued to give a weak wail after every few breaths. Her body was quivering against Grace, but at least it wasn't shaking like it had been before. Grace could feel the wetness on her shoulder and kissed Ella on her soft head.

"Here, baby," she said, trying to shift her so she could wipe her face.

Ella renewed her grip and started to cry again. Grace's heart pretty much cracked in two. Her daughter was traumatized.

"You just had to have your way," she said to her mom, who was stroking Ella's back. "Why didn't you listen to me?"

Her mom flinched. "What?"

"It's not just the grocery store anymore, Mom," she said, crying softly. "Those jackals were willing to pay a thousand dollars for a picture of Ella. Now do you see? My life—Ella's life—isn't normal anymore. *Oh, God.*"

Ella's cries washed over her, and the ache in her chest grew painful. Tears clouded her eyes as she thought of what had happened.

"Oh, baby," she whispered to Ella, soothing her back. "I'm so sorry."

Her mom cuddled closer and hugged Grace gently as her crying renewed.

"I'm sorry, Gracie," her mom said softly. "I didn't know. I didn't know."

When her mom started to cry too, Grace shifted closer to her and pressed her face against her cheek. Her mom never cried.

It truly was the end of the world.

CHAPTER 27

Jordan was eating dinner with his offensive players, shooting the breeze, talking trash about tomorrow's opponents when he heard Coach call his name.

"Yeah, Coach," he said and headed to his table.

Coach was already standing and waiting for him, and the deep grooves around his mouth were pulled into his proverbial frown. He pulled Jordan off to the side. "I'm giving you ten minutes before the team meeting to call Grace. Chaz called me personally to tell me there was some trouble. Don't get alarmed, but it seems Grace and Ella got ganged up on in a grocery store by some fans who'd heard about the tabloid's bounty for a picture of your kid. It's going to make you angry when you see the photos and videos on the web, but I'm trusting you to channel it."

Instant pain shot through his gut. "Are they okay?" He'd thought they were safe from the contest. Grace never took Ella anywhere except the restaurant a few times. Why had she gone to the store?

"They're fine," Coach told him. "Your daughter got scared, no surprise, but a good Samaritan came to their rescue. I know there have been problems at home because of this before, so I wanted you to know."

He fisted his hands at his sides. "I...shit...I know we have a team meeting and curfew." Like everyone else, he'd already checked into the hotel for the night.

"You can't go home for this," Coach said, staring him straight in the eye. "If I make an exception for you, I'll have to do it for everyone. You know I can't. I'm letting you call Grace before the meeting. That's the best I can do."

Jordan nodded and stormed out of the dining room to find somewhere quiet to call Grace. He checked his phone. Why hadn't she called him? She knew he couldn't take any calls until after the team meeting, but still... He thought of Ella, and horrible visions of people trying to touch his daughter filled his mind. He wanted to kill them. All of them.

The lobby was packed with people, so he detoured to the elevator to run up to his room. Coach wouldn't bust his chops if it took him fifteen minutes rather than ten, and besides, he was having trouble caring about anything but Grace and Ella right now. When Jordan reached his room, he called Grace immediately.

She didn't answer, so he texted her.

Hey! Are you guys okay? I just heard. Call me please. Coach gave me fifteen minutes before our team meeting.

He eyed the clock. It wasn't Ella's bedtime yet. Why wasn't she answering?

God, how bad had it been? He texted his publicist to prepare a file for him to review once his meetings were finished. He needed to know exactly what had happened. If only he'd said something to Grace...but he'd feared it would damage this new bond between them. So he'd tabled the discussion, planning to bring it up whenever she suggested taking Ella somewhere other than Marcellos.

He kicked over the garbage can by the desk. "Dammit!"

When Grace didn't call or text him back, he called Meg. She didn't pick up either.

Now he was really worried. Meg had *always* picked up while Grace was on bed rest.

He texted Meg as well, but when ten minutes rolled by without an answer, he finally called Tony, who also didn't pick up. Not that he'd expected it. He was a chef, after all, and Saturday night was his busiest time.

Jordan told himself Grace and Meg had to be busy calming Ella. He charged back downstairs when his time ran out. A few of the other guys asked him what was going on, and he told them what he knew. They all made him feel better. Many of them had families too, and they'd been through the wringer before.

When Jordan got out of the team meeting, he checked his phone. Grace had finally answered.

Sorry I missed you. Was soothing Ella. We're okay, but shaken up. Not going to be able to make the game tomorrow. Don't want to leave her. Get some rest. I'll see you when you get home tomorrow night.

He felt the chill in her message. She damn well knew he could call her after the team meeting. He always did. Curfew didn't mean he had to go to bed right away—it only meant he had to stay in his room. But there was one thing she didn't say, and that worried him most of all. She would guess he'd known about the tabloids' contest.

When he got upstairs, he called her anyway. *Please pick up.* She didn't.

He texted her, pacing across the front of his bed,

worry gripping his gut. *I'm back in my room. Call me. I need to know you and Ella are okay. I love you both. So much.*

She texted him back. *I don't want to do this over the phone. I'm upset, and you have a game.*

He sank onto the bed, his legs giving out from under him. He knew what she meant. God, he knew. He texted her anyway.

Don't give up on us. Please. We've come so far. Let's talk about this.

They were a family. She couldn't just walk away.

She responded. *You knew about the bounty, didn't you?*

He stared at his phone a long time before responding. *Yes. I knew it would upset you. I'd planned to mention if you told me you wanted to take Ella somewhere. But you haven't. I thought I had more time.*

It took her longer to respond than it should have, and he started to sweat. *I wish you had told me. I can't tell you what it felt like to hear her scream like that, to have her nails dig into me in terror. Please. I don't want to do it this way. Let's talk tomorrow.*

He could feel his rage growing, the heat rage through his body. *I know I wasn't there, and I know I should have told you. I'm sorry! That's why I want to talk to you. I want you to take a picture of Ella sleeping and kiss her goodnight for me. It kills me to think about her crying like that and you being so upset. But please don't give up on us. You promised.*

He waited for her to respond. The screen remained blank. He fell back onto the bed, feeling tears gather in his eyes. His phone chimed, and he popped up.

I know I promised, but you weren't there. I love you, but I can't do this. Not to her. She's just a little girl. I'm sorry.

He dropped the phone to the floor and put his head in his hands.

CHAPTER 28

Ella had a horrible night, waking almost every hour whimpering. Grace and her mom took turns rocking her unless she wanted to nurse. As each hour passed, Grace's certainty became more resolute.

She had to protect Ella from the madness surrounding Jordan's life.

Even if it meant leaving Atlanta.

No one would know or care who she was in another city. She and Jordan wouldn't be photographed together anymore. People would forget what she looked like, and as Ella grew older, her daughter would be unrecognizable. No one would ever pay a thousand dollars for a picture of her daughter ever again.

Grace's devastation was complete. She would have to break up with Jordan again.

Her mom didn't say much to her, focusing on helping with Ella and scrubbing the kitchen counters until they sparkled, a sure sign she was upset too. When the guards buzzed her to say Jordan was home like she'd asked them to, she kissed Ella on the cheek. Her daughter hadn't smiled once today. Usually such a happy and carefree baby, she'd been jumping at the slightest sound.

"Be right back, baby," she said, smoothing back the fine hair curling to her forehead.

Her mom took Ella from her, shadows under her eyes. The baby started to cry, and Grace's heart clenched. Her daughter didn't want her to leave the room, even with her mom present.

"I'm going to talk to Jordan," she said, catching her mom's frown. "What? Are you going to tell me not to break up with him?"

She shook her head and tucked Ella closer to her body. "No...it's not for me to decide. In your place, maybe I'd do the same thing. Take your time. Ella and I will be all right."

The baby was crying softly, holding a little hand out to her, and Grace had to force herself to leave the room.

She didn't see Jordan's car coming down the last of the driveway to her house, so she headed to the yellow gate separating their two properties. In all the time she'd lived next door, she'd never gone to his house. On some level, she hadn't wanted to acknowledge that he had this separate place, this separate life. And he must have felt the same way, because he'd never asked her.

When she knocked on the front door, she let out a slow breath. *Hold it together. Just get through this.*

Her chest ached with unshed tears when he opened the door. His blue eyes were bloodshot and filled with anger.

"I just texted you I was home," he said, swallowing thickly. "I wanted to...oh hell."

He pulled her against him, burying his face against her shoulder. She tensed up.

"Don't do this," she whispered. "You're only making it harder."

His arms dropped immediately, and he took a few steps back. *"I'm* making this harder? You're throwing us—our family—away after you promised me we'd face things together. You refused to talk to me last night when I was worried as hell about you and Ella, and then you pretty much fucking broke up with me through a text. How in the hell am *I* making this harder? I didn't do anything but open my heart up to you again and give you everything!"

"Don't swear at me. Please. I can't take that." She pressed her lips together when they started to tremble. There were tears in his eyes despite the anger radiating from him, and she quaked from the force of his emotion.

"I'm sorry, but I'm upset."

She didn't want to postpone this, but perhaps it was best. "Maybe we should talk after you cool down some. It doesn't help that you lost your game."

He cocked a brow. "We didn't lose."

She blinked. "Oh, I assumed—"

"That I couldn't hold it together enough to win? I wasn't going to do that to myself or my team. I shredded Dallas. I don't need to cool down. I want to see Ella, Grace. Did you come up here to tell me I can't? Because if you think I'm angry now, try keeping me from my daughter."

In all the time she'd known him, she'd never seen him like this. "I would never keep you from Ella. I only wanted us to talk first. She woke up just about every hour last night whimpering, and she cries when I leave the room for even a second. She didn't smile all day! I didn't want her to be any more upset. It tore my heart out."

He pounded his chest. "I understand the feeling. All I wanted to do was comfort you both, and you shut me out."

Pain shot through her, and she squeezed her eyes shut. "You didn't tell me about the tabloid bounty—"

"I told you why," he said, his voice hoarse. "Are you going to blame me for this too?"

She knew it wasn't fair, but she wasn't feeling magnanimous right now. "You didn't even come home last night," she whispered. "What does that say?"

"I couldn't come home because I had curfew," Jordan said in a hard tone. "Coach said he couldn't make an exception for me even though I wanted one. Dammit, Grace. You're punishing me for something completely out of my control."

"Did you watch any of the videos on the web?" she shot back, deciding not to correct his language this time. "I'm sure someone videoed us being surrounded by *your* fans. Ella screamed, Jordan. Screamed! Her little fingernails dug into my shirt." She tore back the neckline to show him the red marks on her skin. "Some wonderful older man had to come to our rescue and get us out of there. How can you ask our daughter to go through that again?"

"Why did you even go to the store? Especially when it's crowded like that? Why didn't you take a guard with you? I made a mistake by not saying anything, but you up and ignored the protocols I set in place to protect our family. Dammit, Grace. You're tying my hands behind my back!"

"Stop swearing!" An angry burn shot through her stomach. "Yes, it's partially my fault, and I take full responsibility. I told my mother it wasn't a good time, but she said it was just the grocery store. I didn't push back. She couldn't believe I hadn't taken Ella anywhere except the restaurant. She made me feel like a bad mother, Jordan."

His eyes narrowed. "Your mom would never do that. She knows you're a great mother."

"But she didn't understand what your fame is like." Grace stared him down. "She does now."

"So, what? Are we supposed to keep our daughter in some ivory tower for the rest of her life, away from people and places, all because of one bad moment? I had all night to think about this, and while I want to destroy every one of those people who made her scream, keeping her hidden isn't the answer. That's no kind of life for anyone. We have to figure out a different way."

Oh, God, she was going to have to tell him now. She'd hoped to wait. She crossed her arms to protect herself from his reaction. "I know it's not the way. I think I should take her away from Atlanta and raise her in a different city—one that doesn't care so much about their quarterback."

"No way!" he yelled immediately. "You are not taking my daughter away from me."

"I'm not taking her away," she said, trembling to her toes. "You can see her anytime you want. I swear. But this way, she can grow up and have a more normal life. No one is going to be gunning for a picture of her to win a thousand bucks."

"No!" he said in a hard tone. "I won't allow it."

"Please, listen," she said, reaching out a hand.

"No." He shook his head. "Not this. If you move, I won't see her except in the off season. Dammit, Grace. Don't take away my baby girl. I love her more than anything. Taking her away isn't the answer. She needs her dad. I know. I...grew up without one. It fucking sucks. Don't do that to her."

Tears slid down his face, and she took some deep breaths to quell her own rising urge to cry. His swearing was only making her tremble more, but she knew it was a sign of how upset he was that he couldn't control himself right now. "I know you love her, and I do too.

I know how much it hurt you when your dad left, but you'll still be in Ella's life. It's not the same as it was for you. Jordan, you need to do what's best for her."

He planted his feet. "Being in Ella's life every day *is* the best thing for her, Grace. I know you're a great mom, but I'm a pretty awesome dad. She needs both of us. I don't want Ella to ever think you left because I didn't want her."

She took the punch to her solar plexus. "I would *never* let her think that, Jordan."

"You don't know what kind of things a kid thinks," he growled. "How you blame yourself for your dad not being around. How you think you must have done something to make him leave. I won't have her thinking those things, Grace. Jesus! How did we get to this place? You talking about taking our daughter away? What about us? How can you even talk like this when you say you love me? When you know how much I love you?"

"It's not enough!" she cried. "Do you think this decision is easy for me? I love you too, but I have to protect our daughter—because you can't."

He swiped angrily at the tear that leaked out of his eyes. "We're back to this, are we? I can't protect her— or you—because I'm the cause. That's bullshit, Grace. Other players in the NFL find a way to make this work. Why won't you work with me? It's our life, Grace. It's us and Ella. Our family. I was hoping we were finally getting to a place where you'd believe I want to marry *you*. Not because of Ella. Are you really going to let your fears ruin that?"

So he had planned to ask her. Pain exploded in her heart, but it couldn't matter. She couldn't let it. "You weren't there yesterday," she said again. "You're not hearing anything I say. This is not my fault."

"No, and it's not mine either." He held up a hand.

"I'm not saying yesterday wasn't awful, but why can't we use it as a lesson and agree it won't happen again? I promise not to keep things like tabloid bounties from you."

"And you accuse me of wanting to put her in an ivory tower?" she said, locking her arms tighter across her chest. "You can't have it both ways."

He pinched the bridge of his nose before lowering his hand. "Do you love me?" he asked, locking gazes with her.

The hurt slashed through her, and she squeezed her eyes shut again. "You know I do."

His hands curled around her arms. "Open your eyes and look at me. Do you believe I love you and Ella more than anything? That I would do anything for you? That I want us to be a real family and live in this house?"

Her throat closed, and she made herself shrug. "I know you love us, but this is bigger than that."

He stared into her eyes, as if struggling for words. "I'll leave the NFL and move back to Deadwood with you like you always wanted...if that's what it'll take to keep us together."

Her mouth parted, and she took a step away from him. *"Jordan."*

"If this is the *only* way to keep us together, then I'll do it." He sniffed and wiped his nose. "I would only ask to finish out the playoffs. I...God, I don't want to let my team down."

Her mind was reeling. "I'm not asking you to give up the NFL."

"No, you're not," he said harshly. "But you're not giving me any choices I can live with. I can't live with you moving away with Ella. What you decide about us is your choice. I...would want us to be together."

She took a ragged inhale. "It would kill you not to

play." He'd wither in Deadwood, building houses with her dad. She could see that now.

"It would kill me more not to be a father to my daughter," he said. "I could lose you and survive—I did once—but I can't lose Ella. Can I go see her now? I... Grace, I really need to see her."

Her control was shattering. "Of course you can. I know you don't believe me right now, but I would never keep you from her."

The look he gave her before he walked off cut her to the core. He *didn't* believe her, and after what she'd said to him, she couldn't blame him.

***

When Jordan let himself inside Grace's house—the house he'd built for her and started to think of as theirs—he rapped on the door and called, "I'm coming in."

Meg was holding Ella, bouncing on her feet in a soothing rhythm. "Hello, Jordan," she said gravely, looking as exhausted as Grace.

His daughter immediately let out a wail and reached for him.

"Hi, Meg. Can I hold her?" he asked, feeling tears burn his eyes again.

"Of course," she said, crossing to him.

Ella turned her head to look at him, and from the way she didn't raise her head or smile at him, he could tell she was exhausted too. His heart broke as she gave another weak cry.

When he put her to his chest, he could feel the ache spread. Ella curled her little body into him, and he closed his eyes, rocking her slowly. *Oh, baby. I'm so sorry.*

"How bad was it yesterday?" he asked Meg.

Meg had always given it to him straight, and after hearing Grace talk about moving away with Ella...

"Pretty bad, honey," she said, patting him heavily on

the back. "I'll be in my room if you need me."

"I'll head up to the nursery with her," he said, desperate to have some privacy. He was going to break down now that his little girl was in his arms, and he didn't want an audience. "I'm sorry, Meg."

She leaned her head against his shoulder and ran a hand down Ella's soft head. "It's not your fault, honey. It's just...in all my days, I haven't experienced anything like it. I don't know what to say. But I'm sorry for you guys. This situation... Go be with your daughter."

She patted him on the back, and he started toward the stairs. Before he could climb them, Meg added, "You're a good father, Jordan. Never forget that."

As he walked to the nursery, holding Ella close, he tried to find some peace in Meg's words despite the turmoil swirling inside him. Maybe he should have told Grace about the bounty, but there was no use falling into self-recriminations. He could only do the right thing now, and if being a good father to Ella meant leaving the NFL, he'd do it. However he looked at it, his heart was going to break.

But being Ella's daddy was the most important thing in his life.

He shut the door to the nursery—even though they usually left it open—and sank into the rocker with her. Her little body was warm and heavy, but listless. The pain in his heart spread until he felt tears leak out of his eyes.

"Daddy's so sorry he wasn't there for you and Mommy yesterday," he said hoarsely. "I'm so sorry you got scared. I wish..." His voice broke.

She shifted in his arms and raised her head, gazing at him with those blue eyes he'd given her in the miracle of life. Drool ran down her chin, and her eyes were crusty from crying.

He kissed her cheek and cupped the back of her small head, marveling at how fragile she was. Grace was right. He had put them in danger. What if the fans had gotten more aggressive and hurt Ella? She was too little to protect herself.

"I love you," he told her, smiling at her through tears. "Do you know how much? You've changed my whole life. There isn't anything Daddy wouldn't do for you. Okay? I know you might be too little to understand, but I promise you that I'm always here for you. That you're the most important person in my life. Everything else pales in comparison."

She raised her little hand and patted his cheek, and he pulled her close again, pressing her little face next to his.

"I'm not letting anyone keep us apart," he said hoarsely. "I'm never going to leave you. You're my girl now, and I'm your dad."

He couldn't hold back his tears, so he cried softly while she cuddled against him, vowing he would do whatever it took to stay in her life. Even if it meant giving up the game he'd once loved more than anything.

While he held her, he came to terms with his decision. When Ella finally fell asleep against his chest, he continued to rock her, unable to bear the thought of setting her down in her crib.

The door slowly opened sometime later, and Grace poked her head in.

He whispered, "She's asleep."

She walked hesitantly forward and laid her hand on Ella's head. "I thought she might want to nurse, but maybe we should let her sleep."

He rose with his daughter in his arms, feeling the awkwardness hovering between him and Grace. "I'll get out of your way. If she has another tough night, just text me. I want to help—if that doesn't bother you."

His mind flashed back to the early months after Ella was born, how he'd had to push to help with the night shift. It seemed as if they'd come back full circle.

"Let's hope she sleeps," Grace whispered, and in the soft light, he could see the grooves in her face from exhaustion and stress.

Ella wasn't the only one he was hurting.

"I really am sorry," he whispered, his chest aching. "When I saw her, it all hit me. You're right. She didn't smile at me. She just...lay against me all curled up. It broke my heart, Grace."

She nodded, her face bunching up with grief. "I know."

"I'm sorry I got mad earlier and swore at you," he said, filled with regret. "You caught me off guard, talking about moving. Grace, you need to know. Regardless of what you decide about us, I'm going to leave the NFL. I won't let anything happen to you and Ella. We can talk whenever you want."

He handed Ella over to Grace and stooped to kiss her round cheek.

"I love you, little one," he whispered. "Sweet dreams."

There were tears shining in Grace's eyes when he straightened. He nodded and let himself out quietly.

Meg wasn't downstairs, and Jordan noted the time on the clock in the family room. It was well after ten o'clock. He needed to be at the stadium in the morning to recap how they'd played today. He also needed to talk to Chaz and the other members of the front office about setting up a press conference.

Apparently NFL commentators had even mentioned the incident with his family during the broadcast of today's game, speculating that it had driven him to deliver a punishing defeat to Dallas and get into a fight with one of the defensive linemen who'd tackled him after a play. What no one knew was the asshole had called him out for not being able to defend his family. Jordan had lunged at him, but he'd been pulled back by two of his own players. Otherwise, he would have decked the guy and potentially gotten thrown out of the game.

It was a freaking mess. He'd never shown such bad sportsmanship, and the media had run with the story.

After the game, Chaz had told him the front office was getting requests for interviews about the grocery store altercation with the Rebels' fans. Apparently, a majority of Rebels' fans were up in arms about it and had been sending condolences to Jordan and his family. Media commentators were discussing the ethics of tabloid bounties for children, which was prompting a hot debate about celebrities' privacy. The media had even identified the Good Samaritan, and Jordan planned to call him tomorrow to thank him for looking out for his family.

He hadn't told Grace about any of it because she'd pretty much cold-cocked him with her talk of leaving Atlanta to protect Ella. But he'd have to—even though he was planning on retiring—because he wouldn't keep anything concerning their daughter from her again. Tomorrow was soon enough.

Digging out his phone when he reached his house, he scrolled through the texts he'd received from his Once Upon a Dare brothers. The general theme was the same: were he and the family okay?

He didn't have the energy to respond to everyone individually, so he sent back a group text.

Things are pretty bad, but I'm working on changing that. Tell you more deets when I have them.

Jordan couldn't sleep that night, kept awake by thoughts of leaving the sport he loved, but the memory of Ella's sad, listless body cuddled against his chest was enough to reaffirm there was nothing he wouldn't do for his little girl.

CHAPTER 29

Grace didn't know what to say to Jordan yet, so she left Ella with her mom and drove to Tony's apartment in Midtown after Jordan had left for work. He'd come to the house to say goodbye to Ella, who had thankfully only gotten up once in the middle of the night. The baby had still been asleep when he'd arrived, but Grace had heard Jordan's words loud and clear over the baby monitor.

"Don't worry, sweetheart," he'd said softly. "Daddy's going to take care of everything today."

Was he planning on announcing his retirement? Her stomach was clenched in knots at the idea. Not this soon, surely? After a sleepless night, she was all tied up with indecision. Had she been wrong to suggest that she and Ella move away? Jordan was a good dad, and living in different cities changed things between a parent and a child. His willingness to leave the NFL to stay with Ella had moved her fiercely. With that one move, he was showing her his daughter was truly everything.

And that wasn't the only thing tying her into knots.

After all this time, he wanted to marry her. She'd spent plenty of time sobbing into her pillow over that.

Surely there was some other way for them to stay together as a family—one that wouldn't require Jordan to give up the game he so loved. Tony was one of the people she knew best, and his separation from the situation meant he could give her impartial advice. That was something she desperately needed right now.

When she reached Tony's penthouse, he greeted her with open arms. "I would have come to you," he said, hugging her tightly. "You have enough on your plate right now. I'm surprised reporters didn't follow you here."

"They did," she said, letting him lead her inside. "I ended up having Jordan's driver bring me here." It was her acknowledgment that Jordan had been right about her following the protocols he'd put in place. But her heart had pretty much pounded the whole way considering all the news vans and other cars in hot pursuit after they cleared the gate.

He narrowed his eyes at her. "You should have stayed inside."

She'd thought about it. "Things...got taken care of." The guards had been super angry about the incident, and they'd encouraged her to let them do their jobs. She'd assured them it wouldn't happen again.

"Tempers are running hot about what happened," Tony said. "It's all over the news. Everyone is wondering if the Rebels are going to have a press conference today to address what happened. The local morning news programs have been talking about fans being bullies and tabloids going too far to get pictures of celebrities' kids. A few outraged fans have said they want to punch the people at the grocery store in the face. I share that sentiment."

When they reached Tony's massive kitchen, Grace sank into one of the stainless steel bar chairs in front of the island. "I told Jordan I thought I should take Ella away from Atlanta and move to a different city—one that doesn't care so much about him and his personal life."

Tony's eyes went flat. "You're going to let those bullies make you run? I thought you'd gotten beyond that, bella."

His words confirmed she might have overreacted yesterday. "After thinking about it all night, I'm having doubts."

He put his hands on his hips. "You can't give people like that any power. They're pissants. You would leave Marcellos and the man you love because of this?"

The thought of leaving Marcellos had made her heart seriously hurt, but she'd realized something—she could be a chef anywhere while Jordan was facing the prospect of giving up his career. "I only want to protect my daughter, Tony," she said. "I feel like I'm between a rock and a hard place."

He shook his head. "Blow up the hard place. You don't give in to bullies, Grace. You fight back. You draw better boundaries. You shame people when they act like this. Trust me, the more ethical journalists and Jordan's fans are already doing this. You need to join them."

Hearing people were on her side raised her spirits. Other than the Good Samaritan yesterday, she hadn't thought it possible. "Jordan didn't like my idea either," she said, the taste in her mouth suddenly like bitter almonds. "He said he'd rather leave the NFL than lose Ella—regardless of whether I decide to stay with him."

"Only a rare man would leave the career he loves for his family." Tony set Grace's espresso before her. "If you're questioning your relationship with him, those bullies have won, after all."

"He totally shocked me." Grace's hands were shaking

too much for her to reach for the espresso. "I...I can't bear the thought of us breaking up again. This time it would be for good, but Ella would always keep us tethered together." How could she live with this decision, knowing how much they loved each other, knowing he finally wanted to marry her and have a family with her?

"Then don't break up with him," Tony said, crossing his arms. "Jordan may not be a perfect man, but he's not to blame for what happened. And yet you're thinking about taking everything he loves away from him: you, his daughter, and football."

"I don't see any good choices here," she said, pressing her hand to her heart. "This is my daughter we're talking about. Tony, she screamed. She hasn't smiled. It's...an impossible situation."

"You need to find a better solution," Tony said tightly. "Right now you and Jordan are coming up with impossible choices. Grace. For all of your sakes. How do you think Ella will feel when she gets older and finally learns the truth behind your decisions? Do you think it'll make her happy?"

Her head spun. "I hope she would understand we did it out of love."

"Or she would be sad that you did something that could make everyone so unhappy because of her," Tony said. "It would be a lot to lay on a child."

Grace blinked. "She wouldn't think that." But her daughter might, especially if her mom and dad continued to look at each other with love for the rest of their lives, filled with regret that they could have been a family, but weren't.

"I might," Tony said, giving her a pointed look. "My mother gave up working at an antique shop in our town when she started her family. My father didn't want his wife working outside the home. Family members later told me stories about how happy she'd been working in that little shop filled with beautiful things. I asked her one day why she never went inside that shop anymore, and she said it still made her a little sad. I would never have wanted my mother to make that choice if I'd been old enough to stop her. Neither would Ella."

Her throat clogged with emotion. "Do you really think Jordan and I could shame the media into backing off?"

He made a fist in the air and waved it menacingly. "Yes! I know how much you hate bad language, but sometimes it's the only way to get people's attention. You say 'Fuck you,' to the bullies, and you do as much as you can to prevent them from bothering you again."

Grace flinched at the word. Tony had never used it in her presence after learning about how her first boss had used harsh, demeaning language to bully her. That chef, she realized, had goaded her into leaving a wonderful opportunity—just like Grace had almost let these bullies do to her now. No, she couldn't keep running. It was time to stand her ground.

"I don't know if I can say that, but I understand the force behind the word." Maybe she could muster that.

He gave her a pointed look. "If you can't say it now, you practice saying it until you can. But you don't leave Marcellos, and you don't let Jordan give up football. Most importantly, you don't leave the man you love for the second time, Grace."

Grace firmed her shoulders. "Okay, I need to practice it." She winced. "Fuck."

"That's terrible," Tony said, a slow smile appearing on his face. "Again."

She said it over and over again at his prompts until he clapped his hands. To her shock, she felt a million times lighter—and more empowered.

"Bravo," he said. "Now, find Jordan, Grace. Before he does something he can't undo."

The urgency was rising inside her. "I...don't know whether I can get to him. He's in meetings."

Tony rolled his eyes. "You can get to him. And if anyone gets in your way, you use your word and punch them. Let me show you how to make a fist." He tucked her fingers into her palm and arranged her thumb horizontally over them. "Family is worth fighting for. Love is worth fighting for. Don't ever let anyone make you forget that."

"I'm going to fight, Tony," she said, raising her fist. "For Jordan and me, and for our family." It wouldn't be easy or pleasant, but she couldn't let those bullies take away everything. They'd already hurt her and her family enough.

"Let us go then," Tony said.

She nodded and followed him out with both hands fisted by her side, ready to do battle for the people she loved.

***

The Rebels' owner and Coach didn't like Jordan's plan for how to handle what everyone was calling the grocery store incident. In fact, they were downright pissed.

"Son," Coach said, standing at the edge of his desk in his office, "I know you think you're protecting your family by retiring from the game, but this isn't the way. You're still a Super Bowl winner. No matter where you go, you're going to be famous. Hell, I played ball with some pretty great guys in my time. People still ask them for autographs, and they're bald and fat now."

The fact that Coach had called him 'son' three times in the last half hour while arguing with him didn't unsettle Jordan so much as the stories he and Chaz had told him about marquee players never being able to return to a normal life. He wondered if that would be the case in Deadwood.

"I hear what you're saying," Jordan said, rubbing the back of his neck. "I just don't see another way to protect my family." So far, he hadn't shared Grace's plan to leave Atlanta, not wanting to air their private personal business.

"Let me get Coach Garretty on the line," Coach said. "Or you can take a couple of days off this week to visit him in Ohio. You trust his opinion, right?"

Coach Garretty was one of the most influential people in Jordan's life, but he didn't need to talk to his mentor to know what was right. "Coach Garretty might agree with you and he might not. I respect Coach and both of you guys, but in the end, I have to follow my heart. That's what Coach Garretty taught me, and in this situation, my heart is with my family."

Chaz narrowed his eyes. "If this is about more money..."

"I've told you it's not," Jordan said, fighting his impatience. "You said you wanted to hear my thoughts about what to say to the press, and this is it."

Coach shook his head in frustration, his eyes locked with Chaz's. A knock sounded on the door, and Coach went to open it. One of the assistant coaches leaned in, and the two conferred briefly before Coach straightened.

"Chaz," he said, jerking his head to the hall to get the man to follow him out of the room.

Jordan sat back in his chair and took some deep breaths when they closed the door. Right now, he felt like he was fighting with everyone he cared about: Grace, his team, and himself.

The door opened again, and he looked over, bracing himself for another round of arguments. But his mouth fell open when Grace closed the door behind her. He shot out of his seat.

"Has something happened to Ella?" he asked, putting

his hands on her shoulders, fear washing over him.

"No, nothing's happened to her," she said, her brow wrinkling. "She's okay, Jordan."

He blew out a long breath, adrenaline skyrocketing through his system. "Are you okay then? Why are you here, Grace? You never come here."

She hadn't in ages. The last time was years ago—she'd come to watch him practice because he'd just joined the team and needed some moral support.

Her right hand rose, and he realized it was clenched into a fist. "I want to fight for our family. I don't want you to leave football. I don't want to leave Atlanta. And I don't want to break up with you again."

He stared at her, his heart rapping hard against his chest. "We've gone through this before, Grace," he said, his walls anchored firmly in place. "Are you sure this time? I...I can't go through that again."

"Since you know how much I hate foul language, maybe this will convince you." She took a deep breath. "I plan to tell those bullies from the grocery store and any other ones who bother us to go...fuck themselves."

He was sure his mouth had dropped to the floor, but somehow he managed to choke out, "What did you say?"

Her chest rose with another deep inhalation. "I said they should 'go fuck themselves.'"

His hands cupped her face, and he looked into her vibrant green eyes. "You just said fuck. You *never* say fuck. You never cuss. Holy shit! Are you sure you're okay?"

Maybe she'd cracked under the pressure. He knew how bone-crushing it could be.

Her laugh sounded a little crazy, which concerned him, but then she lifted a shoulder. "I'm fine, I think. Oh, I forgot the other part. I need to raise my fist in the air and say it. Here. Let me try it again. I've been practicing. *Go fuck yourselves.*"

"I can't believe I'm hearing this," he said, running his eyes over her face. She still looked a little pale to him, and her body was trembling. "Are you sure—"

"Yes, I'm sure," she said emphatically. "Whew! All this cussing makes my head swim, but honestly, it feels kind of good. It's like this huge relief every time I say a bad word."

And to prove her point, she let out a whole slew of other words she'd never used before, pretty much blowing his mind.

"Tony had me practice on the way over after we talked," she told him.

Things were starting to make more sense. "You're a fast learner," he said with complete admiration, forced to put her in one of the chairs in front of Coach's desk when she started weaving in place.

"Head between your legs," he said, sinking to the floor in front of her and rubbing her back.

She took deep breaths, and he angled closer to her, worried as hell. Cussing and close to passing out? She was not okay. When she raised her head, there were tears in her eyes, and they pretty much slayed him.

"Grace."

"I *love* you," she said, putting her hand to his cheek. "Jordan, I don't want to give in to these horrible people. I want to find a better way to handle them. Heck...hell, I want to shame them for what they've done to our daughter. Together. I hate that we have to deal with this, but I won't lose you. Not again. I can't believe I almost let that happen."

He rested his forehead against hers. "Oh, Grace. I want to find a better way too, but I just don't see it. Shaming the media and bad fans isn't going to work for everyone. Leaving the NFL might be the only way to make sure it never happens again. That you and Ella are safe. I need you to be safe."

She pulled away. "I might be a little late to the party, but I was wrong to want to cut and run. Tony is right. We don't give in to bullies. We raise our fists and say—"

He put his hand over her mouth. "I don't think I can handle hearing you drop the f bomb one more time today. *I* might pass out."

Her laughter sounded like it had been wrenched from her heart. "Then maybe let me say something else." She grabbed his hands in hers and looked him straight in the eye. "Jordan Dean. Will you marry me?"

He toppled backwards and landed on his backside. "What?"

"I'm proposing to you," she said, trying to smile over the vulnerability clouding her eyes. "I know you told me you finally wanted to ask me, but I want *you* to know how much I want us to be together. That I want to marry you for you—and that means you the football player too. I'm sorry I hurt you last night. Please forgive me."

That she would propose to him after waiting all these years humbled him fiercely. "Oh, Grace," he said, picking himself up off the floor and putting his hand on her knee. "You were scared, and I went...crazy. You and Ella both just mean so much to me. The thought of losing you..."

A tear rolled down her cheek. "I know," she said, digging into her jeans pocket and producing a large masculine-looking ring. "That's why I'm asking you to marry me. Ella is already yours."

He felt tears burn his eyes.

"I was hoping I could be yours too," she said, crying now. "Forever. In the beautiful yellow house you built for us."

She was pretty much squeezing his heart inside his chest. "You're already mine," he said, pulling her out of the chair and into his arms. "And I'm yours, but yes. I want to marry you and live in that house and raise Ella and our family. More than anything."

She smiled through the tears raining down her face as she reached for his hand. "This is Tony's signet ring. It was the best I could do at the last minute." She tried every one of his fingers before laughing harshly. "It doesn't fit any of them."

He brought her to his chest. "That's okay," he told her, thinking about the ring he was going to buy her. "It's probably someone's way of saving my manhood a little—what with you proposing and all."

"I couldn't think of a better way to make you understand why I decided to fight all of a sudden when all I wanted to do yesterday was run."

"I'll need to thank Tony somehow," he said, kissing her on the cheek and then moving to her lips.

She sank into him, and he gave them both what they wanted: the hot, deep, wet, connected kiss that told them disaster had been averted between them and everything was going to be okay again.

"You and Ella are my everything," he whispered against her soft lips, kissing her again.

Her body curled into his, and he luxuriated in running his hands along the sides of her waist and up her back. She moaned into his mouth, and he groaned when her tongue darted out to dance with his.

"As much as I want to make love to you," he said, giving them both a little space, "we're in Coach's office."

Her breath shuddered out. "Right. Cussing and having sex in Coach's office. I don't know if I could take both in the same day."

He laughed. He couldn't help it. "And proposing to me. Don't forget that."

Those green eyes of hers turned luminous. "I couldn't forget that."

"Neither will I," he said softly. "Ever." He eyed the door, wondering how much longer they had before someone interrupted them. Neither Chaz nor Coach were the kind of men to be kept waiting—even if they hoped Grace would help talk their marquee quarterback out of retiring.

"I'm talking to the media this afternoon," he said, holding her gaze. "Do you want me to tell the bullies to 'fuck off' on your behalf and say they should be ashamed of themselves?"

She smiled. "I was hoping to say something along those lines myself while holding your hand, if you're okay with that. I...need to speak for Ella too."

Of course she did. Their beautiful daughter had come into their lives unaware of all the changes she'd make inside them, just by being herself. "I'd be honored to have you by my side, Grace."

And so a few hours later when they faced the press together, they both stood for everything that was important to them: their daughter, their relationship, but most of all love and family.

Epilogue

Jordan and Grace's wedding took place a couple of weeks later on a mild December day right before the holidays in a heated tent filled with family and close friends. Grace had agreed to let Jordan move heaven and earth to make their wedding come together so they could spend Christmas as husband and wife.

Grace's mom held Ella throughout the ceremony and then handed her to Jordan so that he and Grace could walk down the aisle as a family.

This time, Jordan had a wedding ring that fit his finger. Grace's engagement ring was a simple but elegant yellow diamond—according to him, he'd picked it to match her sunny demeanor.

Grace wandered through the crowd with her hand on Jordan's back as he held Ella. She was so happy that her father and brothers were making the effort to embrace Jordan again. Moments ago, her dad had finally said to Jordan, "You did a pretty good job with that house of yours." Since her dad had been the one to build the original, it was high praise indeed. Her mom might have given her a quick wink, and Grace had pretty much smiled unabashedly when they'd left her family to make the rounds with their guests.

When she and Jordan reached the corner reserved for his Once Upon a Dare brothers, she took the baby from him and watched him man-hug every single one of the guys. Her eyes met Natalie's, and she smiled at Blake's wife, who seemed so at home in the midst of all this testosterone.

"I lost a hundred bucks to Brody," Hunter was telling Jordan. "Everyone thought Sam was going to get hitched next."

"If I'd known about the bet," Sam said, giving them all a pointed look, "I could have assured you I haven't met anyone good enough to become Mrs. Garretty yet."

"She'll have to be the sweetest girl alive," Zack said, kicking back his heels and simpering. "Sam won't go just for smart and pretty."

"I thought Natalie was the sweetest girl alive," Blake said, totally deadpan.

All of the guys burst out laughing, and soon Natalie was throwing a few of the party favors on the table at the football players. Ella screeched out at the game, drawing everyone's attention.

"She likes what's going on," Grace explained to some of the more kid-shy football players.

Now that the regular season was over, everyone had flown in for Jordan's bachelor party a few days ago and gotten a chance to meet Ella. Shocking everyone, Ella had taken a fancy to the biggest man in their group—Grant—topping out at six-foot-five and three hundred pounds. Grant had to remind all of them he was the oldest of five kids and had pretty much raised his brothers and sisters after his dad had cut out on them.

Grant approached Ella with a beaming grin. "How's my little girl today? Are you happy your mommy and daddy finally tied the knot?"

Ella lurched forward, gurgling, and he caught her easily, making faces at her.

"Who knew your ugly mutt would make her laugh like that?" Jordan teased. Despite being a giant, Grant was pretty handsome if you asked Grace.

"All the women like me," Grant said, making all the guys start the trash talk. "Hey! Watch your mouths. Little ears."

"No one was cussing, you moron," Brody said, rolling his eyes. "Jordan said he'd punch us if we so much as said 'd-a-r-n' in front of Ella here."

Of course, Grace also had to watch her mouth now that she'd learned the incredible release of energy it provided. Jordan delighted in hearing her use swear words when it was just the two of them. Grace liked to think it was part of her toughening up to handle all the attention that came with Jordan's profession.

Natalie gave Brody a playful punch to the shoulder. "I believe moron is on the list."

"Man!" the wide receiver cried out. "There are way too many rules with you peeps getting hitched and having babies."

Blake put his arm around Natalie. "I know. It's terrible. You should get compensated for being our friends."

Logan snorted and flashed Grace a playful smile. "Don't listen to Brody. But seriously, since Sam's here, who's going to lay down a fresh bet he's the next one to walk down the aisle? I mean seriously, he's getting old."

Sam leaned back in his chair and regarded the group calmly. Of all Jordan's Once Upon a Dare buddies, Sam had always seemed the most mature. And he was in his late thirties, which did make her wonder why he hadn't married yet. Jordan had said Sam was picky, and Grace respected that.

"You're going to find someone great, Sam," Grace said, giving him an encouraging smile. "You're too nice not to."

"Is that how it works?" Sam asked. "You have to be nice? Jordan! Did you know you were nice?"

Her new husband didn't rise to the bait. Instead he put his arm around Grace and looked down at her, smiling. "Some people bring out the best in you. But the one you marry...well, she's the gate to everything."

And then Jordan kissed her right in front of his friends, making her heart beat just a little faster because he was half right.

Their love was the gate to everything.

Dear Reader,

I've been so excited to start this new series, Once Upon a Dare. Since I was a little girl growing up on Nebraska Cornhusker football, I've wanted to write a sports romance, but like everything else I write, it's not a typical story, and certainly not just a romance. Writing about what it means to be pregnant and have a baby and to be parents was an especially dear journey to me. I hope Jordan, Grace, and little Ella warmed your hearts and helped you remember what your gate to everything is.

If you enjoyed this book, please post a review! It helps more readers want to read my story. And when you post one, kindly let me know at readavamiles@gmail.com so I can personally thank you.

To keep up with all my new releases, please sign up for my newsletter at www.avamiles.com. And join our Dare family celebration of fun and inspiration by connecting with me on Facebook.

If you haven't read Blake and Natalie's story yet, you'll want to read A BRIGE TO A BETTER LIFE. And what's coming up? As you might have guessed, Sam Garretty is the next hero to find true love, and he discovers it with hospice nurse, Faith Daniels. Moira and Chase are our next Dare Valley couple in HOME SWEET LOVE. And the next Dare River book will be Shelby and Vander's story called THE FOUNTAIN OF INFINITE WISHES.

Thank you again for reading and being one of the greatest blessings in my life.

Lots of light and joy,
Ava

To learn more about Faith and Sam's story called FINDING FAITH, sign up for my newsletter.

Watch for the next Dare River story, THE FOUNTAIN OF INFINITE WISHES (Shelby & Vander), out later in 2016!

And the very next Dare Valley book called HOME SWEET LOVE (Moira & Chase) will be out in early 2017.

ABOUT THE AUTHOR

USA Today Bestselling Author Ava Miles joined the ranks of beloved storytellers after receiving Nora Roberts' blessing for her use of Ms. Roberts' name in her debut novel, the #1 National Bestseller NORA ROBERTS LAND. A mere six months after her debut in 2013, she'd hit the USA Today Bestseller list and released five books. So far, over a million readers have discovered Ava's stories, which have reached  the #1 spot at Barnes & Noble and ranked in Amazon and iBooks' Top 10. Ava's books have been chosen as Best Books of the Year and Top Editor's Picks and are being translated into multiple languages.

Made in United States
North Haven, CT
26 April 2023

35887652R10195